I Am Woman...

Book One: My Journey, My Tony

Mrs. Anthony

PARTRIDGE

Library of Congress Control Number: 2021921530
ISBN: Hardcover   978-1-5437-6743-8
                  Softcover   978-1-5437-6741-4
                  eBook   978-1-5437-6742-1

Print information available on the last page.

To order additional copies of this book, contact
Toll Free +65 3165 7531 (Singapore)
Toll Free +60 3 3099 4412 (Malaysia)
orders.singapore@partridgepublishing.com

www.partridgepublishing.com/singapore

Contents

Foreword

Hello and thank you for choosing to read this book! I am Dr Shabnam Ardev, a functional medicine practitioner with a master's in nutritional medicine. I list my credentials proudly, for my beloved mother, the author of this book, is the only reason I was able to step out bravely into the challenging world and fulfil my childhood dream to become a doctor. She was even stoic enough to allow me to specialise in a field of medicine that others thought too radical or foreign. Now, more and more experts have to admit that functional medicine is the medicine of the future.

This book was first incepted in the year 2004, and we had quite the team, brainstorming words and ideas, as Mom patiently typed each and every word. My late grandfather, a renowned English and geography teacher, would come up with the most delightful words and phrases while my brother would re-enact certain scenes or create his own sound effects. I would either join him in his efforts or oppose him and declare a sibling war, much to my fatigued mother's chagrin. Writing was often done after hours, once Mom had closed the classroom and grabbed a spot of tea.

Unforeseen circumstances compelled her to put her pen down until recently. Although we no longer have access to the old digital files, she had fortunately kept the old manuscript safe. Though yellowed and sad, that old manuscript has been revived, embellished, and reinforced to convey to you, dear reader, a most spellbinding memoir. The journey that follows is analogous to being out at sea in a vessel, facing unpredictable weather. There is much pain and heartache, but there is also much humour that will make you chuckle aloud and smile.

This story is true to life—I know, for I grew up witnessing and perceiving all that took place in the pages that follow after Mom married. It was in this home that I had all the love and attention of doting grandparents, the dedication and fierce love of a strong mother, the camaraderie and adoration of a cheeky brother, and the pride and love of a father. I am of a very close-knit family; we have laughed and wept together through thick and thin.

I am bursting with pride as I type the conclusion to this foreword—it has taken sheer grit, willpower, and absolute determination for my 64-year-old mother to revisit the past, face many painful memories, and write them down in a colossal effort to compile a memoir that is a true reflection of her journey as a woman. She, who is not computer-savvy, has patiently typed almost every word in this story. I have been actively involved with proofreading, editing, and checking for continuity, in between patient consults. I must say, I am confident that this book has all the makings of an international bestseller.

I know for a fact that my father is very proud of all my mother has achieved and will continue to achieve. She awaits me impatiently to free her seat at the computer for she is all set to get started on her second book.

By the way, I am Dewdrop.

By

Dr Shabnam Ardev d/o Anthony Sammy
Malaysian Medical Council Number: 45080
MBBS IMU (2006)
Dip in Family Medicine (2012)
Master's in Nutritional Medicine (2018)
27 September 2021

Preface

Woman, the Creator's gift to man—she is often perceived as beautiful, gentle, and kind.

Me? I am woman, all right, but most likely one that you would not afford a second glance. I am plain-looking, short, and always seem to have a bad hair day. However, I have been flung full force into the sea of life and challenged many times over—not fair, especially when I can't even swim! How on earth have I kept my head above water?

My seemingly sweet love marriage turned bitter when my beloved Tony allowed himself to be seduced by a shapely bottle of alcohol. Soon, an occasional bottle just wasn't enough to quench his thirst. My wonderfully warm, loving, and diligent Tony slowly let himself be ravaged health-wise. Our family was neglected, and finances took a steep downhill descent.

It is easier for a woman who is naturally soft and giving to remain submissive indefinitely. However, when along her arduous journey, this very woman also has no choice but to don heavy armour of sheer grit and determination to fend for her loved ones, it can take a heavy toll on her spirit. In place of her cheery smile, she wears a gaunt expression of weary resilience coupled with intense fortitude.

I have had to journey deep into the recesses of my heart and soul to gather the facts and summon up the courage to put pen to paper. So much has happened in the life of this tested soul. I feel that I owe sisterhood my story and hopefully give others foresight if their lives are taking a similar turn. I am also sincerely trying to create awareness among those who indulge in more than the occasional drink, believing that life without the intoxication of drink is lacklustre. Woefully, many falsely believe that they can put a stop to drinking, just like that.

I welcome you, dearest reader, to journey with me through these pages as I divulge the story and experiences that have filled my 64 years to the brim. I would be honoured if you deign to laugh and cry with me as I sail across the seas of memories. Be warned that the weather is often far from fair and the seas rather stormy.

So are you ready to join me?

This book is dedicated to my beloved husband, Tony.

Tony,
A man with a heart of gold,
Destined never to grow old,
He lived his life on the brink,
All for the love of drink.

Dear God, who reigns above,
Why did you so test my love?
Couldn't you see I'm merely human,
But wait, is that why you made me woman?

Girlhood

(1957–1977)

Ours was perhaps the smallest in the row of houses that smiled at St John's Hill, Melaka, across the road. Home sweet home boasted only two bedrooms as well as a conjoined sitting and dining area. The kitchen was a tiny one with the bathroom just beside it. We shared the bathroom wall with the neighbouring house. Voices could waft to and fro via this rather thin brick wall, especially when the speaker raised his or her voice.

There was a quaint little garden in the front of our house and a bigger yard behind, with a guava tree. Fragrant white wedding bells gracefully adorned the humble wire fence separating our house from the neighbours on the left. This floral conversation piece was courtesy of Uncle Horace, who seemed to have been born with green fingers. Visitors to both homes often stopped to marvel and gush over the scent and allure of the elegant wedding bells. Uncle Horace would be only too pleased to momentarily leave his orchids and dispense some gardening wisdom. Orchids were his passion, and destroying any of them incurred certain wrath! I had the misfortune of finding this out first-hand! The main gate to our house, however, was so low I sometimes wondered why it was even there. Even I could easily climb over it.

1

Life was blissful in the late 1950s in Melaka despite Dad's solo efforts as breadwinner. Teachers were not paid very much just after Malaya was liberated from colonial rule. However, Dad was highly respected by one and all, right to his last breath. Our neighbours, Uncle Horace and Aunty Iris, had warmly welcomed my blushing newly-wed parents when they first arrived to live next door.

My parents' marriage was an arranged marriage between family friends. Both Dad and Mum hailed from Penang, another Commonwealth settlement. Dad had come to Melaka to serve as a teacher in a secondary school. Mum should have been awarded a gold medal for her skills in cooking, embroidering, and keeping the home spotless. Despite being the firstborn of a reputed doctor in Penang, Mum did not have it easy. Her mother, the queen mother, ruled the brood with an iron ladle! Her words could slice any reluctant vegetable! She was a very orthodox lady who believed that a girl's place was first and foremost in the kitchen.

Mum's would-be mother-in-law had long observed this attractive young girl with aristocratic features who would make an amazing wife for her second son. Dad had no objections, for Mum was also a childhood playmate. It was a marriage between childhood friends.

Rita

The army of children in the house on our left breathed life (and mayhem) into the neighbourhood, and the youngest, Rita, was the icing on my cake. She was a year younger than me, but somehow, I always seemed to be under her command. Where did I go wrong?

'Let's run down the road and see if we can steal some star fruit from Sikluk's tree!' suggested my playmate Rita. Sensing my reluctance, she added, 'Don't worry *lah*! He's gone out. Nobody's going to catch us.'

Meet Rita, the closest I had to a sister when I was about five. She was a little younger to me, but supercharged with bravado. Of course, I ran down the road with my 'guru'—I wasn't going to lose face, and of course, those forbidden fruits were oh-so sweet.

Rita was the youngest of seven siblings. She had four elder brothers and all the attributes of a tomboy. Remember me telling you that the bathrooms of our houses shared a common wall? It was something I found rather hard to digest after a particular incident. One afternoon, while having a bath in our only bathroom, Mum shrieked in horror, 'Hey! There is a hole in the wall! Iris! What are your boys up to?' Mum's shriek of indignant horror successfully permeated the thin wall but paled in comparison to Aunty Iris' thundering threats to blind her guilty sons. The incriminating hole was sheepishly plastered that very evening after Uncle Horace had wielded his trusty cane amid shrieks of instant regret and pleas for mercy. It was a relatively quiet evening after that. Honestly, I never felt safe in the bathroom after that harrowing discovery.

Rita was often found in our home, rummaging determinedly through my treasure chest of toys. I never had many, for Dad was struggling to make ends meet. However, I cherished every simple toy that came my way. Rita, however, was given full leeway to decide which precious toy would be deemed fit for that day. I was only too happy to go with the flow. I felt blessed that she focused her attention on lonesome little me. One could not be too choosy when one's only sibling, the firstborn and male, to boot, had been exported to Penang, way up north, at the behest and decree of the queen mother, my intimidating maternal grandmother. Shiv was lording it over there, living it up!

Rita and I were a sight to behold. The short-haired Rita was usually clad in a vest and a pair of baggy shorts, while I, sporting long pigtails, normally wore a modest knee-length frock. I envied Rita her free-and-easy lifestyle—she was in and out of her bathroom in under three minutes, while I had to endure my long hair being washed every second day, followed by vigorous drying with a rather worn towel. It didn't help when Mum was hard-pressed for time! Tangles were a daily nightmare too, especially when I had to sit in silent anguish while Mum braided my hair. I must admit, though, I rather enjoyed the compliments I received when I was all dressed and my hair neatly braided. I guess those twenty-odd minutes were worth it, especially when Mum worked pretty ribbons into the ends of my thick ebony braids.

Rita always featured in my birthday photographs. She would be eyeing the creatively iced birthday cake, while I would be keeping a watchful eye on her! Evidence of this fatal attraction is perpetuated in my childhood photographs, yellowed over the years but still much treasured. The album is the same, but like the rest of us, it has seen better days.

Rita was my faithful companion and, I thought, my confidante. When not playing in the bedroom I shared with my only sibling, Rita and I could be found under the shade of a little tree in her garden. We would be lost in a world of fantasy, quite oblivious to the frantic cries of our fatigued mothers hoping to enlist our services in domestic chores.

As mentioned before, Rita's father had a passion for gardening. He spent hours tending his plants, especially the orchids. His garden was his kingdom, and he reigned over it with an iron hoe! As soon as he got back from work each evening, he would change into his shorts and singlet and make a beeline for the patch of garden in front of his house. The sight of prized orchids in brilliant hues, cascading from pots on a multi-tiered wooden rack, somehow made one forgive the stench of manure that could otherwise overwhelm the senses.

His no-nonsense demeanour discouraged pesky pixies, garden gnomes, and curious children.

While we were at play under our favourite tree one day, I accidentally knocked over a flower pot placed on some bricks. I panicked, for I knew Rita's father would scream at the sight of the forlorn speckled purple orchid sprawled helplessly on the ground, amid pieces of charcoal, earth, and fragments of the broken flower pot. I looked beseechingly at the only witness to the tragedy. 'Rita, what am I going to do? Your father is going to get really mad! I'm so afraid of him when he shouts! Please, you've got to help me!' I had a vision of short, stocky Uncle Horace suddenly grown seven feet tall, as he was prone to do when furious, looking down on an even shorter me, causing me to shrink to almost nothingness! Heaven help me.

It did. When I looked at Rita, she was suddenly sporting a halo. Comfortingly, she said, 'Never mind, let's just pretend we had nothing to do with it. Come on, let's get out of here fast!' Holding my hand tight, she led the way as we fled from the garden of doom, out of the front gate of her house, to our sanctuary—my house.

We sought refuge sitting on the concrete apron that ran along the far side of my house, away from hawk-eyed enemies—at least for a while. Yes, this was our hideout whenever we had committed an unspeakable crime that would have one of the adults soon hunting us down. Our throbbing legs would be stretched across a narrow drain, the very drain which was also our improvised toilet when the urge was unbearable and the bathrooms or toilets in both homes were all occupied.

While still trying to catch our breath, I looked at my guardian angel. Could I trust her not to snitch on me? As if she had read my mind, or perhaps in response to the pleading look in my eyes, she assured me with 'Cross my heart! I won't tell Daddy you killed his orchid. Hey, come on *lah*! Don't look at me like that! I crossed my heart, remember?'

I wished I could be really, really sure, but, her face barely a few centimetres away from mine, Rita looked straight into my eyes and solemnly vowed, 'I really, really promise not to tell, but you owe me a biggie, all right?' Meekly, I nodded.

I could not help wondering, therefore, how the others in her family still came to know that it was I who had broken the pot in which her father had triumphantly grown that rare orchid. Ever since then, Uncle Horace, in his mud-splattered wellingtons, always gave me a look of disapproval whenever I stepped into his garden. I mentally cancelled my debt to Rita. I owed her nothing!

We continued to be friends, for in a way, I was at her mercy. While she had her team of siblings to replace me within seconds, I had nobody else to turn to in my lonely state. As mentioned earlier, my only sibling, Shiv, was in the north, staying with our maternal grandparents. I too could have secured a fairly prestigious position in the sprawling grounds of Mum's parental abode, being the sole granddaughter until then, but I chose to be in my parents' humble dwelling—this little two-bedroom semi-detached house with a garden in front.

Our pretty little garden was home to numerous flowering plants. The blooms were no match, perhaps, for the exotic orchids next door, but nonetheless, they were appealing in their simplicity and sweet fragrance. I could spend hours sitting on the little blue wooden swing in the garden, admiring the beautiful array of flower pots Mum tenderly nurtured. While the daisies and chrysanthemums lent their lovely colour, the roses and jasmine flowers graciously fragranced the little garden. This was where I could be found, all alone and nursing my wounded heart, whenever Rita discarded me.

When she finally decided I was worthy of her company again, Rita and I would adjourn to the more spacious yard at the back of my house. There, we would climb the sole tree which inhabited the yard. It was a fairly tall guava tree with a few branches comfortably low enough for us to perch on. While she updated me on all the exciting things she had done when away from me and in the company of her siblings, we would reach out to pluck some half-ripe, puny-sized guavas.

'Ouch! Stupid ants!' would be an all-too-familiar exclamation as the two of us frantically tried to beat off the big red ants that had crawled up our legs, daring to eavesdrop on our girlish gossip. The annoying six-legged pests, however, could not deter us from biting into the stomach-ache-promising fruit.

When my father bought his first car and took me for a drive, Rita was, of course, given the honour of sitting beside me. Before we boarded our 'flight', I was determined to elaborate on the assets of the latest model just off the Ford assembly line.

'This is called a Ford Anglia. See, it's got wings!' I proudly exclaimed, pointing to the maroon beauty with a sunny yellow roof. When we got in, I rattled on relentlessly about all the gadgets in front and what wonders they could do. 'See all these buttons? Don't touch them, OK? You don't know what they do. I don't want anybody to damage my daddy's brand-new car!'

I wore a smug look as I presided over the conversation. Dad drove us around the neighbourhood, enthralling us with the car's smooth performance. Rita tried to look impressed, but of course, she was seething with jealousy and defeat. I could tell—she was gritting her teeth! I was thoroughly enjoying my reign—though only twenty minutes long, it was *so* sweet! *Her* daddy, with all his exotic orchids, had no new car to rival *my* daddy's!

All too soon, the magnificent ride was over. The minute we 'touched down', Rita jumped out of the car without any sign of gratitude for the great honour that had been bestowed upon her. When my father (my divine protector), was out of earshot, she stuck her tongue out at me and then started to chant shrilly all the way back to her front door, 'Boaster, boaster, you are a boaster!'. That was the last time *she* rode in *my* father's car!

Shiv Returns

When Shiv turned 6, he was returned to his rightful family. Our maternal grandparents were compelled to return this bundle of mischief after he single-handedly painted a continuous horizontal silver streak right across four newly painted walls of the master bedroom in our grandparents' bungalow in Penang. This great piece of art was discovered when the two workers returned from their lunch break. The can of silver paint was actually meant for the window grilles. Shiv instead had deemed it fit to make his austere grandmother see silver!

Mum and Dad were relieved to have their firstborn home in time to be enrolled at a primary school. Older than me by one whole year, Shiv never failed to remind me of his great seniority. Several times a day, he could be heard admonishing me with 'Don't forget I am older! Just do what I tell you,' or 'I get to choose what I want first.'

Initially, I was in awe. Soon, I was in fear and pain. He was the resident terrorist, and whenever I crossed his path, I was instantly removed, bodily! I learnt quickly who the boss was, and never dared to forget that Shiv reigned supreme. I attributed this to the fact that for too long, he had worn the crown in our maternal grandparents' domain. I missed the days when I knew no fear except for the moments that I crossed the path of Uncle Horace.

Shiv, however, could be loads of fun when he wanted to be. He was self-appointed ringleader of the games we played with the children next door. Rita, her elder brother Teta, Shiv, and I spent a few adventurous years together.

Our favourite haunt was the historical hill across the road. Aspiring mountaineers, the four of us, we climbed this hill daily, weather permitting. It was not a very tall hill, but if you chose to ascend it from the nearer side, just opposite our homes, it was rather steep and challenging. There was an overgrowth of bushes and tall grass, raising the eyebrows of any concerned parents. Our mothers never tired of warning us of the dangers that could be lurking there. Creepy crawlies and snakes had often made their way down the hill and into our compounds. Therefore, we were accustomed to discovering these little creatures and saw fit to make our way into their compounds, returning the favour.

Little did our mothers, or the four of us, realise that the curious projections we used as handholds and footholds were actually the peaks of tombstones! We were aghast with horror when one fine day, grass cutters from the municipality diligently removed a fair extent of the overgrowth on our side of the hill, revealing that our trusty climbing aids were actually tombstones! Rita declared, 'My goodness! We are lucky *lah* that we have not been visited by *pontianak* or evil spirits!'

'Rita, next time, don't play the fool when we are saying the rosary!' chided Teta.

Shiv and I exchanged looks of horror. We silently decided that we would no longer find excuses to miss going to the Sikh temple every Sunday.

You must be wondering if the sight of aged white tombstones deterred us from our daily hill-climbing fix. Perhaps for just a few minutes—after thanking the divine forces that be for saving us in the past, we confidently decided that our protection against ghouls and local banshees was guaranteed for the present and the future. We found that this morbid revelation actually added to the excitement and allure of the great ascent.

The boys would lead the way, like seasoned climbers, while Rita and I struggled to keep pace with them. I was, of course, usually the last one to reach the top, with the hem of my frock covered with love grass. Rita, whose tomboyish attire did not attract the clinging seeds, would laugh at me. Then sensing my dismay, she would sit down sympathetically beside me to help me pick and throw off the love grass one by one. If the evidence was not removed, my mother would guess where I had been, and that would mean trouble for the lot of us!

Once we were on the slope proper of the hill, the four of us would race up and down the rocky terrain, finally adjourning to the fort right at the top. This fort was the ruins of a once-powerful Dutch establishment. The final neck of the slope leading to the entrance of the fort was extra steep, and the rough terrain could put one off. Many a child attempting to run up to the fort had fallen in the attack, bruising knees and elbows—the more 'wounds' they were decorated with, the greater their 'heroism'!

After racing up the slope, the four of us would celebrate our victory at the entrance to the fort, with loud shouts of joy. Sometimes, we purposely shouted at the top of our voices, cheekily challenging our mothers, peacefully napping at home, to hear us! Then we would march into the fort proper to catch our breath.

All that remained of the ancient fort were its whitewashed walls comprised of huge slabs of rock with spaced gaps for daunting black cannons. The mighty cannons had been long removed and transferred instead to the cobbled centre square of the fort proper. They were excellent for us to sit proudly astride on or jump down boisterously from. Truly, not even the most exclusive toy shop could boast of such thrilling toys that could satisfy even the most discerning adventurous child.

Still trying to catch our breath after running across the centre square, the four of us would clamber to the top of the wall of the fort. While Shiv and Teta paced the perimeter of the wall, pretending to be soldiers, Rita and I would perch comfortably for a while on the ledge of a gap. I would be desperately trying to hold down the skirt of my frock if a strong breeze happened to be blowing just then. Rita, clad in her usual vest and shorts, would delight in my windblown misery! She would never be able to understand that traditional Punjabi parents frowned upon girls dressed in shorts. My parents were a little more modern, but they were very filial to their respective parents, all made in India, or Punjab, to be more accurate.

Though generally chatty, even we four would sometimes be at a loss for words while taking in the serene picturesque view of Melaka from the rear end of the fort, which had a sharp drop to the foot of the hill. This yet-to-be-developed part of the town of Melaka, stretching out as far as the eye could see, resolutely embraced the Strait of Malacca. The sea shimmered enticingly in the afternoon sun.

If the mood got to us, the four of us would play hide-and-seek on the hill. We would hide among the bushes surrounding the other three sides of the fort. It was sheer excitement, waiting to be found, as long as we were not discovered by a creepy crawling centipede or a sinister slithering snake! At times like this, I was only too happy to be found quickly!

Development slowly found its way up the slope of our hill. A reservoir was constructed midway on the slope. I shall never forget the time Rita and I adventurously explored the frontiers of the newly built reservoir. 'What a lovely big bowl!' I exclaimed in awe.

'I wonder what's inside it. Look, the door is open!' Rita looked at me. I knew that look.

'No, Rita! Don't even think about it!'

'I knew it! You're a coward *lah*!'

Nobody called me a coward. I was immediately all for the exploration.

The workers had gone home, leaving the door unlatched. Shiv and Teta were perched on the walls of the fort, busy aiming at distant targets with their home-made catapults. Now, I was really curious to see what the big bowl of the reservoir looked like while there was no water in it yet. Besides, we would be one up on the boys. What a delicious thought! Without wasting another minute, Rita and I bravely opened the door and gingerly stepped into the bowl.

It was rather dark and musty inside. Gradually, with the light coming in through the doorway, we could make out the workers' ladders and tools, which lay scattered on the ground. Then we noticed a spiral staircase leading up somewhere. We never discovered where because we soon heard the door shut with a bang. We were instantly plunged into total darkness! We heard the door being latched from the outside, amid the wicked shrieks of laughter of our brothers!

Rita and I started to scream and howl, horrified that water might flow into the mighty bowl any minute! It grew uncomfortably warm inside, and we were both in a panic. We hit the metal door hard with our fists and screamed for dear life. Frightened by our screams, Shiv and Teta finally relented and let us out. Rita and I charged out of the reservoir, tears streaming down our faces. We made a beeline for the foot of the hill, heading straight for the security of our homes. We stayed away from our favourite haunt for a record two weeks.

The four of us also never spared any fruit trees in sight. We were too young then to understand that Sikluk, who lived at the end of the row of houses in our neighbourhood, was intelligence-challenged and that was why he reacted so 'favourably' to our mischief and taunts of 'Sikluk! Sikluk! Come quickly *lah*! We are going to steal your star fruit! Come on, dance like a monkey!'

It thrilled us no end when our taunts annoyed him enough to make him shout unintelligibly as he tried to protect his orchard. We were still on the other side of the fence; thus, his fruits were safe from our clutches. However, he could not understand this, and he felt threatened enough to wave his arms about wildly as he screeched and hooted at us while violently shaking the chain-link fence, perfectly resembling an angered ape in captivity. Sikluk's comical attire of tattered vest and a pair of baggy psychedelic shorts only heightened the thrill of tormenting this rare specimen. We were fully convinced Sikluk was the missing link between man and ape!

Equally thrilling were the times when it had rained. The four of us scooped up tadpoles with our bare hands in the muddy, slimy pools which magically appeared in the wasteland behind our homes after a heavy downpour. It was great fun, competing to see who cupped the most tadpoles, the boys or the girls. After the exciting competition, we dutifully returned the traumatised little creatures to their watery home. We did all that was fun and expected of children our age—6-, 7-, and 8-year-olds.

Whenever my brother and I were sent off to our maternal grandparents' home in the north every school vacation, we really missed Rita and Teta. Sure, we had a couple of uncles and aunts (my mother's rather young cousins) to hang out with, but nothing could match the joy of being with the children next door.

Mum's cousins almost regularly converged on our maternal grandparents' bungalow, with their parents during school vacations. Admittedly it was fun for the first few days that we were together, but the novelty would wear off when this slightly older bunch of adolescents grew condescending. You see, they were practically all academic superstars, and they would flaunt their scholarly status at every possible opportunity. Back home, Shiv and I were the brighter duo, but we never let it affect our friendship with our playmates next door.

The pattern of fostering family ties had been set by our maternal grandfather. As the eldest son who had migrated from Punjab, he had seen to it that his younger siblings were settled down comfortably in nearby towns in Malaya. He himself had arranged their marriages, as expected in a respectable Sikh family. Thankfully, the siblings had fairly sound marriages, and they showed the utmost respect for their eldest sibling by having family reunions during long vacations.

It was quite practical for the three families to put up in the spacious bungalow of our grandparents for the duration of their stay. Our grandmother would not have it any other way, for she rather enjoyed the company of the wives of her younger brothers-in-law. They looked up to her for guidance and advice on crucial family matters, feeding her persona of the family matriarch. Their children, however, deemed it their right to instruct and direct Shiv and me, very much to our displeasure. Here, Shiv was often put in his place. They always wanted to call the cards. Shiv and I were just 'orderlies'. We would count the days till we returned to our domain.

The Move

When Dad and Mum decided to move to a bigger house, my heart broke. Dad was concerned at the seemingly unbecoming behaviour of older boys in the neighbourhood. Their carefree, inconsiderate, and discourteous attitude gave Dad increasing cause to worry. He especially feared that Shiv might be influenced. Furthermore, he thought it only proper that we should have a bigger house with separate bedrooms for Shiv and me, ideally nearer to school. This would reduce the time spent on the road each day, travelling to and fro. Moreover, the house he had viewed was within walking distance from both his school and mine.

Luck was on Dad's side! This newly built house, still available for purchase, even had a bit of extra land, thereby enabling

Mum to pursue her hobby of gardening. Moreover, as the house was off the main road, we would be spared the noise of vehicular traffic. With a heavy heart, I packed all my worldly possessions into three boxes. Every toy, every paper doll, and every handmade necklace of colourful beads held cherished memories of childhood play with Rita.

Too soon, we were saying our goodbyes to our long-time neighbours. Even Aunty Iris had tears in her eyes as she hugged Mum, her culinary consultant. The two women, plump yet attractive, had been mutual sounding boards for grievances and joyous anecdotes. It was obvious the two would never get over each other. I definitely would never forget the neighbours on our left. With heavy hearts but fond memories, we moved.

Shiv and I checked out our new neighbourhood even before the boxes and furniture could be unloaded from the lorry. Heaven help us—we could not find any children our age! Not all the sixteen houses had been occupied yet, and those that were did not seem to hold exciting prospects.

The first week away from our ex-neighbours was so unbearable that my parents went to fetch Rita and Teta to spend the weekend at our new home. We relived old times with a vengeance and bade farewell with promises of more such weekend rendezvous. 'Don't worry, Rita,' I said reassuringly. 'I'll tell Mummy and Daddy that we miss you and Teta so much I just feel like crying. That way, we can pick you both up on Friday and send you home on Sunday.' Was I reassuring myself actually? Dad, however, put his foot firmly down. Rita will never know how much she meant to me. I guess someone who already had more than her fair share of siblings would never understand how it felt to be sisterless.

Life in our new home slowly became interesting. Shiv and I were fascinated when the overgrowth on the land beside our house was cleared. 'Come here quick! Look!' I looked towards where Shiv was pointing and gasped. It was truly an interesting sight to behold. Shiv and I were not going to be devoid of fun after all! These neighbours on the far left were a silent yet intriguing lot. It was up to Shiv and me to break the ice.

One night, at the stroke of midnight, we tiptoed to the master bedroom. When we were sure that Mum and Dad were fast asleep, we quickly parked ourselves at the centre window of Shiv's bedroom, which afforded the best view. Armed with a big powerful torchlight, Shiv shone it, directing it determinedly on *them*. I have yet to see them come alive. So much for living next door to a cemetery!

Adolescence

The years passed. Shiv and I moved on to secondary school. The both of us were not exceptionally bright, but neither did we lack intelligence. We remained in the best class respectively, and with some ups and downs, laughter and tears, schooling was done. During the schooling years, however, our classmates found our home to be a welcoming place.

Mum was all hospitality, and our fellow teenagers were always hungry! Dad, for his part, was more than willing to chauffeur us to designated schools for meetings, debates, and the like. This was perhaps his way of keeping an eye on what we were doing and whose company we were keeping. It suited me fine, for I was often the envy of schoolmates who did not have such accommodating parents. Shiv, however, sometimes resented Dad's overprotective nature, preferring to cycle to tuition classes and tennis practice.

Now it was time to further our studies. Both Shiv and I went through a period of trial and error. Career prospects were debated on; some were appealing while others appeared bleak. Tempers flared when unsolicited advice was offered by know-it-all friends and relatives. Finally, we each embarked on a tertiary course that the elders thought was best and had potential.

Shiv spent a year abroad and later decided that the course that he had pursued was not to his liking. He obstinately returned, determined to graze on local pastures. Of course, some money was lost, but thankfully, not in staggering amounts. We still had a roof over our heads.

Then it was my turn. It was a case of repeat performance except that I came back, abandoning my arts course in response to a crisis at home involving Shiv. His break-up had battered his spirit, and Mum and Dad were having a tough time helping him back on his feet. Realising that Dad and Mum had greater need for my presence at home, I dismissed all plans to resume the course that I had abandoned overseas. Unfortunately, neither could I continue pursuing a course similar to that locally. Hence, I started working.

Slowly but surely, my brother and I found our true callings (or so I would like to believe) in life. Shiv worked away from home as a quality control supervisor in a palm oil processing mill. I, thankfully, was much closer, teaching temporarily in a government school in the mornings and giving tuitions at home in the evenings. With some distance between us, Shiv and I found that we actually missed each other. We also discovered that where we once could not make it through a day without at least a dozen squabbles, we were actually beginning to get along better, treating each other as adults. We gave each other encouragement when it was needed and made it a point to congratulate too, on a task successfully completed.

Our parents were pleasantly amused when Shiv and I began to value each other's opinions on dress sense, mutual friends, and the attributes to look for in our choice of life partners. I was quite sure that they were secretly relieved to find that the squabbling siblings had not only made peace but had also learnt to look to each other for reassurance and enlightenment. During the rare weekends that Shiv could not make it home, it did not surprise my parents at all to hear me say, 'I miss Shiv so much. I wish he would suddenly appear. Weekends just aren't the same without him.'

Shiv, after a few unsuccessful romantic interludes, decided that he would settle for a proposed match after all. However, he wished to get to know the young lady better before committing himself. They met, they saw, and she conquered! Everyone was pleased.

I, for my part, picked up the very friendship that I had actually run away from. He was my former classmate who had revealed his feelings for me much earlier. As we were from different communities, I had been fearful then and even more insistent on leaving for overseas. However, his feelings for me had remained steadfast even during my absence. Furthermore, his unflinching loyalty to my family during moments of despair touched my heart. My parents were all praise for him.

When I asked Shiv for his honest opinion, he said, 'Your suitor is the only friend who has stood by me through thick and thin when my first girlfriend dumped me. When I was ready to give up, he took time off from his own duties to stay constantly by me and give me confidence. It would be hard to find a better person anywhere.' A lot had happened during the two years I had been away, and my young man had proved to be indispensable to the family. I felt duty-bound to give this persevering and noble youth a chance.

Tony

When Dad and Mum celebrated twenty-five years of fairly blissful marriage, Shiv and I stood proudly beside them, smiling for the various cameramen among friends who had been invited to join us in the celebration dinner held at home. We were both romantically involved by then and nurturing thoughts of happy marriages. I was sure that I too one day would be hosting a silver jubilee wedding celebration with my wonderful Tony. Shiv, standing beside his fiancée, gave me a knowing smile.

When the photographs were ready to be viewed, it was hard to believe that our family members could be so photogenic! Dad and Mum, looking regal and younger than their mid-forties, wore peaceful, contented smiles while Shiv wore a cheeky, dimpled one as he stood next to his blushing fiancée. I, bespectacled, and with a slight tendency to be plump, could not believe that the radiant beauty in a blue organza sari was me. With my long hair coiled into a bun at the nape, adorned with a rose, I stood shyly beside my Prince Charming. Of medium height and build, my beloved had the physique of an athlete. He was oblivious of how appealing he could look with his wavy hair and thick moustache. How transforming love could be, and how its promise of a presumably wonderfully magical life ahead could ignite a glow in the heart that could show on the face! I often secretly took out the silver wedding anniversary album to view, and my fingers would lovingly caress these photographs that were surely a preview of a most happy marriage to come.

A few months later, Shiv walked down the aisle with his lovely lady. He was ready to embark on a different journey in life, in a new country, and he wanted his sweetheart beside him. Shiv went first, while his wife honoured the remaining term of her contract with the company she was working for. At the end of her contract, arrangements were made for her to join her anxiously awaiting husband. When we saw her off at the airport, I could swear she was blushing as profusely as she had on her wedding day. Ah, love—the lovebirds were soon reunited thousands of kilometres away, ready to set up home together. With them went the best wishes and blessings of the elders.

Promising Love

The dashing young man who had put the glow on my face had started a new job and was on the first rung of the ladder to success. He declared, 'When love is reciprocated, it is sure to bring good fortune. Your love is going to make me stronger and more determined than ever to succeed and provide you with the best.'

I was deeply touched but attributed his new-found success to his sheer diligence and steadfastness to make it in life. I was very much in awe of him and all that he did and intended to achieve. When he was on the third rung of the ladder to success, he surprised me one evening. 'I have something serious to discuss and wish to do so as soon as possible.' I was alarmed, but something told me not to delay the matter. When we were alone later that same evening, he professed, 'I love you more than I have ever loved anyone. If you are happy with me and have faith and trust in me, will you marry me?'

I was so taken aback, I lost track of the number of rungs that were on that ladder to success! Now, I no longer had to stand back and watch in awe – I was being invited, most lovingly and sincerely, to climb every rung of that ladder with him, beside him. Of course, I said, 'Yes. There is nothing I want more than to be with you for the rest of my life.'

A Clash of Cultures

Dad, Mum, Shiv, and his wife Sil were supportive, but it was not all smooth sailing. As we were from different religious backgrounds, some of the elders on both sides were not exactly thrilled to bits at the thought of us uniting in holy matrimony. Very often, during the course of the months that followed, I was filled with trepidation. Was I making a mistake? Would I be strong enough to smile bravely and weather whatever storms arose? But hey, I had no reason to worry, had I? My beloved constantly reassured me, 'All that matters is that we stand by each other, no matter what, and the elders will surely relent and warm up to us.'

There was much truth in what he said as we were both God-fearing and filial to our elders, except for the fact that we refused to be not married to each other! Furthermore, he had said, 'We will be paying for all the wedding expenses incurred from our own earnings. This will prove how seriously we intend to build a secure future together.' With such a determined and far-sighted husband-to-be, I was probably the luckiest girl on the planet!

In the meanwhile, I tried my utmost best to win over my future in-laws. I visited them when occasion called, in the company of my Prince Charming. I dressed in a manner which would appeal to them every time I did so, which meant donning traditional outfits, mostly. The children in the family warmed up to me almost immediately, eager that I would be tutoring them.

In later years, some of these children would grow closer to me. They seemed to understand me better than their parents did. I, on my part, found them endearing for they were open in their adoration and made no unkind remarks in a foreign tongue that I barely understood. Neither did they utter any unwelcome forecasts. I thanked God that they were too young to be tainted with prejudice.

The elders were doubtful that I would ever be able to speak their language or cook the kind of food that was enjoyed by my young man. They strongly believed that religion would pose a point of contention, especially when children came along. They hinted that I might consider converting, but my Tony insisted he loved me as I was. I was never sure where I stood with them.

My beloved advised me to keep smiling and never reveal that I was affected. He told me to be brave and have full faith in him. He promised that he would handle all matters pertaining to our relationship diplomatically. He assured me that everything would go exactly as we pleased, but for that moment, I had to bear with all that was happening around me, or being said within earshot.

Juggling Two Careers

Busy with my own career, I had also started helping my beloved with the paperwork involved in his job. He inspected damaged vehicles and was required to come up with an estimate of the damage after each inspection. This job required him to entertain managing officials of underwriting firms. As such, he, who had always been against beer and alcohol, had to entertain them with the same. Some of the managers pointed out that he could stand to lose potential sponsors if he did not join them for a drink or two at least. He battled with this advice for a while, and then compromised. We decided that he would draw a line after the second drink, at the most.

My Prince Charming requested that I accompany him during the times I had no tuition classes on. I would sip at a soft drink while he discussed business matters with managing officials. I was reassured by the manner in which my beloved conducted these business-cum-entertainment sessions. He also made a few friends among the managing officials. These same friends were often included in our outings, sometimes to my dismay. They were admittedly courteous and respectful, but as long as they were there, drinks were a necessary feature. This discomfited me.

It slowly dawned upon me that I no longer seemed to have time for my own friends, whom I had unwittingly started to neglect as my relationship progressed. I had not realised that they had been gradually fading into the background when I started to give all my time and attention to my beloved. Before I knew it, he was my only friend.

The Engagement

Our forthcoming engagement distracted me from certain growing anxieties. There was much to do and little time left to complete all tasks necessary in preparation for one of the most important events in my life. Although there was some family discord with regard to traditions to be observed and choice of auspicious dates, I was fairly blissful, perched on cloud nine. As far as I was concerned, things would surely get better. Wasn't that what my Tony always said?

The function, held in my parents' home, was attended by our immediate relatives and some close friends, mainly his. Some snide, even racist remarks were made by certain snobbish relatives from Tony's side of the family. Dad, who had overheard them, maintained a stiff upper lip and did not retort for he wished for his little girl to blissfully exchange engagement rings with her chosen one, and not bitter words with her future in-laws.

After rings were exchanged in the presence of all our guests, a beautiful cake was brought to the tea table by my mum, who was beaming at us with pride. Being a simple and loving lady, she was oblivious to the sinister undercurrents brewing among some of our guests. The double heart-shaped engagement cake, iced with pastel pink and blue flowers, was cut together by Tony and me amid cheers and applause. Mum then expertly divided the rest of the cake and speedily served it to impatient relatives and friends. As they left, most of our guests wished us well and declared that they were eagerly awaiting wedding invitations. While shaking hands with them or returning hugs, I could not help observing that some of our relatives, on both sides, wore somewhat cynical expressions. Perhaps it was only my imagination. It had been a rather hectic day, after all.

Womanhood

(1978–)

The Marriage

'Tony, my darling Tony, today, and until the time I breathe my last, we shall be together. You will be my husband, my guide and the captain of the ship that we shall set sail in, a few hours from now. Tell me that you will always be there, whether the seas are calm or treacherous. I shall be obedient, even subservient, for I know that you are wise and of sound judgement. All I ask is that I shall always have that special place in your heart, and that you will never let go of my hand, which I place most trustingly in yours.'

Nurturing this idyllic vision, I prepared for the most momentous event in my life – my marriage to Tony, my Prince Charming, the most understanding, warm, loving, gallant young man who would make the rest of our lives together as wonderful and peaceful as he possibly could. I would, of course, do my part, to make this union a remarkably compatible one, despite the fact we came from different religious and social backgrounds. As long as he was by my side, no mountain would be too high to climb, or any ocean too deep to cross.

We were wed that beautiful morning, with celebrations that continued late into the evening. It started at the office of the registrar of marriages, followed by a traditional ceremony at the abode of my father-in-law. I had draped a heavy beige sari with a dark-brown border and held a bouquet of flowers. My hair had been neatly carried up in a fetching Japanese knot. I had never received so many admiring glances. My Tony looked dashing in his light-brown suit.

The front of my father-in-law's house had been decorated with lush banana plants tied to the poles of the porch, strings of freshly picked mango leaves, and sprays of fragrant flowers. The ethnic atmosphere was further enhanced by the sound of shrill music from traditional trumpets and the beating of Indian drums, with the music reaching a high-pitched climax at the exact moment that my beloved fastened the symbolic *tali* of matrimony around my neck. Now we were truly man and wife. Somehow, this vibrant ritual overshadowed the rather subdued ceremony held just hours earlier at the registration office.

After a hectic session of being photographed as a couple, and then with relatives and friends, Tony and I settled down on a sofa to catch our breath. We were, however, almost immediately flanked by well-wishers and those who were bent on giving us a dose of good-humoured teasing. After some refreshments, the guests dispersed, promising to attend a grand dinner scheduled to be held later that same evening.

At 7.30 p.m. that evening, Tony and I made a regal entrance into the beautifully decorated reception area of the town hall. For this reception, I was clad in a peacock-green heavy-brocade sari with complementing jewellery. My hairdo, thankfully, had remained intact. Again, I was swamped by compliments. I had never felt so beautiful in my whole 24-plus years! Tony still wore the same light-brown suit but had changed his shirt. He had never looked more fetching.

Seated right at the centre of the banquet table, I shyly looked up and saw that the hall was full to capacity. I felt deeply honoured that so many relatives and friends had turned up to grace this momentous occasion. Among the guests present were some dignitaries, further honouring the families on both sides. The dinner served was declared superb, and nobody was unsmiling. Everything had been well organised and catered for, with no details spared. In his short speech during the reception, Tony expressed his appreciation and gratitude to all those who had, in one way or another, contributed to the success of the proceedings of a most memorable day.

I could not help thinking, however, that the success of the entire occasion was mainly due to Tony, who had once again shown admirable skill in organising receptions. We had all been in awe of him when he had organised Shiv's wedding reception just over a year earlier. Still, Tony and I were sincerely grateful to those members of our respective families who had been supportive of our marriage and obligingly done their part to make it a success.

I recall how, at one point before our marriage, I had commented, 'Tony, our savings are almost depleted! At this rate, we shall have nothing left. Please, don't you think it would be wise to tone down a little?'

Appeasing Two Cultures

With a reassuring smile, he had replied, 'Sweetheart, we have to ensure that none of our elders lose face in any way. The money spent at this juncture is sound investment for a happier and blessed future for the both of us. Let not anyone say that we have not paid homage to our respective cultures. We are still young and have ample time to replenish our savings. For now, we must adhere as closely as possible to all traditional requisites, in the hope that this will ultimately win over the hearts of those family members who still harbour misgivings to our matrimonial alliance.' The wise man had spoken.

We, the newly married couple, were commanded to bide some time in Tony's father's house until certain ceremonies had been carried out. We complied, wanting to start our new life on a happy note and with the blessings of the elders. I found this difficult to explain to my folks, for they were aware that Tony and I had already planned to rent a small house until the time we could afford to buy one. However, not wanting to upset anyone, they let it be. For that matter, Tony's people were also in the know of this, but they placed greater importance on tradition.

We dutifully observed the deemed necessary cultural practices for newly-weds, conducted mainly by a few rather insistent members of Tony's family. Finally, after they were fairly convinced that I was not likely to deprive them of the homage and respect that Tony had duly shown them thus far, they released us to be on our own. I sheepishly wondered if they could sense my relief!

Home Sweet Rented Home

Overwhelmed with joy at the thought of finally being able to set up my home sweet home, though a rented one, I set about the delightful task of decorating the little terrace house with the airs of a professional interior decorator, much to the amusement of my adoring (and diplomatic) husband. If he felt that there was something not in harmony with the prevailing decor, he would hint at it subtly with remarks like 'That vase is beautiful, but perhaps it would look better just next to the television set, don't you think?' and 'Maybe we should lay the rug just beside the bed so you don't catch cold when you step on the floor first thing in the morning. You know how prone you are to sneezing!' My Tony was such a darling.

Dad and Mum, aware that all our savings had been channelled towards the matrimonial conventions and reception, delved deep into their own pockets to enable us to furnish our nest fairly comfortably. Tony was touched by their warm affection. As usual, they had risen to the occasion. Little did he and I know then how often this endearing pair of occasionally feuding warlords would put aside their own differences to help navigate us through the stormy seas that would be challenging our ship.

During the mornings and afternoons of the days that followed, Tony and I pursued our respective careers. He travelled a fair deal, by car, in the course of his duties, which was investigating accidents or thefts of vehicles, besides assessing damage to them. Tony often had to drive to workshops located in towns in the south but tried his best to return the same evening. I would finish cleaning the house, put the clothes out to dry on the line, and proceed to the centre where I tutored students after school. Later, in the evening, Tony would pick me up, and after dinner, we would go home. That was the original plan, but sad to say, there soon came a time that it was hardly adhered to.

As mentioned earlier, Tony's job also entailed entertaining business partners and executive officials of underwriting firms. This had been the case even prior to our engagement, but Tony had then constantly reassured me that the entertaining would be reduced to a minimum once we had tied the knot. While we were courting, I had accompanied him on some of his business outings. Tony would have a drink or two with these key personnel, hoping he could secure more business. He had sometimes chided me if I appeared reluctant to join him. Tony would declare, 'You are my right hand. When you are beside me, I feel more confident. Also, you are my lucky charm! When you are with me, I always get more assignments.' How could I not give in after such charming compliments? Not wishing to disappoint him, I even learnt to nurse a warm brandy. It was supposed to be good for those with a sinus problem.

After marriage, it became almost impossible for me to accompany him on such occasions. Earning from tuitions was mandatory in order to replenish our savings. Also, there was a growing demand for tuitions at home. I fervently hoped and prayed that Tony's business contacts would not be a bad influence on him where drinks were concerned.

While we were still courting and Tony had decided to start his own business, he had been unable to recruit reliable staff. Sensing his despair, I, in my enthusiasm to be indispensable to him, had said, 'Let me help you with the paperwork until you find someone reliable to run your office. I cannot type at lightning speed, but I shall try my best to get your reports ready on time. Just give me a good sample or two to study and follow.' He was deeply touched, for he knew that I had hardly used a typewriter. I had only toyed with Dad's obsolete Remington, which graced his desk in the study.

Each time a report had gone out without a hitch, Tony would thank me repeatedly. He was most appreciative and never failed to tell me, 'I am so grateful to you for all the time and effort you have put in.' This expression of gratitude was almost always followed by an affectionate kiss and a warm hug. It was a triumph for us both when a report was submitted successfully without any amendment required. I was touched by Tony's implicit faith in me; he had so much confidence in my untrained ability. I actually felt important. It was this sheer belief of his in me that saw the initially amateurish-looking reports gradually transform into more professional documents. Goodness, Tony was truly a boost to my ego, although he kept me constantly on my toes!

Busy, Lonely Me

After marriage, I was still in charge of the mounting clerical workload in Tony's office. It was no piece of cake juggling the paperwork and the increasing demand for tuitions. However, I trudged on, smilingly. It was crucial to me that I never complain, or let my husband down. I wanted him to always be proud of me, and need me.

Slowly, however, as the weeks passed, Tony often failed to pick me up as scheduled. Each time I called him from the tuition centre, he promised, 'I'll be there in just a few minutes.' He seldom appeared before at least an hour had passed, and I found it increasingly difficult to keep smiling and pretend that it was nothing to get upset about.

Initially, there would be a few pleasantries exchanged over dinner, but gradually, no conversation would prevail. All that kept going on in my head was 'How many drinks has he had?' I began to suspect that my Tony more often than not exceeded the 'two drinks at the most' limit!

Though I tried very hard to keep my cool, as soon as we had reached home sweet rented home, I could not restrain myself from expressing my disappointment at his tardiness and disregard for the promises he had so solemnly made. 'What is happening, Tony? You promised to reduce the entertainment sessions to a minimum! Why can't you just take your business friends out to lunch or dinner minus the liquor? These drinking sessions are becoming a daily ritual!'

Tony would laughingly respond, 'Relax, sweetheart. There's nothing to get worked up about. It's only a passing phase.' Sensing I was not convinced, he would continue, 'Do you think I enjoy wasting time and hard-earned money on people who may never even reciprocate? The problem is that it is extremely competitive in the business world. Every adjuster out there is trying his best to secure assignments. I have to humour and oblige these insurance company managers and officials so that they give me their full support. How else can I give you all that I so want to give you?' Confused, I wondered if I had been too impulsive, too unreasonable.

During the months that followed, I held my tongue each time that Tony was late. I tried to be more accommodating and tolerant. I had to give him a chance.

Pregnant with Hope

It was a most euphoric moment when, after five months of marriage, the gynaecologist confirmed that the stork would be visiting us towards the end of the year. My joy knew no bounds. Tony was over the moon, and I felt peace welling up within me. 'At last,' I comforted myself, 'this will definitely be a turning point in our marriage. Now, Tony will surely spend more time with me, planning for the future of this precious being growing inside me. This baby will evoke all fatherly instincts within him. Surely, nobody could be more responsible than a would-be father. At last, I shall have him come home early.'

Dad and Mum were beside themselves with excitement. They were going to be grandparents for the first time! Shiv and Sil had decided not to have a child until a little later, for they wished to focus on their respective careers, without distractions of any kind. However, they received the news joyfully and promised to be home before the baby 'landed'! Tony's folks were equally elated and excitedly talked about the baby to come, especially speculating on the baby's gender and looks. Obviously, this baby already had a fan club even before its arrival.

My pregnancy was a delight. I was extremely cheerful and optimistic about the two careers that I handled, often surprising even Tony with my new-found drive. After all, nature had now equipped me well for the battle that would surely be my victory.

I typed Tony's reports cheerfully, hardly complaining if there was too much expected of me, too soon. This sometimes happened when there had been a spate of vehicle thefts and the insurers urgently required the adjuster's reports on his findings. When the completed reports had been neatly compiled, I would hand them over to Tony with a smile. Tony would then sign them and put them into a prepared envelope, to be handed over to the insurers personally, or forwarded by courier. He was probably greatly relieved that I had not transformed into a grumpy mother-to-be with an uncontrollable urge to smother him with woes of morning sickness and battles with vicious varicose veins!

Renewed Joy

My students too found me in a chirpier mood, and I could reach out to them surprisingly more easily than I had ever been able to before. I began to look at each and every student in a new light. I realised in my newly enlightened state that each one of them had started out from infancy to reach this wonderful stage at which they had entered my humble classroom. Now, each parent was relying on me to do my bit in moulding the personality of his/her precious child. Yes, each was a wondrous gift from God.

It thrilled me no end to think that I had been entrusted by the parents of my students to impart knowledge that I deemed fit for them. I thought to myself, 'What a great honour has been bestowed upon me! The mind of each child seated in front of me is pure, uncluttered, and trusting. Just think, I have been chosen to colour each one to the best of my ability. I shall do this most sincerely. Each of these wonderful children is going to leave my classroom with more knowledge, greater understanding of life, and a sense of humour! These are the very qualities I mean to inculcate in the precious child I carry in me.' The child I carried had waved a magic wand, and all students who have stepped into my classroom since that moment of revelation are my children too.

A wise person once said, 'A happy mother means a happy baby.' With this in mind, I held endless chirpy one-sided conversations with my unborn child, assuring him/her that Tony would be reformed by the time he/she arrived. I would play little tunes on the piano, for I had read somewhere that this would soothe the unborn child and perhaps arouse a musical interest in the years to come.

'Mum, tell me, did you also feel excited, or were you terrified as your pregnancy progressed? Did you continue to be active, or did you give up your more vigorous duties? Tell me, Mum, please! Just stop whatever you are doing and sit here, beside me. Tell me everything, please . . .' I would lovingly drag Mum to the sofa and make her sit down while I questioned her endlessly about how she had handled her pregnancies. Mum, nursing a cup of hot tea in her hands, would obligingly answer all my queries, while I listened, spellbound. There were also times that I drove her up the wall when I laughingly disregarded some old wives' tales.

Mum would sagely say, 'Do not stare at the lizards on the wall when they pass by. The baby might end up ugly.' I would giggle and gently chide her for believing such rubbish. Mum's eyes would grow round and fierce, and she would reiterate, 'I mean it! Seriously ugly! Now take this lovely picture of baby Krishna home and hang it right on your bedroom wall. Look at it first thing every morning!' I would subduedly nod and accept her profound advice before the round and fierce eyes led to a sharp pinch on my arm. She refused to let me help in the kitchen with sharp objects or cleaning fish, as these kitchen duties too were frowned upon during pregnancy. Mum cooked nourishing food for me and kept me well fed during the pregnancy. Tony was not forgotten—he was bullied into partaking of nourishing pregnancy foods too. He sometimes questioned Mum jokingly, 'Do you think I am also having a baby?' We all knew he enjoyed the attention.

Nothing could bring me down. Even when Tony still often returned late, I would greet him with a smile. After all, it would not be long now before he would have no choice but be drawn home hours earlier to be with his child—the precious little being that would surely steer us towards calmer seas and sunny skies. The birth of our child would make up for all the heartache and loneliness that I had endured from the start of marriage.

The weeks of pregnancy progressed into months, and I still greeted Tony as cheerfully as I could. At times though, it did cross my mind that when it was time for delivery, Tony might not be available to rush me to the maternity hospital. Dad and Mum harboured similar fears and tactfully conveyed their concern about this matter to Tony. He gave it some thought, and we both discussed ways to overcome it.

The Move Back Home

Also, I sometimes felt suffocated in the house that we rented; the inadequate ventilation was not very conducive to health. This became more apparent as the pregnancy progressed. Tony and I pondered how to solve this as well. We finally decided that it might not be a bad idea to move in with my folks, but only after some necessary renovation to the house.

If we were to renovate the house belonging to Dad and Mum, we would of course have to consult them and seek their permission, and blessings! It would only be fair that we pay the cost of renovation, which would ideally include a classroom (there was a growing demand for tuitions) and an office as well. Moreover, this business wing should not encroach on the privacy of Mum and Dad. Shiv would also have to be respectfully consulted.

When we brought up the matter to Dad and Mum, they were overjoyed, for more importantly than anything else, they could personally ensure the well-being of mother-to-be and, later, the baby. They advised me to seek the permission and blessings of my father-in-law prior to taking such an important step. My parents assured both Tony and me that any money the both of us invested in the existing house would never be a loss.

Tony's father, whose opinion was next sought, declared, 'I have absolutely no objection to the both of you moving in with your folks. It is very obvious that your liberal-minded parents have often regarded your husband, their son-in-law, as more of a son. I have no doubt that my son will be treated like a lord in their house.'

He really bowled me over when he graciously pointed out that while he still had some of his other children and grandchildren living together with him, Dad and Mum had their nest sadly empty. He was aware that Shiv was living abroad and intended to do so for a few more years, at the least. Tony's father felt that my parents should also be given the opportunity to enjoy the company of children and grandchildren to come. My once rather intimidating and seemingly detached father-in-law had become more loving and, thankfully, more understanding and accommodating over the months. I was greatly relieved.

Shiv, my only sibling, expressed relief that his sister would be cared for fully during her pregnancy and first-time motherhood. He was often concerned about the long hours Tony spent on the road, which found me alone in the rented house. Furthermore, Dad and Mum would not be neglected as age caught up, for he planned to remain abroad indefinitely. This way, Shiv could have a clear conscience while he and Sil pursued their ambitions.

Hammering in Culture

Tony and I soon engaged the services of a reliable contractor, and renovations began almost immediately. Again, Tony's elders stressed that certain beliefs had to be observed, such as the hammering in of the first nail during renovation and the shifting of the marital bed from the rented house to our would-be bedroom. I was not supposed to witness these activities, for the safety of the unborn child.

An auspicious date was determined for Tony and me to move into my parents' house. Renovations were still not fully completed, but we had to move in anyway as it was the last auspicious date before my delivery. Midnight often found me stealthily tip-toeing over brick, stone, and cement, to the freezer in the kitchen, to get my supply of ice cubes to crunch! Fortunately, I did not have too many peculiar cravings. If anything, Tony was the one who would suddenly long for a sour mango dipped in soy sauce with slices of red chilli, or a bowl of steaming-hot spicy noodles!

The months passed, and I was almost full-term. I still carried on with my tuition classes and the paperwork for Tony's business. I seemed to have boundless energy, probably fuelled by the positive thoughts of what would be my reward after the delivery. I was on top of the world, and I don't think there could have been a cheerier tutor (or secretary cum typist) in town.

Every review at the maternity clinic was much looked forward to. I would ask my accommodating gynaecologist the hundred and one questions that were on my mind, and he would smilingly answer them. He constantly reassured me that I was going to have a healthy baby and predictably uncomplicated delivery.

Dad and Mum armed themselves with all relevant paraphernalia to cater to the needs of the would-be arrival. I often heard Mum remind Dad, 'I want only the best, the softest, and the most comfortable. This is our first grandchild.' Differences that arose over the choice of colour were soon resolved when an ultrasound revealed that it was a princess who was soon to grace our humble abode. Tony was in seventh heaven while I bade a mental goodbye to Rita, my childhood playmate, whom I had appointed sister in my loneliness.

I believe that Dad heaved a sigh of relief when he learnt that it was a granddaughter on the way, perhaps because he still vividly remembered how Shiv single-handedly, or with a little help from Teta, was able to turn the living room upside down with his simian-like antics! The arrival of a grandson at this point in time might still prove a little too soon. A granddaughter, however, conjured up visions of sweet smiles, pretty ribbons, and delightfully predictable behaviour. He would finally have someone to obediently sit on his knee while he related anecdotes about his historic past.

Tony sometimes had reservations with regard to the unborn child. He occasionally expressed fear that the child might have some form of imperfection. It is not unusual for a first-time parent-to-be to harbour such baseless anxiety. I, though sometimes concerned myself, managed to alleviate such depressing thoughts with optimism instead.

In retrospect, I realise that Tony probably felt guilty that he had often failed to keep his promise to come home early to soothe the mind of the mother of his unborn child. He would often even sleep apart from me, fearful that he might accidentally nudge my abdomen. I tried not to show that I was both hurt and confused by his well-meant act. I had read that pregnancy usually brought a couple closer! I prayed that our daughter would arrive soon. Only she could be a catalyst to Tony's transformation for the better.

D-Day

In the wee hours of one morning, the contractions began, and there was a show of blood. I had been advised to look out for these signs as I was already full-term. Tony had returned home late the night before and had not responded favourably when I tried to awaken him with pleas of 'Wake up, Tony, please wake up! It's time for me to go to the hospital. Please, Tony . . .' When I found my efforts to wake him up were futile, I slowly walked to the adjacent room to inform Mum and Dad. They advised me to let him sleep it off.

Mum and I checked to see that the already-packed bag lacked nothing, while Dad got his car ready. They drove me to the maternity hospital. On the way to the hospital, I felt very excited and confident that very soon, Tony would have no reason at all not to cancel any uncalled-for business-cum-entertaining sessions with potential clients. I truly felt that victory would soon be mine. I was going to deliver my little angel unscathed, with a bit of help from my gynaecologist, of course!

I was prepared for delivery by a friendly nurse. I asked her if she had children of her own. She smiled and obligingly told me about her own experience. I was then shown to the labour room, where I eagerly lay, waiting for the contractions to come more rapidly. Dad and Mum sat with me for a few minutes, and after much reassurance that I would be fine, I managed to convince them to go home. It was almost 4 a.m.! Reluctantly, they did so. I smiled bravely as they walked out, not wishing to reveal that I was a little apprehensive about what to expect. Thinking that everything would soon be over, I strived to keep cheerful.

The Waiting Game

The hours passed, but nothing happened. My gynaecologist came in just after sunrise and did a quick check. He predicted, 'You'll probably go into full labour just after noon. Everything's going to be fine.' With a reassuring smile, he left me in the care of a capable nurse.

At 8 a.m., a tearful Tony arrived. He felt greatly remorseful about not having responded to my attempts to wake him up earlier that morning. He cried, 'I have failed to carry out my responsibility! I shall never be able to forgive myself! I have let you down! I'm so sorry . . .'

I had to assure him repeatedly that I was all right and that neither my parents nor I held any misgivings. I told him that I was actually glad that he had slept through what might have been an ordeal after a whole day's travelling. After an hour or so, I convinced Tony to go home for breakfast. I told him to tell the others not to worry. He reluctantly left but was back by noon with a pleasant surprise.

Shiv and Sil had actually arrived at our house a week before my delivery day. They had left for the capital, which was a two-hour drive up north, just the day before. Now, at noon, a grinning Shiv stood next to Tony! I felt blessed to be loved so much, but wait, did I detect anxiety on both their faces?

I was deeply touched when Tony requested to be beside me in the delivery room at the crucial time. This request, we were told, could be complied with, provided no other woman was in labour on the next delivery bed at that time. Just then, another mother-to-be was wheeled in, and my two gallant knights had to leave the delivery room.

I lay in awe as I heard the whoosh of fluid from the woman's water bag and the almost-instantaneous cry of her baby emerging into the world. Wow! That was quick! Never mind, noon was around the corner. A cleaning lady soon arrived to clean up the area just beside where I lay. 'She is not going to rest for too long after this,' I thought confidently. Well, she did not, but the afterbirth mess she had to clear was caused not by me, but by another two mothers-to-be who came and left with equally enviable whooshes! How I 'whooshed' my turn would come soon.

Tony and Shiv were waiting, and starving, outside. They seemed to have gone on a hunger strike; at least I was on an intravenous drip. When the room was clear, I sent for them and insisted that they go home and have something to eat. I told them to reassure all family members that everything was all right and there was just a slight delay. Reluctantly, they left after I promised them that I would 'wait' for them. With my kind of luck, I thought that was probably what would happen anyway.

At noon, my gynaecologist arrived and conducted another examination. He then decided that he would give me a hand by rupturing my water bag. Now we were getting somewhere, or so I thought. The water slowly seeped out—there was neither whoosh nor contraction. I was perplexed. The nurse could not enlighten me much. It was bad enough that I had skipped breakfast and lunch, but little did I know, I would also be missing tea and dinner! My lips were chapped, and I was a wreck. I was given painkillers but in minimal doses, for the safety of the unborn child.

My gynaecologist looked at the clock. It was almost 10 p.m. I had been in labour for almost twenty-two hours! Wearing a concerned expression, he told the staff to prepare me for a C-section. I panicked for he had told me earlier that he had always advocated normal delivery.

Here She Comes, Finally!

Suddenly, I felt them! The contractions started to come in powerful, painful waves. I alerted the nurse, who immediately alerted the gynaecologist. He swiftly turned around and told me not to push if I could help it. There was no way I could stop pushing. I felt as if my body was being controlled by a greater force. Soon, the gynaecologist announced that I was fully dilated but required an episiotomy to assist the dry delivery. I no longer cared what he had to do. All I wanted was to hold my child in my arms, the sooner the better!

I felt a pressure quickly moving down the birth canal and out of my body. 'All right, here she comes!' the gynaecologist announced, with much relief. I was the one in labour for almost a day, but the gynaecologist was the one who seemed pale and weary.

I had 'landed' my baby girl safely! She sneezed with gusto, and I heard Tony, who stood just outside the labour room, heartily declare, 'That must be my daughter! She sounds just like her mother!' I was exhilarated at the sight of my bonny baby girl. At last, she had arrived, she who would bring much-needed sunshine into our home.

The gynaecologist had discouraged Tony from coming into the room earlier, perhaps because he had anticipated some difficulty in delivering the child. He now assured me that the child was hale and hearty. He instructed the nurse to merely sponge the infant clean because it was rather chilly in the room. Meanwhile, he proceeded to stitch me up. He was amused at how cheerfully I had braced myself throughout what other women might have considered an ordeal. However, he advised me, in a fatherly manner, not to have my second child too soon.

I was then wheeled to my bed in the ward. The nurse smilingly brought a pink bundle to Tony and me. I held the precious, long-awaited sure-bringer of sunshine with triumph, and relief. Tony was beside himself with pride and joy as he admired his newborn daughter. Shiv, who had yet to start his own family, was in raptures over his adorable niece. The duo excitedly called relatives and close friends to inform them of the arrival of the little one. Soon, the proud grandparents came into the room, eager to inspect the new arrival. She was declared flawless! I smiled proudly as I looked at all the happy faces around me and silently thanked God for his benevolence.

The nurse then came in to give me some instructions on how to handle and breastfeed my little girl. She also reminded me of the exhaustion I had undergone in the labour room. I was too excited to sleep, but a wave of peace and calm slowly descended upon me. A new chapter in my life had begun.

Dewdrop

Dewdrop was a sparkling baby who brought endless joy to whoever beheld her. Every morning, after I had attended to her, I would proceed to complete any pending reports that Tony had to submit. I worked speedily so that I could be with my Dewdrop. While I typed away or edited any completed assignment, Tony would lie next to his darling girl, whispering sweet endearments into her infant ear. Later, Mum and Dad would attentively attend to her needs while I tutored and Tony proceeded to his destination for that day.

My beloved husband still travelled a fair bit and seldom returned before nightfall. Occasionally, however, he would give me a pleasant surprise by coming home early to be with Dewdrop and me. On such evenings, I wished I could just wave a magic wand to dismiss my students, just to be with my Tony and Dewdrop. I sincerely cared for my trusting students and needed the income, but it was so rarely that I got a chance to be with Tony, especially this new fatherly Tony.

Tony would sometimes take us for a drive to the seaside, and there, he would gently carry and cuddle Dewdrop, conversing with her in baby language, much to my amusement and delight. She, in response, would coo and gurgle, thoroughly enjoying the full attention her adoring father was giving her. Tony would introduce to Dewdrop the sun, clouds, sea, and horizon. Then suddenly, he would bend down and pick up a fallen twig to lovingly etch her name in the sand on the beach. He also collected seashells, which, later at home, he washed and counted, singly, in a premature attempt to teach her how to count! I watched him contentedly and prayed that this bond, which was forming so beautifully, would endure. God had been bountiful.

As Dewdrop grew, so did Tony's business. He was an honest and trustworthy man, and more companies began to appreciate the shrewd assessments he made in evaluating losses and damage in his field of work. With the increasing load of Tony's paperwork, and an even greater demand for tuitions, I was subjected to considerable strain. Tony, concerned about the stress I was undergoing, insisted that we engage a part-time clerical assistant to ease my workload. However, he requested that I oversee the quality of work done by the future assistant.

Though reluctant at relinquishing part of the workload to a complete stranger, I finally gave in. However, the amount of hand-holding, supervising, editing, and playing the middle-person between the evasive Tony and the exacting and brusque clerk was a different kettle of fish altogether! I often wished I had just carried on doing all the paperwork myself. I was used to his absence from the home office and accustomed to waiting patiently for estimates, photographs, and sketch plans for accidents surveyed. Nobody else was going to extend the same amount of patience and tolerance.

Days, weeks, and months passed swiftly by. Dewdrop was now a precocious toddler, charming her way into everyone's heart. Tony was thrilled at her ability to quickly grasp new words and phrases. His siblings often called and asked us to visit so that Tony's father could spend some time with Dewdrop. He had many other grandchildren, but he found our Dewdrop thoroughly entertaining. She was quite the entertainer.

It warmed my heart tremendously whenever my father-in-law (all six feet of him) would rush to the door, with arms outstretched, to scoop up Dewdrop, lifting her high above his head. She would whoop with delight and ask for a repeat performance. Of course, the doting grandfather was only too happy to oblige. Tony had been right—the elders were slowly relenting.

Tony lorded it in his father's house on those occasions, for Dewdrop would obey all his loving 'commands' to sing a little song, do a quaint dance, make various animal sounds, and the like. All the family members would surround the endearing little performer while she held court! I often found it hard to believe that this lively entertainer was actually ours.

Dressed in pretty frocks, with matching ribbons in her wavy hair, Dewdrop was a veritable doll. Her well-stocked wardrobe boasted a multitude of dresses and frocks of every hue and colour. She had more pairs of shoes when she was three than I had owned in my entire life! Tony, Dad, Mum and even I never returned home from any outing to town without having purchased a little something for her, be it an outfit, a toy, a book, or just a bar of chocolate. How I envied her, but I wished her no less. Her delight was my delight. Tony used to love taking photographs of Dewdrop, who simply loved to pose. The duo complemented each other and together finished rolls of film, while I indulgently arranged all photographs in the increasing number of albums.

Dewdrop often accompanied Tony to town, or just for a drive, while I was busy tutoring. This gave me immense satisfaction, for I felt a part of me was with my beloved Tony. I was willing to work hard but just wanted a happy family.

The Cracks Appear

Soon, unfortunately, I started to have misgivings. Tony would often smell of drink on his return from such outings, and this began to worry me. It worried me even more when, in this state, he would playfully throw Dewdrop up a little too high and then catch her. This game absolutely delighted Dewdrop, but my heart would be in my mouth! Call me a spoilsport or a pessimist, but to me, this kind of amusement was indicative of irresponsibility on the part of Tony. A gnawing fear began to germinate within me. Sleep on such nights was fitful for me.

The months rolled on, and Tony started to drink a little more than I sensed was necessary, or good, for him and the family. Our respective jobs were demanding, and the remuneration was just enough to meet our financial commitments. Tony was returning home late again, and it was taking on a regular pattern. Waiting up for him began taking a toll on my health. Heart-to-heart talks with him were unproductive. I wound up tuition classes even later at night so that I would not pace the floor, wondering if he was, yet again, going to break the promise that he had so solemnly made that very morning to come home on time.

As I locked up the classroom for the night, I would turn around every time I heard the sound of a car or saw the reflection of car lights on the glass pane of the window. Alas, it was only someone else's husband turning his car at the dead end. I would then trudge into the living room, feeling lost, confused, and weary.

Suddenly, Dewdrop would run out from behind the sofa, where she had been hiding and waiting to give me a scare! She would tug at my right arm, pull my hand, and try to 'scratch' away all the red ink marks that I had acquired on my palm during the day's corrections. I would smile again, pick her up in my arms, and take a walk along the quiet road outside. Singing softly to her, I would teach her the words of another new song, even while my eyes strained to spot Tony's car turning into the road leading to our house. All the while, I would be hoping, 'I am sure he will be here any minute now. Maybe, just maybe, he has not touched a single drop tonight . . .' Alas, it was only wishful thinking. I would finally give up, walk back home, and get Dewdrop ready for bed. I would then lie down beside her, often wondering, 'Where have I gone wrong?'

As soon as I heard the familiar toot of Tony's car, I would rush down the stairs, into the living room. Grabbing the key from the ornamental hook behind the door, I would rush to unlock the main gate. Mixed emotions would overwhelm me— relief, knowing that at least he was back home safe and sound, and annoyance, on reflection of the fact that once again, he had gone back on his word. A myriad of questions were at the tip of my tongue, the answers to many of which were by now predictable. However, the minute I saw Tony's tired expression, I would hold my tongue. I only wished, however, that he did not reek of liquor as he approached me.

Tony's returning home well past midnight was almost a daily occurrence. He would have a quick bath and make some remarks on the day's happenings while drying himself. Then he would kiss the sleeping Dewdrop and come downstairs again. Settling down comfortably in front of the television, he would have his warmed-up dinner. If I happened to show even the slightest sign of disapproval, chances were that he would refuse dinner or raise his voice, or sometimes, both. This was the last thing I wanted at that hour for he would then storm off to our room, often absent-mindedly locking me out.

If I made any reference to the incident the next morning, I would be lucky to be given an explanation for his late return the previous night. Even if any explanation was given, I was rarely fully convinced. However, to maintain peace at home, I most often gave him the benefit of the doubt, brushed away my fears, and put on a happy front. 'One day,' I thought, 'one day soon, Tony will realise that these late nights and drinking sessions are not going to boost his health or career. Also, our bank account is never going to flourish if this attitude of his continues.'

Mum and Dad seemed to guess my growing dilemma. They worked cohesively with me to keep our household going and were heaven-sent where Dewdrop was concerned. She had all the attention in the world while I tended to Tony's paperwork and my tuitions. Their cheerful, loving nature kept me going. Also, Tony was lucky that they always tried to see his point of view, sometimes frustrating me! They would always remind me of his positive attributes. Mum and Dad would diplomatically retire to their bedroom before 10 p.m. in order to give us space. I suspect that it hurt them to witness Tony's late and sometimes dishevelled return. How could I tell them about my fears and increasing anxiety that were brought on by Tony's irresponsible attitude? Yes, he was working hard, but definitely not at our marriage!

One Drink Too Many

Tony, once so patient and accommodating, now often lost his temper at the slightest provocation. I was his most frequent target, and once again, to maintain peace and harmony, I would refrain from expressing my opinions or revealing my shattered ego. He became especially irritated if I requested that he forego drink, at least for the day, should we go on a family outing—Tony, Dewdrop, and I.

His initial reaction would be one of hurt and disbelief that I even thought it necessary to make such a request. 'Are you implying that I have a drinking problem? Drink is not a priority for me. I am a family man, fully aware of my responsibilities. Sometimes, I just cannot refuse my friends, and I agree to have a glass. Can I help it if a friend buys another round and that drink parks next to my first? Come on, you yourself have seen it happen when you sometimes accompany me. Anyway, today I shall prove it to you. Get ready, both of you, and let's go.' I chided myself silently for having misjudged him. Was I perhaps unnecessarily harbouring fears that he could not do without drinks?

The outing would be a happy one, with Dewdrop perched on Tony's shoulders. We would visit the zoo or perhaps the butterfly farm, and Dewdrop could be heard squealing and shrieking with delight. It was obvious that the little girl simply adored her indulgent father. I trailed behind, feeling a little apprehensive about whether this was the way it would always be, and hoping that it would.

Tony would sense my unspoken sadness and tell me, as if he could read my mind, 'Don't worry, my darling. Your husband will always be a loving man. I know that your intentions are well meant. I will never let you down. We shall always be together.' With this, he would draw me closer to the both of them, including me in a warm, reassuring threesome hug. I often wished that life, for me at least, could click to a stop at such magical moments. How could I doubt such a sensitive, perceptive jewel of a man?

After a pleasant and hearty meal in a quiet restaurant, we would drive back, with Tony playing my favourite cassette. He would even whole-heartedly join in when the romantic lyrics came along. I would blush and look shyly at him, and we would exchange loving glances, recalling those sweet days of courtship. Ah, if only Tony could always be this way. As soon as we got home and I had given Dewdrop a bath and change, I would settle down beside Tony on the sofa contentedly. Dewdrop would leave play and snuggle up to us. She was not going to let go of Tony that day either. We both loved the man to bits, but with her, I was willing to share! It was as if the little one too realised that such moments were too precious and rare to let go.

Dewdrop and I could consider ourselves really blessed if such a rare day could go untarnished. Sadly, more often than not, during such heavenly moments, the telephone would ring and snap us out of our joint reverie, hurtling us back into harsh reality. Tony would rush to the cursed telephone, reassure the caller that he would see him shortly, and then try to pacify the totally disillusioned me. 'Don't worry, don't fret. I'll be back in a few minutes. We'll visit my folks this evening. Have a short rest before that, OK?' With that, he would get into his car and reverse out of the garage.

Watching him drive off, I would feel dejected and lost. Forcing myself to smile, I would find myself reassuring the puzzled toddler, 'Don't worry, Dewdrop. Daddy will be back soon.' Who was I kidding?

Of course, Tony did not keep his promise. By the time he returned, it would be rather late and he would have had a couple of drinks. I would diplomatically dissuade him from visiting his folks, as he had earlier planned. I did not wish to hear any untoward remark made by any member of his family. I had heard too many such remarks by then, and though the well-meaning folk did not mean to hurt me, I myself felt embarrassed at the thought that they might think me incapable of advising him. Tony would then have his shower, eat his dinner while watching television, and retire for the night.

Very few and far between were the days we actually spent together when Tony did not touch a drop of that dreaded brew. I knew he was most sincere about wanting to be with us and going drink-free sometimes, but he was finding it increasingly difficult to resist the temptation to drink and indulge in some camaraderie at the same time. There were definitely times when some such sessions brought in business, but mostly, they reeked of forebodings.

The weeks turned into months, and the months to years. Tony continued to indulge his friends and immersed himself in their regular sessions. Official work involving investigating, interviewing, surveying, and estimating damages would usually be over by late afternoon. However, Tony would enthusiastically volunteer to have casual meetings with various acquaintances, involving himself in their affairs rather than coming home as promised to help out with Dewdrop while I tutored so that Mum and Dad could have a break.

Tony was often roped in to help organise events and functions for his friends and their contacts. They recognised his skill at managing and networking, and they were only too happy to seek his counsel and assistance. They rewarded his efforts with drinks. I had often thought that if Tony had only charged a service fee for his organisation skills, life might have been easier. When I suggested that he do this instead of settle for drinks as a token of appreciation, he was incredulous. 'What? Charge my friends? Come on, surely you're joking?' I felt really small and kept my opinions to myself, many a time.

Mum and Dad soon realised that Tony was not to be depended upon for Dewdrop. The little girl would eagerly await her father's return. Tony would have promised to return early enough to take her to an open field nearby so that she could ride her new bicycle, but sadly, she was often left waiting. I would open the classroom door and see her look out for her father's car in vain. My heart would be close to breaking. Then I would see Dad, the doting grandfather, hoist the bicycle into the boot of the car. Dewdrop would squeal and eagerly hop in. Dad would give me a reassuring grin, despite his aching arthritic knee, and drive her to the field.

Mum would be watching me watch Dad with a knowing smile. Mum and Dad did not mean to take over Tony's role, but he left them no choice. They voluntarily went all out to make sure Dewdrop lacked nothing, while I determinedly threw myself into tutoring. I would open my classroom door before 3.00 p.m. and wind up only after 9.30 p.m. The tuitions provided financial security and kept me fully occupied. If Tony even appeared at 7.00 p.m., he would soon be off within the hour.

Dewdrop turned five and was in pre-school. Precocious as ever, she amused us all with her antics and remarks. Tony and I were proud parents but often felt awkward when well-meaning friends and relatives asked us why Dewdrop had no sibling. I felt guilty. Of course, I wanted Dewdrop to have a sibling, but I was stressed with the workload I myself had voluntarily taken on, from years ago—the paperwork, courtesy of Tony, and my increasing number of tuition classes. But more honestly, how could I tell anyone my fears that I might not be able to go through another pregnancy with Tony behaving the way he did?

One afternoon, while I was passing Dewdrop's bedroom, I heard her talking to herself. I was startled, and concerned. When I gently probed, Dewdrop admitted that she had an imaginary playmate, with whom she would discuss what outfit to dress her Barbie doll in, or what snack to prepare with her play dough. Her colourful menagerie, moulded somewhat awkwardly, but lovingly, from plasticine, also sadly lacked an admiring audience. Watching her race her toy cars to one end of the room and then run to the other end to race them back again, all by herself, I became angry with myself. How could I have been so selfish in fearing that I would not be able to handle another pregnancy while Tony still had to be reformed permanently? I had not considered my poor little daughter's lonely state! Dewdrop was undeniably the most wonderful gift that Tony had given me, but he had yet to give himself to us.

Growing Distant

Tony was on the road almost daily, but instead of returning home after his investigations had been completed, he would drop by at the club or a pub to have a beer or two. Meaning to stay for just an hour at the most, he would get so caught up in an interesting conversation the hours would simply fly. He would then call, apologise profusely for the delay, and try to make it up to me by taking me out to supper. If I was in a forgiving mood, I would accept the invitation, but if I was not, I would remind him, 'Look, Tony, I'm not superhuman to keep accepting your excuses for coming home late! I have also given my best for the day. Forget about me, what about Dewdrop? Is it so hard to make just a little time for our only child?'

At such times, Tony either would try harder to pacify me or would return home, have a quick shower, and make a fast exit without saying a word. The forbidding expression he wore on his face at such tense moments was to become a common feature in the months to come. The telephone calls once made to apologise for his delay and so clear the air were no longer granted to me. I was left behind, mostly because I had dared to assert myself.

I sadly realised that I was playing a losing game. If I wanted him to spend even the minimal time with Dewdrop and me, I had to accept him as he was, on his terms. Otherwise, it seemed as if he was slipping away from me, from Dewdrop. I did not wish to confine him to the cage of matrimony, but surely, I had the right to make some demands of him and his time, if not for me, at least for Dewdrop. I still hoped for a breakthrough—my marriage would yet be a happy, lasting one.

My chance finally came (or so I thought) when Tony left his then business partner to join a new company. I had an even more important role to play here, and Tony was to face greater challenge in his work. The workload for me was going to increase further, but I was prepared to undertake all extra duties, with the help of a more competent and accommodating part-time typist. Yes, this typist would have to cope better with Tony's sudden onslaught of reports and, perhaps, periods of no investigation carried out. Sometimes, even I was snapped at if I tried to clarify a point or two in a report that he wished to be attended to quickly. I was really trying hard so that it would not have to be redone. Many a time, amendments had to be made because of oversight on Tony's part.

Another Baby, Another Chance

Dewdrop was thrilled when Tony announced that he was planning his work in such a way that he could spend a little more time at home. She was also on cloud nine because her long-awaited sibling was finally on the way!

Yes, we were going to have another baby. Once, again, I felt a surge of confidence well up within me. I was more cheerful than I had been for a long time. I prayed hard that with a second child and a more promising job, Tony would find stronger anchorage at home. My parents fervently prayed for the same outcome. They loved us so much that they were prepared to babysit all over again, but hopefully, in a cheerier ambience.

Tony, perhaps inwardly aware himself that he was going off track a little too often for everyone's comfort, looked upon the pending arrival of his second child as pivotal in motivating him towards greater family solidarity. He had sheepishly admitted this once, in one of his more sober moments. This declaration had been a boost to my waning spirit at that time.

With the knowledge that another child was on the way, Tony worked at his investigations with renewed vigour. This was most reassuring and heart-warming. He also made more sincere attempts, with a little prompting on my part, to spend quality time with Dewdrop. She and I saw sunnier Sundays and a few brighter weekdays as well. Yes, things were going to be fine—I could feel it in my 30ish bones! I had been a fool to put off a second pregnancy for so long!

I honestly think that I was at my best when giving tuition during pregnancy. If I had even suspected this to be so when I was carrying Dewdrop, it was now confirmed when I was pregnant for the second time. I felt elated and developed even greater rapport with my students. I began to look at things more often from a younger person's point of view. I became aware that children just entering their teens could be wonderfully refreshing and entertaining! I was really going to enjoy my own children's company in the years to come.

Valentine's Day was the expected day of delivery for our second child. During the seventh month, the gynaecologist conducted an ultrasound to check if all was fine with the foetus.

I was amused when he literally jumped off his revolving stool to tell his nurse to get Tony in quickly.

Tony soon appeared, looking anxious. 'Is everything all right, Doc?'

The gynaecologist caught Tony by the arm and pulled him towards the monitor. 'There, there it is! Can you see it?' he exclaimed, pointing excitedly at something on the screen. Lying on my side, I could not make out what exactly they were looking at and what the excitement was all about. However, I was sure it was something positive, judging from the broad smile on his face.

'I'm not sure what it is I'm supposed to be looking for, Doc,' was Tony's perplexed response.

'Come on, can't you see the testicles?' the gynaecologist asked Tony, in disbelief, pointing again more closely. 'You're going to have a son, young man!' Tony was stunned momentarily. Then he drew nearer to the screen, as if to ascertain the phenomenon.

'I'm going to have a son! I can't believe it!' Tony turned to look at me, as if waiting for me to confirm it further. I too could not believe what I had just heard.

God is great. Earlier, we had both decided that we would not have more than two children, even if the second child happened to be another girl. When we had expressed this wish to the gynaecologist, he had not been too pleased. He personally felt that we should have more than two, thereby increasing the chances of having both a girl and a boy. When we were still adamant, he had frowned, but he did not pursue the matter. Now, everyone was smiling.

Back home, the news of a forthcoming grandson was music to my parents' ears. This would be their second male grandchild, for Shiv and Sil were already the proud parents of a charming toddler, Ritchie. Dad, who had once shuddered at the thought of impish little boys, had been rather taken in by this 'imported' grandson with a winsome smile!

Tony's father's eyes shone at the prospect of yet another addition to the family, and male at that! He fondly started referring to the little one I carried within me as Boss!

As my pregnancy advanced, so did my expectations. Sadly, real life does not boast the trimmings of a fairy tale. Tony tried his best to please both me and Dewdrop but often fell short. I tried not to feel overly disheartened when he still kept late hours, or if hardly a day passed that he had not had at least a few drinks.

I told myself, and Dewdrop, 'A little boy, perhaps, will be the key to Daddy's transformation. Just wait, my darling Dewdrop . . .' She could not fully comprehend what I had implied, but nonetheless, she gave me a very warm and reassuring smile as she rested her small palm on my protruding belly. Dewdrop too was eagerly awaiting the arrival of her baby brother, already a few days overdue. The gynaecologist had advised induced labour should there be further delay.

Wriggles

Wriggles was nine days late. We did not know it then, but our Wriggles was often to delay in most of his endeavours in the years to come! He finally made his appearance after one false alarm, but I went through relatively shorter hours of labour compared to Dewdrop's birth. He was born just a minute before teatime, at 3.59 p.m. Teatime, with cake or cookies, became his signature meal of the day from the time he was tall enough to sit at the dining table.

The same experienced gynaecologist helped to deliver this baby, whose appearance somewhat startled me. His skin was peeling as a result of being a 'mature' baby. He looked most wrinkled and wise, as though he had been through a lot in life already! The actual 'product' virtually had to wriggle out of his 'cocoon'!

Family members on both sides came to welcome this new long-awaited arrival warmly at the maternity hospital. I recall vividly a most amusing yet overwhelming incident that occurred the first time that Tony and I were alone with our little boy. Having made sure that nobody else was around, Tony, rather sheepishly, lifted up the fold of his newborn's diaper to reassure himself that he had actually fathered a son! Honestly, I did not know whether to laugh or cry.

Back home, Dewdrop and Wriggles were a sight to behold. She kept examining him, to inspect if everything was in place and to make sure that we had not been short-changed! Never having seen a male child so closely before, she was bewildered by what was between his legs and feared that something which should actually have been within had accidentally slipped out! We were beside ourselves with laughter.

The Giving Grandparents

I caught a twinkle of amusement in Dad's eyes, and I predicted that he was going to have loads of fun during his years of retirement. If, earlier, he had been at a loss as to what his recent status of a pensioner held for him in the future, it was obvious at that moment that these two grandchildren were his newly acquired career. Little did he know then that it was to be a full-time job!

Dewdrop had just started schooling then, and I had to adjust to a hectic daily schedule. Dad and Mum were highly supportive, and they practically took over the management of the two children. Tony and I viewed this positively, for it would have been impossible to find better child-minders anywhere else. This arrangement suited everyone just fine. Dad and Mum appreciated the fact that their nest was once again filled with happy little chirps. They planned their daily routine well to accommodate the needs of the little scholar and the unsteady toddler.

Tony was immensely grateful to his doting parents-in-law. He was on the road more often than before, and he grew tired more easily. I was greatly relieved that I could continue with my two jobs, without having to feel guilty. We really needed to build up finances. My children were safe, happy, and healthy. I did not have to worry about cooking interesting meals for the children, for Mum provided very nourishing meals, to the best of her culinary skills. Dad lovingly guided Dewdrop with her homework and encouraged her to read as much as she could. It was a happy family that lived in our humble home, but still, Tony was hardly around.

I was up to my neck in tuitions and supervising investigation reports. I chose to be in this situation knowingly, for I was determined to earn enough to allow my two children to pursue their future ambitions. They gave a significant meaning to my otherwise rather lonely marriage, and I wanted to provide them with the best. Tony claimed he was trying to make more time for his family, but sadly, the nature of his job, as well as an obvious lack of willpower, posed growing obstacles.

If we were lucky, Tony would take us out on the occasional outing with his friends and their families. While the children frolicked on the beach or in a park, the wives and mothers sat and exchanged notes on their children and spouses. The described antics of children were both enlightening and heart-warming, but the discussions on husbands and drinking habits were rather alarming.

I did not contribute much to these discussions, for Tony and I had, from before, agreed that whatever happened between us was always to be regarded as strictly personal, confidential, and even sacred—they were never to leave the confines of our home. Furthermore, while other husbands just stuck together in a group drinking and cracking jokes only meant for male ears, Tony would still stride over to the ladies' group and ask, 'Ladies, are you comfortable? Can I get any of you anything? Coffee? Ice cream, perhaps?'

Tony would come over to where I was seated and give me a warm hug. I would be the envy of every woman in the group when he enquired, 'Are you all right, darling? Anything I can get you? You always do everything for me. Let me get you something, at least . . .'

Tingling with pride, I would assure him I was fine. Watching Tony leave our table, the other ladies would declare that I was extremely fortunate to have married such a gem of a man! I thought so too, but nevertheless, I could not deny that there was a foreboding lurking in my heart: 'Oh, God, please never let my Tony become like the other uncaring husbands and fathers.'

Tony would then join the children in their play for a brief spell, much to their delight. They would squeal and scream as he tried to imitate them. Tony was, I had always felt, a little boy at heart—a gullible, vulnerable, and naive one. He could never put on the airs of arrogance and superiority that his friends seemed to exude. I could see through their false sincerity, but my trusting Tony was oblivious and refused to believe that his friends were not as sincere as he was. Tony longed to be accepted by them, so he went all out to impress them.

My sweet, simple, sincere gem of a Tony was driving too close to a dangerous bend, cheered on by others who did not really care what his outcome could be. They wanted their jobs done, and they did not have an ounce of his well-being at heart.

Ram

However, one kind friend did have Tony's and our family's best interests at heart. This man, Ram, saw to it that the children and I got some family time with Tony. Ram was a very close friend to the family and a self-appointed younger brother to me. He collaborated with Mum and Dad to plan an exciting overseas vacation for us. He was far-sighted enough to plan this a few months in advance so we could take advantage of Dewdrop's school festive break.

That festive break, Dad and Mum encouraged Tony and me to go for a holiday with the children. They big-heartedly gave us a cash gift to motivate us towards taking off on a family holiday. Wriggles and Dewdrop were thrilled at the thought of going overseas. The destination chosen was not very distant, but nonetheless, a very popular one with tourists travelling on a budget. Medan and Lake Toba were where we were headed, accompanied by Ram.

Ram had once assisted Tony in his job. He looked up to Tony very much but was not too keen on continuing with surveying. They had also enjoyed drinking together for a while, with other friends, but Ram soon left for a more satisfying career. I suspected that he had found it hard to turn down Tony's constant invitations to drink.

The efficient Ram organised the entire holiday and lovingly helped with the children. At Changi Airport, Dewdrop and Wriggles excitedly ran up and down the duty-free arcade, trying hard to get the adults to buy them some items that caught their fancy. Tony obliged the best he could, while Ram picked up the rest! The generous Uncle Ram was flanked on either side by a grateful child. The still-single Ram was on top of the world, probably imagining what life would be like when he settled down and had his own family.

When we boarded the plane, I was very excited for the children. Wriggles, sadly, decided to fall asleep just as the plane was taxiing prior to the take-off! So much for his first plane ride! Dewdrop, however, was in awe of all that she saw from her seat by the window. As I looked at her from my seat, I prayed that my children would see many more days as happy as that one. I also noticed that Tony had started his holiday with a drink.

The three days spent on the Indonesian getaway were a pleasant change from mundane routine. We visited several picturesque towns on the itinerary. Each was quaint in its own way. Berastagi was especially pleasant, with its cool air and horse-drawn carriages. As we rode in a carriage, we looked admiringly at the clean little cobbled roads and souvenir-decked stalls around us. The children happily munched the delicious roasted groundnuts that appealed to the adults as well.

The Tumultuous Lake

The idyllic holiday was soon to take an alarming turn. Tony insisted on doing something foolhardy while we were in the hotel on the brink of Lake Toba. Lake Toba is the largest crater lake in the world and is located in North Sumatra, Indonesia. The lake occupies the caldera (cauldron-like crater) of a super-volcano. It is a very scenic sight and was the highlight of our family vacation. Swimming in the lake proper was discouraged, for the depth drops off very quickly and it is estimated to be as deep as 500 metres. Also, the volcanic crater had its own strong currents.

Tony got into the hotel pool, which was cordoned off from the lake, for the safety of hotel guests, and slipped under the safety cord to enter the prohibited zone. I watched, with my heart in my mouth, for Tony was not a swimmer! He held on to the safety cord behind him, for support, but I was still fearful, for he had downed a couple of beers while relaxing in the room earlier. Thrilled, he beckoned to Dewdrop to join him. Dewdrop had started taking swimming lessons, and she was a fairly good swimmer for her age. I could see that she was just waiting for an invitation to slip into the rippling deep-blue waters. I tried to protest, but neither would listen. A boat sped very close past them, the driver of which shouted at them to get back to safety. Dewdrop, oblivious of the close shave, was screaming with delight next to her father.

I turned around and spotted Ram, who was watching them in great trepidation. He too called loudly that Tony and Dewdrop get back to the cordoned area of the pool, but it was to no avail. Ram gave a loud sigh of frustration and stood beside me, where I was keeping an eye on Wriggles, in the children's pool. With bated breath, we watched the daring duo tempt fate. They were holding on tight to the cord, but they were in a very dangerous zone.

'What on earth has happened to the Tony I knew before he got married? He has changed so much! He used to advise me against drinks and taking risks. Look at him now! He is jeopardising not only his own life, but his daughter's as well. Haven't you tried to talk to him? How can you just remain quiet while he does what he wants all the time? Haven't you got a

right? Come on, you're his wife and the mother of his children!'
Ram snapped at me, driving me to tears.

'What can I say, Ram? Do you think I have not tried? You
have known us for so many years. Initially, I thought I could
win him over with love. Now, love is taken for granted. If I
open my mouth to check him or query his actions, I am silenced.
He threatens to walk out, taking the children with him. I have
even pointed out to him that, perhaps, that would be the right
thing to do, except that I go with him. I have even admitted
that perhaps it was a big mistake to have moved in with my
folks, but when he cools down, he immediately confesses that
moving in with them was the most sensible thing we could have
done. What would you do if you were in my shoes?'

Before Ram could answer, we heard shouts of encouragement
followed by peals of laughter. Encouraged by Tony, Dewdrop
had swum a few metres out into the cold, inky waters and back
again. My heart nearly stopped beating when a passing ferry
missed Dewdrop by mere inches! At this point, Dewdrop grew
very much aware of the danger she was in. Visibly shaken, she
swam back to the safety of the hotel pool. Tony mutely followed
suit.

Unknown to Ram and me, Wriggles had witnessed his
sister's close shave. He tried to leave the children's pool to get
to his sister. I pulled him back and hugged him tight, fearful
that he would slip into the pool proper. Thank God it was our

last day in Indonesia. There was greater security in mundane routine.

The Loving Siblings

Wriggles and Dewdrop were inseparable playmates once Dewdrop's homework had been attended to. Often, Dewdrop would have a strong urge to abandon her homework and join Wriggles in his homework-free zone populated by Lego pieces and Ghostbuster vehicles, slathered with very convincing slime. Unfortunately for poor Dewdrop, her hawk-eyed mother would step out of the classroom just then, swoop down on her, and direct her immediate flight back to her desk!

Wriggles would watch such 'cruel' scenes in puzzled dismay, perhaps subconsciously thankful that he had been spared. Little did my baby boy know that similar ordeals loomed for him too, on the distant horizon.

Tony would often say that I pushed Dewdrop too hard, but when she brought home a report card that would please even the most discerning parent, he would smile with pride. Dewdrop was *his* clever daughter! I would smile too, because I had made him smile. Anyway, Dewdrop was in a very competitive class, and she had to get used to the pace. We lived in very challenging times.

At such times, Wriggles would be told by his father that he also had to make his parents proud. While Dewdrop sneered discreetly at the stricken Wriggles, her mother, as was her style, would second such academic expectations! Wriggles, daunted, would seek refuge behind the sofa until the clouds of great expectations had drifted well away. Dad, seated in his usual armchair, would peer over the rims of his glasses, highly amused. Such precious moments were the essence of our family life.

Tony's Turmoil

The number of my students steadily grew. It was a blessing, for Tony was encountering a few problems with his partner, who was becoming rather overbearing. Tony would try to meet the deadline and handle the assignment to the best of his ability. Yet he became a target for brutal criticism. Frustrated, he would march out of the office, to try to rectify the so-called oversight. I would watch him silently, fully aware that anything I said might touch a sensitive nerve. I knew, however, that I would be the one hurting at the end of such a day. Tony would return home late that night, not without drink. God, how I wished he had never taken on such a job!

A couple of years passed in like manner. Dewdrop was Tony's little helper when he needed a glass of water or a towel. This was when I was busy tutoring in the classroom, adjoining our dining room. Otherwise, I was willingly at his beck and call—not because he demanded it, but because I was just so happy that he was at home, with his family. I just needed to make sure that everything was done to make him comfortable and happy—so comfortable and happy that he would not need a drink to feel cheerful and relaxed.

Now, more than ever, I desperately wanted a happy home. I owed it to my two little soldiers. Together, we were on a crusade. We had to win this battle, no matter how long or tiresome. Even if our hearts ached when Tony uttered angry and hurtful words, mistaking our anxiety and concern for interference, we would bravely take them in our stride. He did not mean them really, as was proved the next morning, when, after sufficient sleep, he would be most remorseful and ask for forgiveness.

There were times when I felt Tony was slipping away from us, but I would quickly pull myself together. I would try some other strategy to help him out of the rut he was undeniably getting into. Our crusade simply had to succeed.

The Two Scholars

'Tring . . . tring!' rang the trishaw bell, announcing the punctual arrival of the trishaw man. Wriggles was still at the breakfast table, being coaxed to hurry. Kindergarten class commenced at nine sharp, and he had yet to finish his glass of milk. Socks and shoes would then face a vigorous battle with his reluctant feet, which, more often than not, tried to wriggle out.

Finally, after hugs and quick pecks on his cheeks from family members within easy reach, Wriggles would be pedalled away by the patient trishaw man. Craning his neck, he would turn and lovingly wave to me until the trishaw turned to the left at the junction and I was out of sight.

This was a daily ritual on school days. The trishaw man's services had been enlisted to send Wriggles to kindergarten as Tony often left to attend to his fieldwork after dropping Dewdrop off at school. Besides, Wriggles had learnt from the mischievous Dewdrop what adventures a 5-year-old might encounter while seated in a bumpy, seat-belt-free three-wheeler, allowing an unrestricted 360° view.

With the duo away at school, I would briskly attend to a few personal chores and get on with the office work. Amid editing reports, answering calls, and opening new files, I would prepare lessons for the day's tuition classes, as well as correct work that had been submitted by my students. Fortunately, Dad and Mum did the marketing, and they had taken over all other household affairs. I had enlisted the services of a part-time cleaner to assist with the general cleanliness of the house.

Moving in with my folks had indeed been a blessing. The children were never neglected, nor did they lack anything. Tony and I were able to pursue our respective careers, free of any worry about the well-being of Dewdrop and Wriggles. Both our jobs were demanding in their own ways. How much we earned all depended on how much effort we put in. Tony seemed to be more settled and determined to succeed in his career after Wriggles turned five. He still drank almost every day, but he was returning home relatively earlier. I was most thankful for this blessing.

Tony Tries

This arrangement also allowed Tony to join his friends for a couple of squash games, twice a week. I was glad that Tony, who had once been athletic, had a revived interest in exercise. After a good sweat, Tony would have a beer or two and return home, feeling healthier and happier. I was glad, for the exercise seemed to do him good, and at the same time, he was able to enjoy a little camaraderie with his fellow squash players. On squash evenings, he would return home fairly early and even offer to help the slightly nervous Dewdrop with her revision. Wriggles would quickly busy himself with a toy, hoping that his father would not try to educate him next!

Whenever I emerged from the classroom to witness such a cosy scene, I could barely stop myself from running to Tony and throwing my arms around him. So grateful was I that he was spending time with Dewdrop and Wriggles. Moments like this were golden and rare, and God was smiling down graciously upon me. An evening like this would also, most likely, end pleasantly for me, over a shared supper with Tony, or a television programme viewed together. As Tony lovingly put his arm around me, on the sofa, I blissfully thought, 'This is what I want in my marriage—a very considerate and loving husband spending time with his children and me. We mean more to him than the world outside, we mean more to him than his friends, his drinks . . .'

I was also thankful to my lucky stars that things were running smoothly at home and that Tony never considered Dad and Mum to be threats to his relationship with the children. They were not rivals competing for the children's affection, but family, united in their aim to provide the best for the growing children.

The doting maternal grandparents confessed that they found immense joy in the company of the ever-entertaining Dewdrop and the bent-on-taking-his-own-sweet-time Wriggles. The aging couple also found great satisfaction in knowing that they were needed and that their efforts were most appreciated by Tony, who often told them so. Truly, there was a very beautiful bond between Tony and my parents.

The Trouble with Tony

Life plodded on. The children were busy with schoolwork and some extra-curricular activities like music and art. Tony would give a hand in ferrying them to and from such classes, if he happened to be in town. Otherwise, Dad would be the 'minister of transport', making sure that Dewdrop and Wriggles were punctual for their respective classes. He was also always on time to pick them up afterwards. I would be confined within the walls of my classroom after schools were dismissed for the day, until past nine at night. It was only during these hours that students could attend private tuition classes.

It was extremely stressful for me during the times when Tony, promising to return home on time to drive either child to his or her relevant class, would show no sign of turning up. I would have to leave my students unattended while I tried desperately to get him on his handphone. If I managed to contact him, he would assure me that he was already on his way home to keep his promise. Dewdrop, or Wriggles, already ten to fifteen minutes late, would be getting into Dad's car when Tony would finally show up, hastily turn his car round and determinedly re-usher the child into his own car.

I would be totally at a loss, for I had no idea why he was that late, or if he would be keeping his promise to bring the child home after class. Also, I would sheepishly have to face Dad, who was equally at a loss. No exchange of words was required here; it was a scene that was becoming rather recurrent. The already-tense situation was further aggravated by the fact that Tony would often drive at breakneck speed from wherever he had been earlier, just to honour his word. Even worse, Tony would often have visited the club and had a drink or two.

Apprehensive that something untoward might occur while he was rushing, I diplomatically suggested to Tony that it might be better if Dad, who usually happened to be free in the afternoons and evenings, took over the responsibility of ferrying the children to and from their respective music and art classes. Initially, Tony protested, declaring that it was his duty and responsibility as a father to do so. I then tactfully explained to him that it was not becoming for a student to be often late for class or left waiting for transport home afterwards. Besides, Dewdrop was often both fearful and tearful minutes after the end of class, thinking that her father had forgotten all about picking her up.

Finally, we compromised. If Tony happened to be home at the time that Dewdrop or Wriggles had to attend such a class, he would drive the child there himself. If not, Dad would oblige. Who would be picking the child up after class would be decided only on the relevant day. I did not tell Tony then that I found it hard to concentrate on my tuitions when he subjected me to such suspense and tension. I was often at wits' end, juggling four sessions of tuition classes (with at least fifteen students in each) and arranging for the children to be ferried here and there. I could not bring myself to hurt Tony's feelings or let him feel that I thought he sadly lacked a sense of responsibility.

I tried my best not to let Tony feel that I had no faith in him, for even the slightest hint of my declining confidence in him would upset him tremendously. I feared that this would make him drink even more. However, I also did not want the children to be late for their classes or be reprimanded by the teacher for turning up late. I was deeply concerned about

Dewdrop's 'phobia' and did not want it to grow. I thanked God that Dad and Mum, now aware that I was confronting a mounting problem, gave me their full support in attending to the needs of the children. At times like these, my two feuding warlords laid their own battleaxes on the ground. They realised the growing complexity of my daily dilemma with Tony.

The Cracks Deepen

Tony was clearly in the wrong profession, but he clung to it tenaciously. He was convinced that his integrity and acumen in assessing damage to accident vehicles would stand him in good stead eventually. Alas, his partner continued to make life extremely difficult for him; he would pick on trivial matters and criticise Tony insensitively. He would also purposely delay payment. The delay in payment took on a regular pattern, and later, this very issue was to become a bone of contention between Tony and his unreasonable partner.

To me, it had been obvious from much earlier that the calculating director-cum-partner was preying on Tony's trusting and noble nature. When I had attempted to point this out to Tony, he would browbeat me, stubbornly insisting that there was some profit to be made, though nothing too big to shout about. It was then that I painfully realised, 'This is Tony's identity, an identity he is not willing to surrender for anything. We are running the office and business at a loss! We are never going to get anywhere if Tony refuses to acknowledge the fact that the terms of contract are all wrong, and his attitude, unrealistic.'

How and when on earth were we to break even when Tony's partner had imposed a 20 per cent claim on our gross collection? What about petrol and film processing expenses incurred, not to mention maintenance of Tony's vehicle and expenses for hotel accommodation? Tony's cases, more often than not, required him to stay overnight, more than two hundred kilometres away from home. Many a time, just to save cost, Tony would drive back home late at night. Exhausted, he would stop for a drink or two. He would cite exhaustion as an excuse for drinking in such situations.

I felt like a loser, again and again. Was this ordeal never going to end? My earnings from tuitions were being channelled to cover the costs of running the office, such as paying the part-time clerk, purchasing stationery, printing letterheads and continuation sheets for reports, as well as paying postage and courier charges.

Tony simply refused to acknowledge the fact that it was a no-win situation that he had contracted himself into! Each time I tried to make him see the light, he would put on a defensive front—an armour so impenetrable I just could not reach him, let alone reason! At times, he was even compelled to take on a few freelance cases to make ends meet. He was very uncomfortable when handling such assignments and took on only the very minimal; it was not the regular thing to do, but he had no choice.

I often had to hold my tongue when settling his accumulated bills at the joints that he frequented with alarming regularity. If I even dared to point out the increasing drink expenses, he would tell me that that was definitely the last time he would burden me with his personal expenses. He also, rather unkindly, remarked, 'If only my partner sent me payment due to me on time, I would never have to turn to you! This money,' he would stress, 'is *my own* hard-earned income, and I can do with it as I please!'

Remarks of this nature were like dagger stabs, for in reality, the money that was due was actually money that had been advanced from tuition earnings, to run the whole show. However, in all fairness to my Tony, the minute we were in receipt of a cheque for payment due to us, he would cash it and dutifully hand the money over to me to make necessary payments. He would take for himself only what was needed to meet his personal expenses, including bills for drinks at the club and squash court I. Sad to say, this amount was rather substantial, but I often had to hold my tongue.

Turbulence

This scenario continued for a couple of years. Our savings were nothing to shout about, and Tony's position was stagnant.

The only change, slowly but menacingly emerging, was Tony's shortness of temper and diminishing sensitivity towards those around, particularly me. At the slightest admonishment regarding his almost daily drinking, even later into the night and now including squash days, he would become verbally near-hostile, even threatening to leave the house.

Our arguments, once confined to our bedroom (at Tony's request), now often followed Tony's flight: down the stairs, through the living room, to his getaway car. He would turn a stubbornly deaf ear to my pleas to stay, even if only for just long enough for the two of us to discuss the issue amicably. Fuming, he would drive away with a vengeance, tyres screeching.

The manner in which he drove off really frightened the rest of us, who could only stand and stare, dumbfounded. Dewdrop and Wriggles would both have been shaken up, their happy play abandoned. The anger displayed minutes earlier would have jarred them out of the pleasant occupation they had been engrossed in. Dad and Mum, sipping their afternoon tea and within earshot, would have hurried towards me yet kept their distance, mindful that they might be considered intrusive.

I had requested Dad and Mum not to get involved, no matter how hurt they might feel or how strong their parental instinct might be to protect me. Still hurting and angry with Tony and myself, for bringing up the matter of his drinking, I would turn to look at my bewildered parents, asking them, 'Where have I gone wrong again? Has he stopped loving me?

I beg of you to be honest and not spare my feelings—I really want to know, to change if I have to so that I can recover the Tony I once knew, the Tony who had assured me that never a tear would he let me shed if I accepted him . . .'

How I missed that Tony! How I missed the tranquillity that prevailed whenever he had been around, and how I longed for Tony to help me with all the increasing responsibilities as the children grew. I had thought that marriage was about sharing and caring. It did not matter if we had no material assets or blue chips in the stock market; it did not even matter if I had to work even harder. All I wanted was a husband who could hold the family together and, perhaps, provide some companionship in my rather lonely marriage. Was that asking too much?

Lost at Sea

One fine day, Tony returned from the capital, looking down in the dumps. I had just closed the classroom and walked into the living room, when I saw his dejected expression. He turned to me and said, 'We need to talk.' I could sense it was something really serious. It had been ages since he had seemed this disturbed. If he wanted to actually talk, I doubted it was to do with drinking! We went out to have supper, and he never touched a drop. This was most unusual. Then he dropped the bomb: 'I do not know how you are going to take this, but it is something I have decided. I . . . . I'm quitting my job. I'm sorry to let you and the children down.'

93

What he had thought would upset me was actually music to my ears! Tony was leaving the very job that had turned my life into a nightmare! I was absolutely thrilled, and I was definitely not going to hide my feelings. At last, Tony had seen the light! At last, he was returning to us, his family. At last, the drinking was going to stop—well, maybe not at once, but I was sure it would not be long before Tony would cut down, and then, God willing, he might even give it up completely! The prospect was most elating, and I felt cheerful after a long, long time.

Tony was obviously relieved that I had taken the news in a positive spirit. He was, however, embarrassed about having to leave me to bear all expenses indefinitely, until he secured a new job. I tactfully pointed out, 'Look, in the past, when your payment cheque arrived, there was not a cent to spare after commitments had been catered for. Perhaps now, we shall be able to save a little, for there will be no more office expenses incurred henceforth. I shall work harder in the classroom, and the earnings from tuition classes should see us through until you find a new job.' I had a hearty supper that evening, followed by a long-forsaken deep sleep.

We did not know what nature of work would appeal to Tony next, but it was obvious that the line he had been earlier in was all wrong. In the meanwhile, he was going to take up a case against his ex-partner, suing him for accumulated payment long due to him. The whole procedure would take some time, but if the outcome was favourable, we would be able to recover what was long overdue. Tony himself admitted that his previous job had made him lose direction of his goals and caused him to neglect his duties to his long-suffering wife and children. I was touched and hopeful, truly hopeful.

Tony expressed a wish to venture into business, leaving him with more time for us and allowing him room for self-improvement. I promised him, 'I will give you my full support. I will take over all financial responsibilities, without any complaint, allowing you enough time to find your niche in life.'

A Fleeting Calm

Tony, with tears in his eyes, confessed, 'You know, my dearest, I have often, in the past, felt miserable after a tiff with you. I have always been aware that you have only been standing up for what is good for our children. Deep down, I have never stopped loving you. On the contrary, I have admired your guts and resilience. We both know how I have often raised my voice, using it as a weapon to silence you, despite knowing that you were pointing out facts. I have also abused your trust many a time, and I'm sincerely sorry. I have often wondered how you could tolerate the way I've been treating you all this while.'

I could not believe what I was hearing! He continued, 'Dad and Mum have never interfered but instead have given you, my wife, proper guidance. They have also more than made up for the love that I have often failed to give to our children, owing to my selfish and hectic lifestyle. I am most relieved and thankful to God that you have all stood steadfastly by me. Please continue to stand by me. I need your support more than ever.'

I cried with Tony and hugged him as if I would never let go. My original Tony had been recovered! Dad and Mum would be overjoyed. The children's father had come home, to stay.

The days that followed my captain's realisation of how he had been dangerously steering our ship off course were among the happiest in my marriage. Up with the rising sun, Tony would be bright and eager, ready to chauffeur Dewdrop to school after joining the rest of us for morning prayers. Mum and Dad looked greatly reassured, and Dad, who led us in prayer, always ended it with the hope that the Almighty would guide Tony to greener pastures.

As I gazed at my husband, I saw remorse in his eyes. The captain was truly such a wonderful man. I felt a shudder down my spine when I realised how I had nearly lost him. Now, I really had to be there for him. After all, it had taken a lot for him to confess that he had never really stopped loving me; it had just irked him whenever I pointed what wrong he had done. Now, there would no longer be any bone for contention; our ship should cross the seven seas in fairer weather.

Wriggles, craning his neck from the trishaw, now waved happily to the two of us as he left for kindergarten. He was a little more cheerful each morning, for Tony would joke with him, good-naturedly teasing him as he struggled through the rigmarole of getting ready for kindergarten. Wriggles had seldom seen his father in a playful mood, and he was pleasantly surprised that Tony could be such fun.

In the past, I had often sensed that Wriggles was rather uncomfortable whenever Tony was around. Tony had a tendency to come down a little hard on Wriggles, often reducing the little boy to tears. Tony wanted his son to be rough and tough, with a little more boisterousness in him, but poor Wriggles was not yet ready to take on the world! He never liked to be hurried; he believed, as was obvious from his delayed arrival into the world, that one ought to take one's time to savour every minute and do things comfortably, *slowly*.

After Wriggles had left, Tony would have a workout on the treadmill, followed by a little weight training or perhaps an invigorating session with the bull-worker. 'This is more like it,' I thought to myself, reassured that my husband now had his two feet more firmly on the ground. I was beginning to fall in love with my dashing Tony all over again.

Feeling rejuvenated and recharged, Tony would then shower and get ready to take on the world! After making a few calls, Tony would head to town to meet up with potential contacts in the business field. Lunch would usually be at home, followed by a news update on television. When Dewdrop had eaten lunch and had a short rest, Tony would embark on a homework check with his nervous daughter. He would later have a short siesta followed by a cup of tea, sipped while teaching the silently amused Wriggles how to count on a colourful plastic ball-frame.

Evenings would find Tony at the squash centre, raring to take on a challenge, fuelled by the energising workout earlier that morning. Having played a couple of sets, he would call to tell me that he would soon be home. After a beer or two, he usually kept his word about returning home before my tuitions were done for the day. He often even waited for me to have dinner together with him. At such times, my heart would overflow with love for him. I fervently prayed that he would always be this way.

'Shall we go for a drive with Dewdrop and Wriggles after class is over tonight?' was a Friday afternoon suggestion always welcomed with shrieks of delight from the children. Tony was a most adored and appreciated father whenever he came up with such brilliant proposals.

'Come on, Ma, say yes, please, *please*,' Dewdrop would pipe up, eager not to let go of such a golden opportunity. Simultaneously, there would be an imploring tug at my sleeve, courtesy of the hopeful little Wriggles.

'Only if your homework has been completed, all right?' I would reply, wondering whether Dewdrop would be able to finish all her assignments by 9.00 p.m.

At 9.00 p.m., when the last class was over, I would enter the house proper to find that Dewdrop had already accomplished her urgent assignments, leaving the less-urgent tasks for the weekend. With hope written all over their eager faces, the children would rush into my arms when I nodded that we had a date! Tony would already be reversing his car out of the garage.

We would then go for a drive, listening to lively music from the player, much to the delight of the children. I thanked God that this was all it took to evoke happiness in the hearts of the two simple children he had blessed us with. We were most fortunate that they had never made demands that were unreasonable or beyond our means.

If it was not too late, Tony would stop at a roadside stall where we could enjoy delicious groundnut porridge. As was his style, Wriggles would take his own sweet time to finish his bowl of thick, warm porridge, playing with the popular local dessert, rather than swallowing it. He would lift a spoon of the porridge a little higher and be enthralled by the way it slithered, like a little white snake, down the edge of the spoon, back into the bowl again. Repeating the captivating performance, he would be lost in his fantasy world until brought back to earth, with a jump by his father. Tony, though highly amused, would pretend to be irritated and threaten him with 'Wriggles, if you do not hurry up, I shall finish off what's left in your bowl! See, my spoon is ready! Here I come . . .'

Dewdrop would nearly fall off her wooden stool, laughing at this threat, while Wriggles, no longer of the opinion that his father could be fun, scowled while he struggled to scoop the endangered porridge a little faster. We would return home with a light heart, all of us, and turn in for a peaceful night's rest.

Frenemies

Almost a week had passed in blissful manner, when one day, at noon, Tony received a phone call from a close friend. When the call was over, Tony sat me down to discuss something that had been in the pipeline. It was a business venture involving the import of novelty items from overseas. Apparently, the prospects of a business of this nature had been considered for quite some time already by this close friend of Tony's. Unfortunately, the close friend, a professional in the medical field, had been unable to embark on the venture previously because it would have required him to be actively involved. He had been aware for some time already that Tony was unhappy with his job, and now that Tony had resigned from the same, the said gentleman was of the opinion that Tony would be an ideal business partner. He strongly felt that Tony possessed the energy and drive needed to make the venture a success. Furthermore, Tony was assertive and had a flair for public relations, again essential qualities which could only help a business to flourish. I was stumped.

I did not wish to be a wet blanket, but I felt that Tony should not rush into anything without first giving the matter considerable thought. I was prepared for him to take his time to study the market well and enter the field that appealed to him most, after having sought the advice of those who were already in the field chosen. Tony, not to be deterred, threw his trump card on the table: 'Look, I am not required to invest even a dollar in this potential venture! All I am required to invest are my time, energy, and grit. You have to admit that I could never encounter a better deal anywhere else!'

What could I say? It was on the tip of my tongue to protest further, but I knew that if I had told Tony just then what I truly feared, he would most probably have become distraught and possibly angry. I felt that I was not yet ready to give up my newly found happiness, for I could already see dark clouds looming in the not-too-distant horizon. This friend of Tony's, although an undeniably warm and genial man, had a passion for drink, and Tony had only just reduced his usual quota.

Tony and his business partner, after some speculations derived from a random study of the local market, made a brief trip overseas to scout for some novelty items. On their return, they launched a commodity, which even I thought would be a sure hit. It was put on promotion in shopping centres in a few towns, and initially, a fair number of units were sold. However, many of those who bought the product were mainly obliging friends. Later, sales dropped and, slowly, came to a standstill. The remaining stock in the storeroom was finally distributed among relatives and friends.

The undaunted duo made another brave attempt to succeed in the business world. This time they got wind, from abroad, of the demand for a substantial number of units of a certain commodity. This was a product manufactured locally, deemed to fetch a handsome price overseas.

With much gusto, Tony would leave home early each morning, with hope in his heart, but fatigue evident in his bloodshot eyes. He was most determined to make *this* venture, at least, a roaring success. My heart ached for him. It had now become a question of his self-esteem, for when the last venture had fizzled out, some cynics among his so-called friends had not hesitated to make derogatory remarks.

Tony had been promised a share of the ensuing profits from the new venture; his partner had fully assured him of the same. He was kept very busy for several weeks, carting samples of the commodity to and fro. We, at home, prayed every morning that God would be kind enough to let Tony reap the rewards for his hard work. Tony, out with his partner, returned home every night, staggering and reeking of liquor.

The finished product was soon shipped out. Weeks passed. No reference was made to this export. Months passed, and when, one fine day, I tactfully asked Tony about the progress made with reference to the said project, he snapped at me, 'You will be the first to know when the profits start to pour in!' Hurt, I questioned him no more. I never did learn the outcome of that transaction, but I did learn this—often, those who have stood supportively behind their loved ones during the hour of trial and tribulation are the last, if ever, to know what exactly transpired between the key players.

Tony Withdraws

Busying myself with my tuition classes, I tried my very best not to interfere in Tony's attempted enterprises. I noted, however, that he drank more, perhaps to forget the pain of failure and disappointment. He always returned late, wearing a look of disillusionment. I tried to reach out to him but often found the smell of liquor overbearing and his attitude, foreboding.

I experienced a rather embarrassing incident one evening, when Tony came home earlier than usual. I was just about to wind up class, at almost 9.00 p.m., when Tony, obviously under the influence of a fair bit of alcohol, stumbled, absent-mindedly, into my classroom full of students of rather impressionable age. These discriminating, sniggering teenagers found it highly amusing that their seemingly disciplined, no-nonsense tutor had apparently failed to command discipline at home! How I had wished, at that crucial moment, for the floor to just crack open and swallow me! Never had I felt so mortified!

The Vintage Itch

While still looking for his niche in life, Tony found something interesting to occupy himself with, temporarily. Encouraged by a doctor friend, Tony quickly became engrossed in a vintage motoring club. With his zest, he was soon actively involved in the events organised by this enterprising body. I could not help smiling, watching the enthusiastic and rejuvenated Tony help organise a series of treasure hunts, rallies, and weekend getaways. It was such a relief to see him bright and chirpy again.

The children and I occasionally accompanied Tony for a weekend getaway. Some outstanding events were even given coverage by the media, sending Tony over the moon. He often drove home, on separate occasions, a spectacular vintage car, proudly parking it on the vacant strip of land in front of our house. Each time Tony brought home such a celebrity, he would announce its arrival with the unmistakable toot of a vintage horn. The neighbours too secretly delighted in viewing the 'old gals' from behind their window curtains. Curious to see which model it was each time, they would watch with envy as Tony stepped comfortably in and out of yet another gleaming, regal, well-maintained model of the past. My Tony too looked no less dashing in his sunglasses and sports cap perched fetchingly on his head.

Dewdrop would need no invitation to slide smugly behind the wheel to get the feel! She would then direct the spellbound

Wriggles to climb onto the still-warm bonnet while Tony, the ever-obliging cameraman, clicked away. I mentally made a note to get another photo album. More photographs would soon have to be added to the growing collection of memorabilia of the vintage car era!

It was wonderful to see Tony cheerful again, but once more, drinks were an integral part at the end of each and every event. It seemed to me that everyone Tony knew, knew how to drink!

The 'Hot' Roll Era

The weeks passed with no reference made any longer to the alliance between Tony and his previous novelty business partner. One afternoon, when Tony was on his way out, Mum called out to him to have lunch. Tony, in a hurry to meet someone, requested Mum, 'Please roll up a bit of fried sardine in a chapati. I'll eat while driving. I'm already late!'

Mum obliged, making him three such rolls. Later that evening, on his return, Tony proposed to Mum that it might be a good idea to start a hot-snack business. My tired, just-after-tuition ears could not believe what they had heard!

Tony then explained that he had given one of the three home-made sardine rolls to the friend he had gone out to meet, and it had been declared extremely delicious. The same friend had jokingly suggested, 'You might consider marketing it!'

To Tony, it was no laughing matter. He was all out to do business, but no longer did he desire to do so with friends; this time it had to be with good-old, reliable family members. I did not know whether to feel flattered or shattered!

Tony spent the next few days trying to get me to agree to let him go ahead with his business plan for marketing hot, home-made chapati rolls, preferably with a variety of fillings. Each attempt of his got me heated up, and I was quite ready to grill him. However, I managed to keep my cool.

One Sunday, Tony took the children and me on a drive to a nearby town to discuss this brainwave of his with another friend who, he assumed, would also be interested in selling these sure-to-be-a-hit snacks as well.

On the way, Tony spoke excitedly. 'We'll invest in little oven-like food warmers, just like those used in pubs, to keep curry puffs and other snacks warm. They'll help keep the prepared rolls warm and appetising. I'm also planning to promote the rolls in as many schools as possible!' he enthused.

My head was in a whirl—Tony was moving too fast! I was no business entrepreneur, but even I knew that in business, one had to tread slowly and carefully. To take leaps was to ask for trouble. I asked Tony, 'Who is expected to prepare these few hundred rolls each and every single day?'

He replied, 'Why, we, the family, of course! We shall be the ones doing it initially, and later, Mum can impart the finer art of perfecting them to the wives of the two friends I have in mind.'

'I don't know if Mum will like that,' I remarked. 'You know how she treasures her recipes.'

'For me, she'll do anything!' Tony confidently shut me up.

I had to admit he had a point there. All the same, I was stupefied by the very thought that we, the family (Dad, Mum, Tony, and I), would have to be up in the wee hours of the morning, first kneading huge quantities of dough, then rolling out the dough to make the chapati, cooking the chapati evenly, and finally, stuffing the prepared chapati with various fillings. The fillings, of course, would not have fallen from the heavens—these too would have had to be laboured over, even earlier! Rolling up each chapati after putting in some filling presumably would be the least laborious task of the entire process of the proposed chapati roll venture.

Now, myriad questions plagued my mind. What about transport arrangements for these much-clamoured-about chapati rolls? What about clearance from the Health Department, not to mention approval from the heads of schools? Who was to sell these snacks in the many schools that Tony had in mind? Would canteen operators fall in line? Who would manage the financial accounting for this widespread business? It was just too much for me to even imagine!

Also, how on earth would my aging mother, with her much-wailed-about rheumatism and arthritis, cope with such a colossal task? Her varicose veins too were definitely not going to take this news sitting down! However, these were still the least of our problems. How was I going to persuade my mother, the queen of secret recipes, to share her preciously guarded recipe for chapati rolls with two total strangers? Mum would probably oblige her beloved son-in-law, but I might never hear the end of it!

The journey to Tony's friend's house was the longest I had ever made. Visions of our sleep-deprived family members slaving over hot chapati rolls in the stuffy kitchen, with frayed nerves and flaring tempers, were conjured in my mind. The questions I was dying to get answers to remained unanswered, for I never dared to ask Tony. I was afraid that he might get worked up and mistake my fears for pessimism, or worse, sheer laziness. He might then drive recklessly, in a fit of temper. I did not want to endanger anybody.

The journey, which I thought would never end, finally did. We reached our destination and the matter of chapati rolls was soon being discussed enthusiastically, but only by Tony. Tony's friend, of whom he had been so confident, asked exactly the same questions that had plagued my mind.

A brother-in-law of Tony's friend, who happened to be there, was not very encouraging either. Also, Mum need not have feared that her recipe would no longer be a secret—the rather arrogant wife of Tony's friend scoffed at the very thought of slaving in the kitchen for several hours every morning, losing sleep over chapati rolls! God had indeed been merciful.

Sensing great disappointment in the dejected Tony, his friend gallantly offered to treat us all to dinner, preceded by drinks. I did not dare to show even the slightest sign of disapproval. It was bad enough that Tony's hot chapatis had rolled away. It would be unwise to stop his gallant friend from soothing his ruffled feathers. I braced myself for a long drive back that night, trying to mentally recall the route home—I was definitely driving.

The Call of the Wild

A week after the chapati roll venture had flattened out, the jungle invaded our home! Before I could shut the front door to the wild, the jungle creepers had successfully entered and entwined my Tony. I dared not stand between the still-smarting Tony and the enticing call of the wild.

Another friend of Tony's, the proud, rugged owner of a formidable 4WD, had made several trips into the wild, ferrying nature lovers. This friend was of the opinion that taking such enthusiasts of nature to explore the country's flora and fauna in the hardy vehicle could prove lucrative. However, he needed a co-driver. He needed someone energetic and vibrant, someone who was not afraid of being bitten by mosquitoes. No prize for guessing who fitted the bill.

The adventurer made Tony an offer, and Tony, ever ready for an adventure, was thrilled at the prospect. He felt that this would be a good way to leave the company of friends who, with time to spare after work, whiled away hours drinking at the pubs. Several also displayed a tendency to get involved in brawls after having had a drink too many.

I suspected that Tony, in a pensive mood, had realised that he was being rather unreasonable spending hard-earned remuneration on drink. Being of generous nature, he was also wont to buy drinks for those in his company, a habit which was not very wallet-friendly.

Switching to jungle trekking gave Tony a different perspective on life. The children and I were soon introduced to the intimidating machine on four monstrously oversized wheels. I was not too keen on looking down at the rest of mankind, seated in a vehicle so high off the ground. I also found it rather attention-fetching, especially in the city itself, for one could not travel unnoticed.

Dewdrop and Wriggles, however, found it absolutely thrilling and whooped with delightful joy each time Tony drove up and down highland areas on the outskirts of the city. He needed getting used to handling and manoeuvring the 4WD, and this was best done in the encouraging and supportive company of his family. Each time he practised, I prayed that the excitable duo, seated behind, would not get too familiar with being driven in such a formidable vehicle. When Tony hinted about taking the children into the wild during the next school vacation, I shuddered, and my prayers became even more fervent. Creepy crawlies were not on my list of best friends.

Soon, the much-anticipated expeditions began. Prior to each expedition, Tony would buy cuts of fresh meat and marinate these juicy chops with pounded spices. The marinated pieces would then be wrapped in plastic film and packed in polystyrene boxes containing ice to keep them fresh until barbecued. The cook-out was to be conducted in some peaceful clearing in the forest, with a gurgling brook nearby. Choice fruits and vegetables for making salad would also be purchased, with a bottle of favoured dressing. Of course, there would be cartons of fruit juice and the inevitable cans of beer. How I envied Tony his new vocation—I too felt like fleeing my classroom to head for a little rest and recreation. It was just too bad that I had built my own Alcatraz!

Jungle trekking persisted for a couple of months, with Tony's initial enthusiasm slowly waning. The monsoon rains did not favour this project too much, and often, Tony and his friend had to diplomatically persuade their nature-loving clients to temporarily abandon the comfort of the 4WD and 'enjoy' wading across a newly formed body of water, while driver and co-driver gallantly pushed the monstrous vehicle with all their might. This had to be done because of the muddy nature of the terrain, which denied the vehicle necessary grip.

Furthermore, the frequent company of a certain young lady who made Tony's friend's heart beat a little faster did not augur well with Tony. My Tony, you see, was strictly a one-woman man who found it extremely hard to condone infidelity in marriage. This, I must stress, was a quality I found most reassuring and endearing in my beloved husband—he truly was a rare gem. This extramarital affair would often be a reason for a sudden trip to the wild, with the baffled Tony finding out only en route, when the femme fatale suddenly appeared at the last post of civilisation, on the edge of the wild. That was the last time Tony was co-driver to the adventurer.

The Spicy Siblings

'Blood is thicker than water,' goes the familiar adage. That is what I told myself when next, Tony decided he would give his eldest sibling a hand in running his restaurant. The brothers had off and on been estranged, owing to frequent differences of opinion and recurring personality clashes. I did not consider this a wise move and declared it so. However, I was told, in no uncertain terms, 'Wives can easily be replaced, but brothers are born only once.' I had no choice but to step back and say a silent prayer for Tony—I could not bear to see him disillusioned yet again.

Tony stepped confidently into the already established restaurant, charged with ideas on how to improve the entire set-up. In all his earlier ventures, Tony had not been the one holding the reins. This time, however, with his elder sibling mostly away, running another restaurant or scouting for workers overseas, Tony, in full brotherly dedication, took firm steps to motivate the existing staff and introduce new techniques in hospitality.

Most of the kitchen and service staff took an immediate liking to Tony's genial approach, a characteristic applauded initially even by his father, who spent many hours each morning exercising surveillance over the running of the restaurant. For the first two months, there was favourable feedback, even excitement. Tony woke up early each morning, bubbling with ideas on how to further enhance business and impress even the most discerning patrons. I was beginning to feel that I might have been a trifle over-pessimistic, after all. It did not take too long, however, to prove that my initial fears were not entirely unfounded.

Remuneration, or rather, the gross lack of it, seemed to be the issue of dispute. This greatly dampened Tony's enthusiasm, for he had confidently assured me, 'Sweetheart, with the income from my managerial position at my brother's restaurant, I shall bear certain financial responsibilities. You have borne them long enough, and they shall now be my sole responsibility. Dewdrop is a promising student, and being in upper secondary, she will soon need financial backing for tertiary education. It is now necessary for you to put aside some of your earnings for this purpose.'

I was beginning to feel more secure, slowly but surely. At long last, my darling Tony was beginning to show far-sightedness. I was relieved that I was no longer the only one worrying about the children's future. Tony's sibling, however, appeared to have started taking his services for granted after the first couple of months. Tony, in frustration, spoke his mind, perhaps a little too bluntly. This was not taken kindly by the offended sibling, and soon, Tony's father was caught in the middle. I felt sorry for the elderly man.

It had always been a cause of heartache for Tony, apparently even from childhood, that his father had shown a tendency to share his firstborn's points of view. This dispute put Tony in a bad light and made him feel that he was up against a mountain. Tired and broken in spirit, Tony called it a day. Family relations became much strained, never again to be what they had been before.

The Pub of Woes

While still recovering from the blow he had received, Tony sometimes frequented a certain new pub in a recently developed sector of the city. One evening, the elderly proprietor confided in Tony that his presence was badly needed in his own hometown, where renovations were being carried out to his original establishment. This soft-spoken, even fatherly, gentleman was anxious about the said renovations, but at the same time, rather reluctant to leave the newly opened local business in the hands of his freshly recruited staff.

Tony, determined to help me with the family budget and feeling guilty that he was still drinking despite the fact that he had not yet secured a steady job, requested that he be considered for the temporary post of manager while the proprietor attended to matters in his hometown. The man, who had already taken to my affable Tony, heaved a sigh of relief and immediately asked Tony, 'My dear young man, when can you step in?'

That evening, after classes were over, Tony insisted that I accompany him to the said pub. Sensing that I might not take well the news of his becoming manager of a pub, Tony probably felt that it would be best for the proprietor himself to break the news to me. When the proprietor informed me of Tony's appointment, I could not have burst with enthusiasm, even for dear life! I was, in fact, taken completely by surprise, having had no inkling whatsoever of what had transpired between the two men earlier that day.

I was unable to speak my mind without appearing to be too dominating and unsupportive of my husband. How was I to express the fears that were almost immediately welling up inside me? How could I tell the kindly gentleman that my intuition was impelling me to forbid Tony to take on the very job that could open the doors to self-destruction? Horrifying thoughts of my disillusioned, frustrated, and misunderstood Tony drinking away when temptation was all around him filled my anxious mind.

I was still in a daze when I suddenly realised that the two men were already shaking hands and calling it a deal! They then celebrated the new appointment with a round of drinks, offering even me a sherry, presumably to soothe my nerves. When we drove home, Tony did all the talking, while I did all the worrying, silently.

Eager to attract more patrons to the pub, Tony decided to boost business by adding new tantalising delights to the list of snacks already on the menu. Tony, with the consent of the proprietor, engaged the services of a part-time cook, a man who was no mean hand at whipping up mouth-watering snacks. This move attracted to the pub more drinkers, who were always ready to nibble on something savoury or spicy while downing beers. Business flourished, and Tony was commended.

Pleased that his sincere efforts were finally being appreciated, Tony went a step further. Having sought the permission of the proprietor once more, Tony instructed the bartender not to allow drinks to be ordered on credit anymore. This was because many of the regular patrons had yet to settle their dues for drinks consumed at the pub.

The total sum that had yet to be settled was a staggering amount, and these patrons had become rather relaxed, perhaps encouraged by the fact that the proprietor was hardly to be seen. He was still away most of the time, supervising renovations to his original establishment in his hometown. Tony felt that these inconsiderate patrons were taking advantage of the patient proprietor and thought that it would be in the best interests of the establishment to disallow drinks to be sold on credit.

Needless to say, the very same people who had once commended Tony on a job well done now began to sing a different tune. Upset at no longer being allowed to drink on credit, they started to talk ill of Tony behind his back. Tony, in the meanwhile, oblivious to the storm that was brewing slowly, kept on serving with dedication.

Enter the Viper

He soon struck up friendship with a young man who had started to frequent the pub. This suave personality had come to know of the legal case that Tony had taken up against his former partner. Also aware of Tony's desire to earn enough to enable the academically promising Dewdrop to pursue tertiary education, he targeted my gullible and trusting Tony. Although years younger than my Tony, who was now in his early forties, the consumptive lanky character possessed the craftiness of a wily old fox.

Tony one day invited his newly found friend home for lunch. The first time he stepped into our house, I saw red. He seemed uncomfortable and tended to avoid the eyes of the person he was talking to; this did not augur well. I had been brought up to believe that sincere and honest people always looked straight at the person being addressed. Perhaps I was instinctively prejudiced, but Wriggles too, for some unknown reason, took an instant dislike to this dubious character. Our combined spontaneous observation forewarned me of lurking danger.

By the grace of God, things looked more promising on the home front. Dewdrop did us proud at the end of that somewhat long and dragging year, bringing in much required sunshine. Tony, who had insisted on accompanying her when she went to school to get her results, was ecstatic over her straight-A achievement, once again!

The minute he returned to the car, where Wriggles and I were anxiously waiting, he gave me a warm hug, gushing, 'Thank you, sweetheart, thank you! I'm so proud of our little girl! I have sometimes declared that you are too hard on the children, but you have always believed that they are capable of high achievements. You have been steadfastly steering them in that direction, although I have sometimes made harsh remarks. Please know that deep down, I have always appreciated what you do for the family. Thank you again!' Well, that was refreshing and certainly long overdue! I too was proud of Dewdrop and

Wriggles. They were good, obedient children, but as scholars, they still needed a little prodding occasionally. Academic competition was stiff; only the crème de la crème was afforded scholarships.

Tony now began to feel the growing pressure to get ready the means for Dewdrop's future academic pursuits. He said, 'It's a blessing that Wriggles is still only in primary school, and we can concentrate on Dewdrop's education first. We have to seriously consider ways to raise money before Dewdrop's next public examination. That will be the deciding factor for the course which will determine her entire future. Two years is not too distant a time.' I could not agree more.

The Lingering Limp

Tony's workout and squash had taken a backseat over the past several months. He found it rather painful to run during squash, and he had thought it wise to give up the game temporarily. He thought he would use the same hours, twice a week, to give more attention to his managerial duties at the pub and, at the same time, be on the alert for greener pastures.

Tony came home early one afternoon, something which was rare, for his work at the pub hardly saw him home before midnight. He was walking with a limp and was obviously in great pain. Tony had especially started to complain more about the pain in his left calf after he had started his stint at the pub.

Dad, Mum, and I were very concerned about Tony's left calf, which sometimes appeared to be rather swollen. Tony attributed this malady mainly to standing long hours at the pub.

The Viper Strikes

It was during this vulnerable time in Tony's life that the conniving young man, to whom Wriggles and I had taken an instant dislike, struck. Like a viper, he sank his deadly fangs into my trusting husband. The 'venom' began to act, and one day, Tony fell prey. He took me completely by surprise on a Sunday evening when he suddenly asked me, 'Have you any savings set aside for a rainy day?'

It was something very unlike Tony to ask of me; he was the same one who had not so long ago advised me, 'Much as you love me, never disclose if there is any cash in reserve.' I had been stumped at this sudden bit of advice but immediately saw the wisdom when he further explained, 'You know that I am still looking for a job or business opportunity, and in the course of doing so, I might feel tempted to use up any savings we may have, as an investment in a venture. I have this fear—what if it proves to be an unwise investment? At least, if we have some savings put aside, we will be able to carry on respectably, without having to borrow money from anyone.' It made sense, and I was impressed at his far-sightedness.

Why, therefore, did Tony suddenly want to know about my savings? I asked him, 'Why do you ask? What do you have in mind? I have to know, for what I have saved so far is just a nominal amount, intended to enable Dewdrop to enter college, or pay towards any urgent medical expenses that might arise.'

Tony then disclosed, 'Remember my friend, the one I recently brought home to lunch?' Of course, I remembered the sleazy character that Wriggles and I had taken an instant dislike to!

Tony continued, unsuspectingly, 'You know, sweetheart, he is really intelligent. He is worldly wise and has impressive business acumen. He has a share in an up-and-coming venture, and you know what? He is graciously offering me a chance to enjoy part of the revenue that is expected to pour in soon! I can't believe that he is offering me a share! You see, darling, this venture is actually open only to those of a particular race to which we do not belong. As such, any amount of money which we decide to put in can only be invested under the name of this philanthropic friend. I'm so glad that he came into my life!'

'But you have only known him these past few weeks!' I protested. 'How can you be so convinced of his sincerity?'

Tony, sensing my hesitation and feeling a little hurt, added, 'Well, it is entirely up to us whether we are prepared to place absolute trust in him. I, for one, am very sure that he has only our best interests at heart. He knows what I have been through and what I am still undergoing. He is also aware of how hard you are working to sustain the family until I find a good and permanent job. He has convinced me that investing in this venture is the best way for me to contribute to the family. This will actually be extra income once I have found another job!'

Tony was most eager to invest in the promising venture, despite the absence of concrete documents. It was wholly based on trust. I was aghast, my intuition screaming that he stop and listen to reason. I protested, but Tony persistently implored. I declared that I did not have much savings, but Tony beseeched that we borrow the rest from a close family friend or even Dad.

I was at wits' end. What was I supposed to do? There were tears in my husband's eyes as he professed how much it meant to him, as a man, to be able to provide for his family. He had tried everything he possibly could have tried to make it in this world, but sadly, nothing had proved successful. He had met only with failure in every venture undertaken thus far.

Tony also disclosed that things were not going smoothly then at the pub; many of those who had been refused drink on credit had badmouthed him to the proprietor. He added dismally that he would not be surprised if the same kindly gentleman, by now presumably misled, terminated his services at the end of that very month. Tony pleaded that he needed something to back him up, and to him, this offer seemed most opportune. I had never seen my Tony so dejected. I had a mental image of my savings account dwindling to zero.

The Victorious Viper

I withdrew my savings, but it was not sufficient to meet even a third of the amount asked for. I sheepishly brought the matter up to my father, who was relying on his monthly pension. After my parents had given the matter some thought, Dad withdrew the entire gratuity that he had deposited in the bank, to enable my hopeful Tony to meet the amount required.

Dad and I both had misgivings with regard to the get-rich-quick scheme that our Tony was about to embark on with the smooth-talking personality, but there was no way that Tony could be convinced not to do so. We were sceptical, but Tony was so broken in spirit that any reluctance on our part might have shattered him completely. We did not have money to spare, but we wanted to spare Tony any further anguish.

I was deeply touched by the love that Dad and Mum had for Tony. Tony, on his part, was profuse in his gratitude, even to the extent of admitting that his own folks would never have made such a magnanimous gesture. He shed tears of gratitude, mingled with relief, and left the house with his head held high. We could merely watch and hope for the best. I now had to make sure that my tuitions never stopped, not even during the school holidays. I could not let Dad and Mum down—they had just handed over all their savings and put their complete trust in both Tony and me.

Pub No More

As predicted by Tony, the misled proprietor of the pub terminated his services with effect from the end of that month. The patrons who had been instrumental in effecting this wore smug looks. Tony, aware for several weeks that a storm was brewing, had become worked up, taking to drink to relieve his stress and tension. Sensing that he would not be around in the pub much longer, he started to give some of the back-stabbers a piece of his mind. He felt that he had nothing more to lose. Also, he had tolerated more than his fair share of ingratitude from some of the staff, one of whom had been eyeing his position. His last few weeks at the pub left me on edge—Tony by then had already been involved in a few brawls and come home with bruises and a dented vehicle.

I was greatly relieved to see the end of Tony's stint at the pub. The job had wrought nothing but sleepless nights for both Tony and me. Tony had seldom got home before 2.00 a.m., and I could never sleep until I knew that he was back home, safe and sound. I also wished to make sure that he had at least eaten some kind of dinner. To make matters worse, all the drinking had started to take its toll on Tony's health. His leg had never looked so swollen, and his limp was rather pronounced. Still, Tony managed to smile; he was optimistic about the investment he had recently made under the name of his benevolent friend.

The Viper Strikes Again

The new venture that Tony had invested in proved lucrative initially. It impressively yielded a dividend of a few hundred within two weeks, making it look as if I might have to eat humble pie! 'Should this favourable trend continue, why, you might even be able to cut down on your tuitions!' Tony confidently announced. I was not so sure, however, if I ever wanted to take such a risk. Tuitions had been the only reliable source of income for us for nearly two decades. Besides, I had never had to look for students—they had always looked for me.

Soon, the viper strongly advised my elated Tony to increase his investment in order to procure even bigger dividends. This time, both Dad and I stood determinedly firm against further investment. Neither of us had a cent to spare, and we did not wish to incur any debts. Tony felt rather let down, but he was fully aware that we had no more resources.

When no dividend was issued during the weeks that followed, I became disgruntled. Tony conveyed my irritation to the viper, who tried to prove his integrity by handing over a few pieces of gold jewellery as collateral until the next dividend was issued. I told Tony, in no uncertain terms, 'I smell a rat, and I am not comfortable with the idea of keeping someone else's jewellery in our house.' I did not have to live with the discomfort for long.

The very next day, the viper called on us sheepishly, requesting that we implicitly trust him without holding on to collateral; he needed to pacify his infuriated wife for the jewellery belonged to her. Tony, being the gem he was, instantly obliged him. I shook my head sadly, now uncomfortably aware that we had nothing to hold on to until the dividends were delivered. This was becoming a no-win situation.

The Viper Vanishes

Dad and I grew increasingly dubious about the whole scheme when still no dividend made an appearance. One fine day, Tony received news that the viper had suddenly left the company he had been working for, leaving no inkling whatsoever of his new whereabouts! Tony was completely shattered, and he did not know how to break the news to us. Finally, unable to hold it back any longer, he broke down and told us his trusted friend had let him down—yes, the viper had struck!

In desperation, Tony went looking for him all over the city, checking every possible haunt of his. I too went with Tony a few times, driving him to these haunts. Tony's left leg was often badly swollen, causing him to wince with pain when alighting from the car.

We finally managed to meet the deceitful man's wife, who, though sympathetic on hearing our plight, could do nothing to ease our situation. She claimed that she herself was having problems with him and was even contemplating divorce. It did not augur well either when she disclosed that her husband had hoodwinked several other trusting friends, leaving her to face much embarrassment. She herself was planning to leave the city as soon as possible.

The Disillusioned Tony

Tony, by then, had lost all confidence in mankind, and he feared that he might do something drastic if he happened to be alone with the person who had cheated his family of their life savings. He found it hard to face Dad, Mum, and me each morning, though we did our best to reassure him that we had not the slightest doubt that he had been most sincere in wanting to do something gainful, with speedy results. I comforted him, 'Please, Tony, don't give up hope—the case taken up against your ex-partner for overdue payments will probably be in your favour.' This cheered him up a little, but he still did not give up trying to locate the viper.

Tony would often return home late, having had too much to drink and wallowing in self-pity. At times, he would not talk much to Dad and Mum. To make it less awkward for him, as soon as they heard his car at the gate, they would adjourn to their own room to watch television. This allowed him the privacy that he needed to be with his wife and children.

Sadly though, Tony did not seem to want to have much to do with the children or me either. He often became agitated if the children or I approached him regarding any matter. I could not help feeling, at this point, that the fact that I earned fairly well further upset his already battered ego.

It had never mattered to me, from the very start of our relationship, who earned more. As far as I was concerned, all earnings were meant for the family. I was neither counting nor comparing; why was he? Was he feeling neglected? Was he keeping away from me because I was kept busy in the classroom? If so, I had asked him many a time, 'Would you rather I end the evening tuition sessions at 7.30 p.m. instead of 9.00 p.m.?'

He had responded, 'We should be grateful to God that there is demand for tuitions even until 9.00 p.m. It would be foolish for us to turn away good luck. Moreover, we need every cent we can earn for the future of our children.'

Catch-22

When I expressed despair over Tony's drinking and late nights, especially when he was barely able to walk without a limp, he sheepishly explained, 'Look, I feel rather uncomfortable, just sitting down in this armchair, watching television, while you slog for hours in the classroom. Hearing the strain in your voice while you are teaching further pricks my conscience. That is why I often go out in the evenings.' It looked like I was in a no-win situation here too.

I tactfully pointed out to Tony, 'Since you have time to spare at the moment, you could, perhaps, try to spend some quality time with the children. They hardly have your attention.

'You could,' I further proposed, 'give Dewdrop a hand with her revision, questioning her on prepared topics. Even Wriggles could do with a little guidance from you. His handwriting needs improvement. You know how the very sight of it, even in passing, drives you berserk! Wriggles may respond more positively to your hand guiding his, lovingly and patiently, while writing, rather than to angry threats coming from an irritated you.' I had noticed that Tony's threatening tone had an unintended adverse effect on the rather withdrawn 7-year-old.

I suspected that Tony's rather short temper had been the result of all the recent frustrations that had been his lot, as well as the increasing pain in his left leg, which seemed to impede mobility. I had tried, with much diplomacy, to convince Tony to see a doctor, but he had vehemently protested. He did, however, finally admit, 'Drink might have perhaps contributed a little to my condition. Anyway, I promise to cut it down, soon.' I wondered if that would ever be possible.

Tony tried to comply with my suggestions regarding the children and, in spending time with them, also cut down his drinking. However, after a few days of trying to fall in line, he was again distracted by those very friends whom he had often bought drinks for. They kept on making calls, wondering what had been keeping him away. I knew this for sure, for many a time, I had picked up the extension line, thinking that it was a call from the parent of a student. On hearing the familiar sickening voices, I could predict what was going to happen next.

Drink, Denial, and Disappointment

One did not have to be a genius to comprehend what was going on and what the next move would be. I was upset, for it was obvious that the period away from drink had helped the swelling of Tony's left calf to subside considerably. He began to show uneasiness when I pointed out, 'See how much better your leg has become with a break from drinking! The swelling has gone down tremendously and you do not limp so much.'

'Look, if I don't go and show my face, they'll think I'm hen-pecked,' he would answer in an irritated manner. Seeing my face fall, he would quickly put an arm around me and give the excuse that his friends might have news of the viper, or his whereabouts. Then, Tony would quickly drive off, without further hindrance from me. This was because during such times, my classes were in session, and I could not spend too much time arguing with him. In retrospect, I wonder how on earth I had carried on teaching or remained sane.

The swelling on Tony's left calf made a comeback, together with his late nights. I felt like banging my head on the wall! Was he never going to come to his senses? However, I had to hold my tongue, for just then, there was news that the pending court issue had finally been resolved.

The verdict broke my Tony. His crafty ex-partner had wangled his way out of making any payment due to him! He had instead magnified the issue of Tony having investigated a few cases freelance. Tony's retort was that he had been left no other alternative, considering he had been denied payment rightfully due to him for far too long. The heartless man was determined not to pay Tony a cent. Bent on teaching Tony a lesson for having dared to take him to court, he had used sly play with words to convince the court to close the case. Tony felt his world collapse.

I was at a loss. How was I to comfort him? Now, there was not even a whiff of any good news in the offing. Life had dealt my naive and gullible husband too many blows too soon in succession.

Viper Tracking

After a few days of trying to drink away his problems in the company of those who lent him an ear in exchange for drinks, Tony, with his calf hideously swollen and eyes sunken, swore vengeance on the viper once again. He spent a number of evenings at various pubs, fishing for information. One evening, he learnt that the wife of the viper had left her job. Tony decided to call on her that very night.

I went with Tony, at his request. We drove to the other end of town, to the last known address of the couple, when classes were over. He explained to me, 'I do not want to alarm the already troubled wife by appearing alone. She may not even open the door if she sees a man. She will be more comfortable if she sees you with me.' I was happy to be of some assistance. At least, I got to spend an evening with him and remain in the loop.

Unfortunately, we were unable to meet her, for the house was locked up. A neighbour, however, disclosed that the couple we were looking for had moved to the capital. The same neighbour also mentioned that we were not the only anxious people looking for the dodgy couple.

Tony had a back-up plan. He decided we would drive to the house of the elderly parents of the viper early the following morning. When I asked him why he had not thought of this before, he replied, 'I did not wish to burden his parents with a problem that did not concern them. They have very often received news of the misdeeds of their youngest son. He is obviously the black sheep of the family.' Tony had learnt all this from acquaintances of the viper whom he had questioned during the last few evenings at the various pubs he had visited. He continued, 'However, now the time has come for me to involve them and tell them what their deceitful son has done. After all, my elderly father-in-law's money is at stake here!'

I believed that this might be the only step left for us to take. Tony had to be allowed his say. He felt that he needed to tell the parents how their son had convinced him to part with the life savings of his elderly father-in-law and trusting wife. Tony was not going to leave any stone unturned in his attempt to retrieve the capital of the investment he had made with the viper. It might have been more tolerable had it simply been his own hard-earned money. Here, his self-esteem and personal integrity were at stake.

Salt and Prejudice

Early the next morning, we drove to the house of the elderly couple. They lived on the outskirts, far from the hustle and bustle of the city. We alighted from our car and knocked on the door of the half-brick, half-wooden bungalow. The mother of the culprit opened the door and bade us enter. She was warm and motherly. We immediately felt at ease, and hope was revived.

On listening to Tony's tale of woe, she was most sympathetic. 'I have no doubt that my prodigal son has caused you untold misery. It is not the first time such a sad story has reached my ears, and I doubt it will be the last. Please wait here for a minute.' Saying that, she entered the adjacent room, to inform her husband of our predicament.

However, things took a downward turn. We were startled to hear angry shouts and verbal abuse. I had expected an elderly man to appear and at least lend a ready ear, like his wife, and comfort my clearly distraught and sickly-looking Tony. My poor husband was taken aback and further shattered when the old man stormed out of the room, waving his fist angrily at him! He declared, 'I do not wish to hear anything that has to do with that scoundrel! Why did you trust him? What were you thinking then? You and your entire race are the same! You spend your time and money drinking and fall for get-rich-quick schemes!'

I was stunned! Tony had earlier told me that this elderly man had once been the headmaster of a school. What kind of education had he received, or even imparted? He literally chased us out, shouting, 'Get out of my house! Don't you ever dare to show yourselves here again!' His wife, highly embarrassed, tried to calm down her agitated husband, but to no avail. Tony and I left that house, disoriented, never to forget the reception we had been given. We would never be able to live it down. The sum we had lost was substantial, the faith that we had lost in mankind, immeasurable.

Tony never fully recovered from the unkind and totally unexpected blow dealt by the angry father of the very man who had connived to con him of his family's savings. This is why I shall never be able to fathom the following episode that took place barely a few days after the nastiness displayed at the home of the elderly couple.

Getting wind that the viper had been seen in a town up north where his wife had just reported for duty in a certain office, the seething Tony got on the viper's trail, almost immediately. I was shaken up. Tony's health had further deteriorated, owing to even more drinking, and he was always muttering, 'I am personally going to set that bastard right the minute I see him, no matter where or when!'

I feared the worst. One evening, Tony insisted on driving up to the town where the viper was believed to be hiding. He planned to wait outside the office of the culprit's wife and keep vigil. The viper was sure to turn up at the office to pick up his wife, for between them then, they had only one car left. Tony had learnt this from the same person who had disclosed the earlier bit of information.

Once Bitten, Still Not Shy

I was concerned that Tony might not be able to withstand the long drive up to the north and back again without adverse effects on his health. To make it worse, he had even lost his appetite. I was torn apart between my commitment to my husband for better or for worse and my duties in the classroom, especially when crucial examinations were approaching. Tony decided for me when he said, 'We cannot both throw caution to the wind. I am driving up alone, and I do not wish to return empty-handed. I mean to settle the matter, even if it takes a few days. You stay behind and hold the fort.'

I shall never forget the two days that Tony was away. As promised, I attended to the family and my tuition classes, but it would be a lie to say that I conducted all my duties nonchalantly. Every time the telephone rang, I would run to pick up the receiver. Dad, Mum, Dewdrop, and Wriggles could never have guessed what trepidations I felt. They knew that I was anxious, but how could I tell them to what extent my fears were? If they knew that Tony was courting danger, they too would be on edge.

I was greatly relieved when, on the second day, Tony called. On hearing that he had encountered the viper and that they had discussed the issue calmly, I did not know whether to feel happy or angry. I was much perplexed. Tony had left in such a vengeful mood, but on the telephone, he had referred to the 'bastard' by his name and had even sounded very sympathetic! My intuition told me that the viper had sunk his fangs into Tony yet again. I would not know the details until Tony's return home. I had a most fitful sleep that night. Now, I had lost my appetite.

Mystical Viper?

On Tony's return late the next morning, he appeared fatigued. I noticed that he had a glazed look in his eyes. He also reeked of alcohol. The glazed look, however, was not one that was associated with drink. Dad, Mum, and I were very puzzled. The children were at school, and I badly wanted to know what exactly had transpired between my husband and the viper! 'Tell me what happened,' I started. 'I have been in suspense long enough!'

Tony, looking rather sheepish, replied, 'I have a very bad headache. If you don't mind, I'll tell you later.' He had a quick shower but refused to eat anything. Then he went up to our room, lay down on the bed, and soon fell into a deep sleep. I was most irritated, knowing that I would not be able to concentrate on anything that day until all the questions plaguing me had been answered. Now, as usual, I would have to bite my tongue and wait. There was a sick, gnawing feeling inside me.

I proceeded to unpack Tony's overnight bag. I found no money, but an obscure piece of thermal paper. I looked harder and was aghast to discover that it was a credit card receipt showing a five-figure sum charged to Tony's credit card for the purchase of some jewellery! I grew incensed. What had he done now? The only reason I had agreed to him having a credit card was to allow him to easily stay in hotels overnight when he was delayed during outstation investigations. He had sworn he would never use it to purchase alcohol or any other items. I could not recall any discussion between Tony and me that would involve such a substantial purchase involving jewellery. Who was this expensive trinket for, and why did it involve my husband's credit card?

We had both heard bad tidings about credit card purchases and had vowed never to allow ourselves to be subjected to the torment of settling credit card debts. According to a friend with first-hand experience, failure to settle a credit card debt within a month resulted in exorbitant interest! What, then, was this all about? Had he so quickly forgotten how alarmed he had been when told how a credit card debt often had a crippling effect?

I got my answers soon enough, for Tony suddenly called for me. With my heart pounding in my chest forebodingly and my thoughts in a whirl, I raced up the stairs. At last, I was going to get to the bottom of all this!

Credit Card Caper

When I entered the room, Tony was brushing his hair. He told me to sit down on the bed. I was getting angry, for this was undoubtedly indicative of an impending unwelcome confession. Tony knelt down before me and put his hand on my knee, as if to calm me down. He began, 'I managed to track down my friend without too much trouble. He was surprised to see me but did not try to run away. Instead, he bought me a drink and shed tears of remorse for having let our family down. He was very apologetic and has assured me that he is going to make good the deal that was earlier agreed upon. However, to do this, he needed another sum of money.'

I was about to protest, when Tony silenced me with a gesture. He went on, 'My friend desperately needed to replace his wife's gold, which he had sold. She had to be appeased enough to take a loan from her current employer on his behalf. Hence, he asked to be allowed to make the purchase using my credit card first as his has been declined. With that loan from his wife's company, he will be able to increase his investments to recover our capital. He will also make good on my credit card debt and any interest it may incur.'

'Really, Tony? Do you really believe this man is sincere? Do you not remember what the neighbours said about him? What his own father said? I am shocked at what you have just told me!'

Who was going to explain to Tony the additional folly he had newly committed? I certainly could give Tony no credit for what he had done with his card!

Tony did not leave the house that entire day. He even attended to the children when they got home from school. He spoke to them cheerfully, sounding hopeful of better days to come. I was not so easily convinced.

That evening, after classes were over, I chose to have dinner alone. After the children had gone to bed, I made an excuse about feeling under the weather and retired to our room upstairs. It was close to 11.00 p.m., but I could not sleep. I felt most disturbed. When I had confided in Dad earlier that evening about Tony's revived trust in the viper, Dad, who had been standing close to his bed, felt his knees go weak, and he had to quickly sit down. My fears were then confirmed.

I could not bear to be near Tony. I felt very let down by the captain of our ship. How could he have allowed this to happen? When was he ever going to come to his senses? Why was he so drawn to the pubs, which were the haunts of such conmen? Why was God punishing me? Did Tony really believe that the viper, the very same viper who had devoured all our savings, was actually going to clear the entire debt taken on his name? I greatly doubted the viper would even pay the monthly interest on the same! How could Tony have been so gullible after all the anguish that the viper had inflicted upon him and the rest of the family?

I was jerked out of my rueful ruminations when Tony suddenly called out to me. Reluctantly, I got out of bed and trudged downstairs to see what the great captain could possibly want now.

Redundant Realisation

'My headache has finally gone and I can think clearly now. What have I done? That bastard brainwashed me into purchasing a gold necklace with my credit card! He must have doped me!'

Was I hearing things? What was this now? I looked at Tony in disbelief. He seemed wide awake now; the glazed look had completely disappeared! He had voiced the very thing that had been lurking in my mind. The viper was certainly one who could stoop low enough to do such evil! He had most likely slipped some powder into Tony's wonderful drink prior to taking him shopping! This best explained the whole situation, but what could be done now?

Tony made a few more trips to the north, travelling by coach. His calf was persistently swollen, but he still refused to seek medical attention. The trips, each time, proved unfruitful, instead incurring further expenses on travelling and accommodation. Tony would assure me, prior to each trip, that he would not have any drink with the viper, but I suspected the viper still managed to strike. The characteristic glazed look was all Tony brought back home after each trip. No further loans were mentioned, but neither was it disclosed if any repayment had been made at all to the credit card company.

I shuddered at the thought of how this venture was going to end. I had a gnawing feeling that I would probably find myself paying up all the debts incurred for the loans taken from Dad and the credit card company! It might have been acceptable if there had been documented evidence of money invested in Tony's own name, but here, most unfortunately, there was nothing but thin air and accumulating interest.

I was unable to speak of my despair to anyone, except Dad and Mum. The children could sense there was something amiss, especially the perceptive Dewdrop, but I did not wish to elaborate. Instead, I said, 'Dewdrop, you just focus on your studies to secure a bright future. This will give Daddy and me something to smile about and look forward to.'

It would have made the children smile brightly if Tony at least returned home early each evening, even if only to sit in front of the television. They would have felt a lot more secure in the knowledge that their daddy, with a limp, was safe at home until he felt better and had a good job. Coming home early would also mean not whiling away so many hours at the pub, which was clearly second home to the lost and still unemployed Tony. His trips to the north, on the trail of the venomous viper, had come to a frustrating and unrewarding end.

Merciless Macau

It was at yet another pub that Tony heard of a local dance troupe that was scheduled to perform in Macau. One of the star performers, who frequented the same pub, invited Tony to join them on the trip, even if only to visit the religious landmarks.

Tony at first merely toyed with the idea, but as the date of departure neared, he gave it more serious thought. Sheepishly, he requested, 'I know we are tight, but do you think you can manage this? It will probably do me a world of good and steer me in a spiritual direction.'

Already at wits' end but still hoping for a miracle, I encouraged Tony to go. If anything, it would be a change from his predictable, miserable routine. The first collection of tuition fee for that month was partly used to purchase a ticket for his flight, while the rest was converted into American dollars. Tony was soon on his way, hopefully, to spiritual enlightenment.

Tony called home on his arrival at Macau. After that, we heard nothing further. On Tony's return, five days later, he appeared rather disillusioned. He brought home only a small bag of gifts, but a big load of woe. The members of the troupe had embarked on a pilgrimage to a greatly revered shrine, leaving him behind. Tony had not even been informed about the proposed pilgrimage, which had taken off from a hotel.

While all the members of the dance troupe had been staying in that hotel, Tony, at the invitation of a kind priest, had put up in a room in a church complex. Tony never got over how his star performer friend in the party of pilgrims had let him down, more so after he had even lent him some money. Having done so, Tony himself had run short of cash to buy certain souvenirs he had admired. However, Tony had at least managed to procure a lovely statuette of the Lady of Fatima, from Macau.

The beautiful white porcelain statuette of the Lady of Fatima stood graciously atop the vertical file cabinet in Tony's office.

Reeling and Remorseful

Many a time when I entered his office, I would find Tony in prayer, holding both hands of the statuette, as if seeking strength from her, to help him forgive all those who had sinned against him and destroyed his faith and trust in mankind. Tony had sometimes, in his sober moments in the morning, shed tears at how the world had played him out. He would hold me really tight and confess, 'The only peace I have ever known is in this home. The only true love and compassion I have ever been shown unconditionally is that showered upon me by you, my children, and my in-laws . . .' Tears would well up in my eyes when he described those of us at home as givers, and the rest, takers.

My Tony respected all religions, and the rest of us at home had equally open minds. 'God,' Tony had often declared, 'is one. Look out of any window, and you will still see the same sun,' is what Tony would tell Dewdrop and Wriggles. As they listened, enthralled, he would continue, 'God is like the sun shining radiantly upon one and all. In God's eyes, all are equal and deserving of his benevolence. Religion was originally created by man, and this has unfortunately segregated the peoples of the world. *All* religions are good, and their aim is to discipline mankind in the way of life. They all preach the necessity to lead life righteously and peacefully. Only then will there be peace in this world and, hopefully, no wars.'

The children, hardly ever having seen their father so passionate about a subject, would gaze in awe at their father as he continued, 'Wars actually stem from quarrels, which, in turn, have stemmed from disrespect of the opinions of others, or their rights. You two must always respect all people and religions. Look at your mother and me—have you ever known us to be reluctant to enter a church, temple, or any other place of worship? We may not visit the church or temple very often, but we do have family prayers at home. I want you to be like us and like your grandparents. They have accepted me most lovingly, though I am of a different faith. They have respected me and allowed me to worship as I please. This has given me great peace of mind, and in return, I have learnt to respect not only their faith, but all faiths that preach the correct path of life.'

He stumped us all when he further added, 'I have but one major weakness. You know what I am talking about, but believe me, I am trying my best to overcome this only evil in my entire being. Please, all of you, continue to stand by me, for I really need your love and support.'

The children understood what their dear father was trying to tell them. They ran into his open arms to give him warm loving hugs and assured him of their unfailing presence by his side. I prayed that God would give us enough strength to never disappoint Tony.

145

Those seated in the car with Tony often saw him bow his head in respect to any place of worship en route, be it a Hindu, Buddhist, or Sikh temple, church, or mosque. Even a simple shrine would be acknowledged. Tony practised what he preached, which was respect for all religions and faiths. Wriggles followed suit, while Dewdrop would say a silent prayer. I offered a prayer of thanks. My Tony had enlightened our children beautifully.

The Promising Pilgrimage

Tony was still unemployed when, three months later, some friends of a different faith discussed plans for a pilgrimage to a temple in the south of India. This pilgrimage demanded gruelling preparation. Aspiring pilgrims would have to abstain for a whole month from meat, alcohol, and sex, prior to embarkation. Tony was eager to go on this pilgrimage with his group of friends of that particular faith. He knew it was going to be quite a challenge, but he wished to undertake it. He felt greatly motivated and felt that this time he would surely succeed. Needless to say, I was all for it and gave him my full support.

It was a miracle! Tony surprised one and all with his successful abstinence during the preparatory period for the pilgrimage. I had never experienced such a wonderful month! Tony was mostly at home, giving his full attention to the children. He was alert to their every need and remained completely calm, even when Wriggles cheekily tested his limits!

I was in my element in the classroom, teaching cheerfully and even joking more with my students. I was at my happiest with the non-drinking Tony, who was safely seated in the living room, with the rest of the family. It was such an immense relief knowing that I would be spared the sight of my Tony returning home in a stupor after drinking for hours in a pub.

Tony graciously spent a little time with Dad and Mum each evening, giving insight into the future. 'Things will definitely change for the better for each and every one of us, on my return. I am confident that this strict fast and the approaching pilgrimage will be most beneficial to me spiritually,' he assured the elderly couple. He was certain that the enlightenment that would befall him soon would guide him towards the best vocation, on his return. He started to look upon the period of unemployment, thus far, as one of trials and tribulations.

One night, I had enthusiastically asked, 'Tony, do you think it would be possible for you to make this way of life a regular pattern on your return from the pilgrimage?'

He had answered, in mock disbelief, 'What? No sex? No meat? How could you be so cruel?' He then laughed and hugged me tight. The naughty boy—of course he knew what I had meant.

After the month of preparation, during which certain traditional garb of the colour black had been purchased, the 'long-suffering' group left for the south of India. They were to be away for a period of slightly over a week, during which time they were to pay homage to a much-revered ancient temple on a hill. There had been hearsay that the ascent to the temple was a precarious one, and that was why the would-be pilgrims had been strongly advised to observe the strict fast. It had been advocated to keep the body light and nimble, as well as to invoke the blessings of the gods. The objective of the pilgrimage was to atone for all past transgressions committed, intentionally or unintentionally.

While Tony and the other pilgrims were away, we at home prayed that all was well with them. We fervently prayed also that the Tony who returned from the pilgrimage would bc a transformed and more resolute man. Many have said that this particular pilgrimage, if performed with utmost sincerity, discipline, and faith, leaves no prayer unanswered.

I was hopeful that Tony, on his return, would completely give up drinking. 'Having been free from the influence of alcohol for well over a month, and feeling healthy and refreshed,' I remarked to the family, 'Tony should not find it too difficult to put a complete stop to drinking on his return.'

Dad chipped in, 'Yes, he should be able to give it up after a whole month's abstinence. He has seen for himself how the swelling on his left calf has subsided.'

Mum assured me, 'The joy and relief on our faces will surely have meant something to him. The children have never been so comfortable with their father!'

I anxiously awaited Tony's return, impatient for confirmation of my optimistic expectations. I did not wait alone; Dad, Mum, and the children harboured similar hopes.

Tony called from the capital one evening to say that he was back and would soon reach home. He was arriving by taxi. The family eagerly awaited his return. Mum, despite her aching arm, made her way to the kitchen to prepare the evening meal. She stopped to ask me, 'Is he still vegetarian?'

As soon as Tony stepped into the house, her question was answered and all our hopes, shattered. Tony reeked of alcohol.

Life returned to what it had been before the period of abstinence in preparation for the 'pilgrimage of a lifetime'.

Nonchalance in New Zealand

Enter Shiv. Yes, my only sibling, Shiv, stepped in next. One fine day, he made a telephone call from Wellington, New Zealand. I was the one who answered that call. After the normal exchange of pleasantries, Shiv enquired especially about Tony. 'Has he been gainfully employed anywhere as yet? If not, I shall be happy to send him a ticket to fly over to New Zealand to check out the prospects of a business in collaboration with me,' he offered.

I was apprehensive about what answer to give for I feared what might transpire if Tony actually accepted the offer. Shiv had completely laid off drinking for at least two years, while my Tony was comfortable with using drink as a crutch! How, then, would the twain meet? I tried to put this across diplomatically to my darling brother, but he was ready to shoot me down. He wondered aloud, 'Why do you women always choose to stand in the way of your man's progress?'

I could not believe my ears! This coming from the same brother who had once told me that I should perhaps stop helping my non-reciprocating husband with his career—he had even suggested that I teach him a lesson and stop his progress by refusing to take on all his paperwork! Shiv, observing a change for the worse in Tony each time he visited, had remarked, 'You, my dear sister, are far too patient and subservient—more than is good for you! Look at what is happening to Tony! Once conscientious, diligent, and responsible, he has grown very complacent. It's all because of drinking! You have been tolerant to a fault, and he has taken you for granted!'

Now, this no-longer-drinking brother of mine was accusing me of being a hindrance! Why were men so fickle? Not wanting to challenge the volatile Shiv, I backed off and let Tony decide for himself. Shiv had told me in no uncertain terms that he was the one financing the trip—intervention at this point would have been disastrous.

The Kiwis won. Wellington was Tony's next destination. He left for the airport in the capital, armed with bags carrying an assortment of eatables that he thought should please Shiv and prove to be a hit in the market overseas. I had accompanied him when he went scouting for local delicacies that would appeal to the Kiwi palate. I must admit, however, that I had not been very enthusiastic. Tony guessed the reason for my dampened enthusiasm and assured me, 'If I do drink in New Zealand, I will keep it to a minimum. I promise not to upset Shiv. I know he's trying to help.' I could only pray and keep my fingers crossed. Tony was driven to the airport by a friend.

Shiv called to inform us of Tony's safe arrival in Wellington. It was Tony's first trip to New Zealand, and he was extremely cheerful when he spoke on the telephone for a few minutes. He promised to call again in a day or two. He was not sure then how long his stay would be, but he had hinted before departure that if Shiv needed him to, he was prepared to stay back indefinitely. He hoped to send some revenue home to us this way.

Only three days after Tony's departure, Shiv called and asked to speak to me. Dad had picked up the receiver, and when he called out for me, I sensed from the tone of Dad's voice that something had upset him. I walked with a heavy heart to take the receiver from Dad's hand. This was not going to be good.

Sure enough, Shiv went into a symphony of complaints about Tony's drinking. Apparently, Shiv had introduced Tony to a fellow Malaysian who had visited his mini-market. The two had struck it off immediately, promising to meet up later for a drink. This rendezvous ended in one drink too many, causing Tony to turn up late at a function specially held in his honour at the home of a relative. I was forced to keep the receiver a safe distance from my ear as Shiv shouted from the other end of the world, 'Do you realise how embarrassing it was for me? Your husband had the cheek to shrug off the whole episode!'

To add fuel to the fire, my ever-cordial Tony had made good friends with two young foreign entrepreneurs across the road. They were Shiv's business rivals but had become Tony's drinking buddies. That was the last straw for Shiv. Sighing heavily, he told me, 'I will give your husband a week's grace to think matters over and get his priorities right. I have spent a fair bit of money in the hope that he and I can work hand in glove as business partners, to supplement the income of both our families. I hate to say this, but I don't think your husband knows the meaning of responsibility and gratitude anymore. I wanted to be there for him, and you, as he had once been there for me, but he is living in a different world . . .'

Shiv's words hurt me badly, but they were undeniably true. I swallowed my pride and apologised for all the pain and hurt inflicted upon him by Tony. My fears had not been unfounded.

Thanking him for graciously giving Tony another chance, I put the receiver down.

Tony, his pride wounded, did not wish to be doled out a second chance. He must have been completely put off by Shiv's fiery threat, for he pulled a fast one on him, claiming that I had called while Shiv had been out, imploring Tony to come home quickly because I was finding it hard to manage without him!

I, who had done no such thing, was shocked to receive a sudden call from Shiv. He asked me furiously, 'If you felt that you would find it difficult to manage without him, why the hell did you agree for him to come to New Zealand? Do you know how much money I have lost? Do you even care how much humiliation I have undergone?'

I was stunned. I tried to clear my name, but I could not get a word in edge-wise. Every word I uttered seemed to aggravate the situation. Finally, I gave up and asked to speak to Tony, hoping to clarify the matter. A very infuriated Shiv replied, 'Forget it. Your darling husband is already on the flight home! I truly hope you are happy now. I really don't see how he is ever going to come up in life. I'm so angry with him that I'll shoot him the next time I see him! I can never forgive him!'

With that, Shiv slammed the phone down. I was quaking with shock at his murderous remark. Shuddering, I tried to attribute his threat to the intense frustration, humiliation, and financial loss that Tony had put him through.

Men never learn, do they? Shiv ought to have known by then that he had lost his lustre to Tony the day he had stopped drinking. I had tried so hard to explain tactfully to Shiv that Tony was far from ready for the big plans that Shiv had envisioned for them both, but Shiv had turned a deaf ear to everything I had said during that first phone call, labelling me a hindrance. If only he had given some consideration to my words, this rather ugly episode in our lives might have been prevented.

Delayed and Disgruntled

The New Zealand-returned Tony had nothing *new* to tell me. He was sullen the evening he got back because I had failed to personally pick him up from the airport. I had been informed by Sil that Tony had wanted me to be at the airport at 7.00 p.m. when he arrived. I had not gone personally because the adventurer had called earlier that day, to have a casual word with Tony.

On learning that Tony was arriving that evening, he grabbed the opportunity to do something to regain Tony's favour. The adventurer was still feeling guilty about the 4WD misadventure and was hoping to redeem himself by gallantly offering to fetch Tony home from the airport. I agreed and thanked him, relieved that I did not have to cancel and reschedule tuition classes. Also, I was too worn out then, mentally, to listen to yet another song of woe.

Unfortunately, the adventurer had ungallantly fallen asleep in his vehicle at the airport car park while waiting for Tony to arrive. He only woke up at 9.00 p.m., by which time Tony had already made his way to a public phone to give me a piece of his mind. The minute Tony heard my voice, he barked, 'If you didn't want to pick me up, you could have sent someone else. Your brother has brainwashed you, hasn't he?'

Again, I was being unjustly accused! I tried to explain to Tony how the adventurer had assured me that he would be met on time, but it was all in vain. Furious, he too slammed the phone on me. Apparently, phone-slamming was a New Zealand trend!

Thankfully, the adventurer had spotted Tony making for the taxi stand. He managed to appease him a little on the long drive home, but it took me almost two weeks to convince Tony that I was still on his side. It was painfully ironic—I was the one who had been *shot* by both brother and husband, but here I was, trying my utmost to pacify one and wondering when on earth I would be able to pacify the other! I dared not tell the wounded Tony that Shiv had threatened to shoot him on sight the next time they met. Neither did I tell Tony that Shiv would never forgive him for having caused him much financial loss and mental anguish, not to mention humiliation.

The Frail Father

During the period of strained relationship between Tony and me, his father fell ill. Seriously diabetic, the elderly man had been hospitalised off and on in various specialist centres. The last time he had been hospitalised, it was in another town, about an hour's drive away. Hence, Tony and I had not been able to visit him as often as we would have liked to. However, we planned to visit him, with the children, as soon as we could.

It was a festive season break when Tony and I took the children on a drive south, to visit their ailing paternal grandfather. When he saw us enter his room, he lovingly beckoned us to his bedside. As we drew nearer to him, it saddened me to see his condition. He smiled bravely, but it was obvious that he was pale and had lost considerable weight. The twinkle in his eyes had vanished. Despite his illness, his thick silver-grey hair was sleek and he was clean-shaven. My beloved father-in-law had always been meticulous about his appearance.

Although it was an effort for him to talk to the few relatives who were already standing by his bed, Tony's father's commanding voice still dominated the conversation. He even managed to joke a little with Wriggles when he held his arms out to embrace both the children. I smiled. I had always had this comforting suspicion that he had an extra-soft spot for Tony's children, although he already had a tribe of other grandchildren!

Sitting up, propped by pillows, he fed each of us a purple grape. It was an endearing habit of Tony's father to feed his family members something or the other with his own hand when overwhelmed with love. He tried to smile as though all was well, but there were tears in his eyes. Little did anyone know then that it would be the last time he would ever feed us.

As we drove home after the visit, Dewdrop asked Tony, 'Daddy, when will Grandpa come home? I want to visit him at home again.'

Wriggles cheekily added, 'Will there be any more grapes? That one was so sweet! Mummy, why can't you buy grapes like those?'

'Your grandpa is very ill. I just hope he recovers,' responded Tony sadly.

Tragedy and Tribulations

The death of my dear father-in-law was a big blow to Tony. The news came later that night itself. Although Tony had braced himself for such a moment, he still broke down and cried. I tried to comfort him, but I also sensed he needed space. There was an upheaval of emotions swirling in his heart and mind. There had been much unspoken love between father and son, but now it was too late to utter words that might have bridged the gap.

Tony had often tried not to show how much his father's favouritism towards his elder siblings affected him, but we at home knew otherwise. Tears would well up in Tony's eyes whenever anything he suggested to his father was put on hold, to be subjected first to the approval of his elder siblings. Only then would Tony's father even consider his suggestion.

I often felt that if Tony did not drink prior to calling on his father, the elderly man might have taken him a little more seriously. With the passage of time, Tony's nephews and nieces too seemed to have diminishing respect for their uncle. I realised sadly how drink had eroded Tony's lustre over the years. My heart bled for Tony.

It had been important to Tony that he too contribute towards the hospital expenses incurred when his ailing father had been warded in. We did not have much savings but gave ungrudgingly what we could. Tony and I could not help wishing that his father had spent a little more time with us and the children.

There was a stage when we had volunteered to look after Tony's father in our own home, but the elderly man had declined the offer, citing that both Tony and I had too much on our hands already, career-wise. I guessed he was more comfortable in his own home, communicating in his mother tongue.

Furthermore, Tony had a widowed sister-in-law who doted on his father and made sure that he ate his meals on time.

She unfailingly administered his medication as well. After her husband's death, this sister-in-law had made it a point to be more of a daughter than a daughter-in-law to Tony's father. This was because my kind father-in-law had not had the heart to send her back to her own country, where tradition would have rendered her a harbinger of misfortune at any wedding or other auspicious occasion. Although Tony's siblings and their spouses sometimes resented the love that their father showered upon this foreigner, he paid no heed.

In this country, in his house, she was still treated with respect and had never known want for anything. Hers had been an arranged marriage to Tony's elder brother, and on his untimely demise, my father-in-law had felt responsible for the welfare of this young bride, widowed at only 26. She had no children; hence, her father-in-law, her benefactor, was her world. She was also deeply religious, another factor in her favour. The death of Tony's father broke her completely. Her wails were the loudest in the house.

There was not a single dry eye at the funeral of the grand old man. Dewdrop even fainted, both from grief and the stuffy atmosphere pervading the house. Many members of the family on Tony's side, and some relatives, sensed that things would probably never be the same again.

My mother-in-law had died in her early thirties, but my father-in-law had never remarried. He had been both father and mother to the seven children that his wife had borne him.

Now that the patriarch had breathed his last, it remained to be seen if the family members would still be close to one another. Already, during his lifetime, there had been much feuding. Sibling rivalry had often been evident even during normal family gatherings.

The funeral proved no different. The siblings quarrelled among themselves as to who should pay for what, with each one grumbling about how much he or she had already contributed. Tony, watching from a distance, felt sickened by their endless squabbling and bickering, even at their own father's funeral.

A doctor friend, observing Tony from a distance, pulled me aside and told me, 'Your husband doesn't look too good. I strongly advise you to get him to seek medical attention as soon as possible.' I felt disturbed, but meekly nodded. Another doctor standing within earshot seconded his opinion. Alarmed, I took a good look at Tony standing not too far away—his face was indeed unusually dark and his eyes, bloodshot. These two doctors had not even seen Tony's swollen left calf, for he was clad in long pants.

As the cortege left from the house for the cemetery, I shed many tears—for my deceased father-in-law as well as for my ailing Tony. Dewdrop and Wriggles, walking on either side of me, squeezed my hands to comfort me. I really needed them more than ever now—my Tony was more ill than we had ever imagined.

Bloody Beginnings

'Tony! Tony! What's this in the washbasin? Is it blood?' I shrieked in alarm, staring at a bright red stain in the washbasin.

'What?' asked Tony in retort, making his way back quickly to the washbasin in the upstairs bathroom. He had just finished brushing his teeth and was in our bedroom. Looking at the washbasin, he said, 'Oh, this is normal. It's been like this for a while. I think I just need to take vitamin C. Stop looking so worried! It's just my gums. They've been bleeding more than usual when I brush my teeth—that's all. Relax, OK?'

As he returned to the bedroom, I followed him, feeling troubled. As I proceeded to make our bed, something on Tony's pillow caught my eye. Pointing at a reddish-brown stain on his pillowcase, I almost cried, 'Don't tell me you've been brushing your teeth here as well!'

Tony was at a loss for words. I saw his face fall and his mouth open. Obviously, Tony was also shocked at the sight of blood on his white pillowcase. Then putting on a brave front, he forced a smile and clung tenaciously to his earlier explanation about his gums bleeding. I could not help feeling that he was actually trying to convince himself.

'Tony, listen to me, please. I don't have a good feeling about these stains. Please, if not for my sake, at least for the sake of Dewdrop and Wriggles, let me take you to someone who can help you. Please, please, this time don't refuse. Your friends at your father's funeral pointed out to me that you look far from healthy. I felt as if they were accusing me of not taking good enough care of you. You know how often I have begged you to seek medical attention. Please, Tony, now, at least, comply . . .' I took both his hands in mine and looked into his eyes pleadingly.

He turned away. Trying to compromise, he said, 'I tell you what. Let me take vitamin C regularly for a week. You could also give me some fresh orange juice every morning, as soon as I get up. Then, if the bleeding persists, I might agree. However, it has nothing to do with drink. Knowing you, I think that's what you're actually trying to point out.'

It did not matter if he was accusing me. At least, I had got him to compromise.

A week passed with a glass of freshly squeezed orange juice greeting Tony every morning. A further daily dose of vitamin C followed at breakfast. Tony now got out of bed only after the children had left for school. He had not yet fully got over his father's demise less than a month before, and he was often restless in his sleep. As such, I let him get up at his own leisure.

Tony was constantly in pain; his swollen left calf greatly impeded movement. His darkening complexion alarmed me, and his bloodshot eyes did not help ease my anxiety the least bit. Dad and Mum were also growing more concerned. Tony was finding it increasingly difficult to walk, even if only from his car to the front door of our house. It seemed to be quite a struggle, for, on nearing the door, he would quickly sit on the doorstep to talk to Pluto, our pet dog. He would carry on for a few minutes, much to the amusement of Wriggles! Pluto would disdainfully turn away and settle down in the other direction. Even he knew fully well that Tony had actually sat down there because he was in too much pain then to take even one more step.

I could barely hold back my tears at the sight of my agonised Tony. To think that this was the same man who had been wielding a squash racket with such gusto, raring for a challenge, just a little over a year back! What had he become? Would he ever again be what he was before, before drink enslaved him?

Shocked and Shaken

Very early one morning, Tony suddenly woke me up. He had just come out of the bathroom, and there was blood trickling down one side of his mouth. I quickly sat up. Before I could exclaim, he asked, 'When can we see a doctor? Please make an appointment, and please, will you accompany me?' I looked into Tony's eyes—I had never seen Tony so shaken up. Holding my hands, he continued, 'I am afraid of what I may have to hear. I need you next to me, please.' Of course, I was going to be there with him, for him. I thanked God that Tony had finally come to his senses.

Arrangements were made almost immediately for Tony to see a local physician reputed to be among the best in our city. The appointment was fixed for 2.30 p.m. I requested Dad to stand in for me during the 3.00 p.m. tuition session, until I returned from the clinic. I had decided to give the students a test paper to work on until I got back. I prayed hard that Tony would not suddenly decide to cancel the appointment. He had been rather quiet morning that whole morning, and I just wished I knew what he was thinking about.

During lunch, Tony did not touch anything that was even mildly hot or spicy. This was quite a departure from the norm, for Tony enjoyed extra-spicy food. He requested, 'Please try to keep the food less spicy and, if possible, chilli-free as well. My stomach has been acting up of late.' I looked up quickly at Mum, who was just about to defend her cooking! Thankfully, I managed to stop her in time. I feared that she would point out that it was not the food responsible for Tony's sorry state, but drink. The last thing I needed just then was a difference of opinions.

We had to leave for the clinic before Dewdrop returned from school. Before we left, however, Tony kissed Wriggles and said, 'Pray for my health, won't you, son?'

Tony looked rather worried, even nervous, as we drove to the clinic for his appointment. We both knew, deep down, that the doctor would probably have something negative to say about Tony's condition. Not many words were exchanged during the drive there.

We did not have to wait too long to see the doctor. He examined Tony carefully, starting with his eyes and proceeding to his abdomen, which appeared to be distended. He also took a good look at Tony's swollen left calf. During the examination, the doctor asked Tony a few questions. Then he sat down to talk to both Tony and me. Tony had started to look uncomfortable.

'I'm afraid that your liver is damaged to a considerable extent. It would be advisable for you to lay off drink completely. If you don't,' the doctor added rather solemnly, 'your condition could deteriorate even further, very quickly.' Then he prescribed some medication, saying, 'This medicine is not a buffer against alcohol, which means you must not take it presuming you can carry on drinking. It is meant to protect the remaining part of the ailing liver. Mind you, this can only be achieved if you totally refrain from drink, even beer.' We thanked him and left.

Depressing Denial

Tony was silent on the way home, and he looked rather depressed. I did not discuss the matter, for I thought it would be wiser to give him some space. He needed to do some serious thinking. Also, I did not wish to repeat what he had obviously not liked the sound of. The advice had come from a medical professional, not a nagging wife or any other overly concerned member of the family. All cards had been laid clearly on the table. If he did not see good enough reason now to quit drink, he was never, ever going to!

When we reached home, my students were already working quietly on the test paper. Dad joined the rest of us in the living room, where Mum and the children were already anxiously waiting to hear what the doctor had said. Thinking it would be better for Tony himself to tell them what he wished to disclose, I excused myself and entered the classroom. I thought it would be easier for Tony to break the rather disturbing news to them if I were not around.

However, before the class in session could be dismissed, I heard Tony driving off in his car. Startled, I returned to the living room to find out where he had gone. Mum and Dad were watching Wriggles complete a puzzle, while Dewdrop was at the dining table, bent over her homework. 'Where's Daddy gone?' I asked her.

Looking up, she replied, 'He said he had to meet someone and would be back in a couple of hours.'

Dad, Mum, and the children were behaving as usual—I gathered that Tony had not told them about the doctor's findings, or if he had, it was probably only to an extent that would not cause the family anxiety over his drinking. I sighed and threw my hands up in despair!

That evening, Tony returned earlier than he normally did. Nevertheless, it was obvious that it had not been a drink-free evening. I just could not understand why he was still being so adamant about not giving up the cursed brew! His foolhardiness was surely going to get the better of him.

As Tony's dinner was being warmed up, he called out to Mum, 'Please remember that I do not want any chilli or spicy food!'

The Truth Is Out!

I was within earshot, and no longer able to tolerate this injustice, I challenged Tony, 'I do not recall the doctor saying anything about food that is to be avoided. Why pick on the food when it is drink that you should totally abstain from? What are you trying to prove, Tony?' Without waiting for an answer, I continued, 'You heard what the doctor said about giving up drink completely if you wish to salvage the little that is left of your liver!'

Unable to contain my pain and frustration any longer with regard to Tony's indifferent attitude, I went on, 'To make things worse, you haven't even told the family the truth about your condition! I just don't know what to make of you—you don't even care for your own wife and children! We don't deserve to be treated like this. Don't you feel, even in the slightest, that you owe it to your family, at least now, to look after your health and give up drinking? When on earth are you going to come to your senses?'

Tony glared at me with bloodshot eyes. For a moment, I thought he was going to strike me. I did not care anymore. The truth had to come out. I had held my tongue for far too long. Not one to raise his hands in the presence of the elders and our children, Tony stormed upstairs, entered our bedroom, and slammed the door shut, locking me out for the night.

I then turned to my alarmed parents to tell them myself what the doctor had told both Tony and me earlier that day. Dewdrop and Wriggles, who had never seen their mother so worked up before, listened intently too. It was best that all at home be made aware of Tony's deteriorating condition. Deep within our hearts, each one of us loved Tony as much as ever, but his indifference to his own health and the well-being of his family was hard to accept or forgive. Though none of us dared to say it out loud, we each wondered if he would ever be able to give up what seemed to have become the utmost priority in his life.

As I tried to get some sleep on the sofa that night, I could not help feeling sorry for myself and the children. I felt terribly let down as I allowed myself to go down memory lane.

Recounting Sweeter Times

Tony had vowed, during early courtship, 'If you promise to be mine, I'll never let you shed a tear or feel regret.' Had he forgotten? He had made this solemn promise at a temple we had visited on an auspicious day. I had returned from overseas a few months earlier, and though Tony had revealed his feelings for me even before I had left for further studies, I had not reciprocated.

I was quite sure then that my elders would not approve of our relationship. Furthermore, I was determined to pursue further education. My return had been unscheduled and premature: things had not been very conducive at home. During my absence, Tony had given Dad and Mum his full support in every way, winning them over completely with his sincerity and dedication.

I had left an admirer behind, in the country where I had been studying, but he could never hold a candle to the gallant Tony. Tony was fully aware of the existence of a rival, for I had never hidden this from my family. Knowing also that I had not exactly been over the moon in the said relationship, Tony probably felt that he still stood a chance to win my heart.

Tony had taken me to the temple that morning of the auspicious day to beg for this chance. There, he had reached out for my hand, and holding it tightly in his own, he had vowed that if I only gave him a chance, he would make it a priority to always keep me happy. What had happened to that vow to never let me shed a tear?

I had enjoyed far better days when Tony had not started drinking even beer. Then we had often spent a pleasant evening out at the movies, without any desire to get the outing over with quickly. It had both flattered and touched me when I had asked, 'Don't you feel the need to join your other friends? I'm sure they are more exciting.'

Tony had answered, without any hesitation whatsoever, 'No, I don't need them. *You* are my best friend.'

Those were the times when I could actually relax and look forward to some tasty fare at a nearby hawkers' centre, followed by an iced concoction of mixed fruit delights. Tony would have the same; in fact, he would be the one to suggest the cooling, refreshing dessert—a bowl of mixed fruits hidden in a little mountain of shaved ice topped with syrup and cream, resembling a snow-capped mountain. He always ordered only one, so that we would be 'forced' to share. We would dig into it eagerly, each holding a spoon.

When Tony had first started to have a beer or two in the company of those he had hoped would help promote business, he would make sure that such sessions did not become a regular affair. Then he had determinedly made time for exercise and a few rounds of badminton with friends who also valued fitness and good health. Happy hours with business acquaintances had been just a weekly affair.

It had been during such a calm and reassuring period that we had tied the knot. I did not feel threatened, for Tony had always stressed, 'A family-minded responsible man should never drink more than is necessary. In fact, once business has picked up and shows a steady trend, I may give up drinking altogether.' I was bowled over.

Tony cited certain ex-business associates who had drunk more than was good for them, or their respective families, thereby destroying all that they had struggled to establish. He had declared, 'Never should a man put the happiness and security of his family at stake.' Mine was a thinking man—level-headed and far-sighted. I was at peace.

Fractured Promises

Later, sadly, Tony had slowly, unwittingly increased his intake of beer and the frequency of its consumption. This coincided with the period that Tony's partner had started to harass him. As if that was not enough for me to contend with at the time, a friend of Tony's remarked, 'Hey, Tony, you've gained a lot of weight! That's a beer belly that you're sporting! Why don't you switch to whisky instead?' Tony felt slighted. He had always valued his good physique.

At first, I had not been too worried, for it was a known fact that Tony, in an amateurish attempt to drink whisky a few years back, had developed very bad rashes. He had sworn then never to go near whisky again. Unfortunately, Tony, reassured by a drinking doctor friend that he had probably developed greater tolerance to whisky after all the years of drinking, decided to give the evil spirit a second chance. Tony soon found a new master, who slowly but surely ravaged his liver.

Back to Reality

The shrill whistle from the electric kettle in the kitchen woke me up from a rather fitful sleep on the sofa. It was early in the morning. When I entered the kitchen to make a cup of tea, I saw Tony already there, taking his medication out of its foil. I was about to caution him against taking it on an empty stomach, when he walked to the opposite counter and picked up a plate, which had been hidden from view. As he turned around, I saw on it two slices of bread and a slice of cheese, already removed from its plastic wrap. I did not have to say anything at all. Perhaps giving him a piece of my mind the previous evening had hit home after all.

Much was still left to be seen. I prayed hard that Tony would not forget what the doctor had said about the medicine; it was not meant to be taken as a buffer against drinking, but to prevent further damage to the remaining part of the liver which was still functioning. Drinking while on the drug would be great folly.

The Reliable Tony

My beloved husband had been a whiz at getting accident and damaged vehicles repaired at workshops during his career as a loss adjuster. His job had ensured that he perpetually enjoyed a good rapport with the owners of reputable workshops. I say 'reputable' because Tony was a man of integrity. He was not one to dance to the tune of unscrupulous workshop operators, who, with intent to make quick money, preferred to work hand in glove with loss adjusters who were willing to close an eye to exorbitant charges for parts replaced and labour provided. Both parties, of course, expected a share from the surcharge.

Tony had a conscience, and he never relished surveying damaged vehicles that had been assigned to be repaired at such workshops. The money-motivated workshop operators too had never felt comfortable if Tony happened to be the adjuster assigned to assess damage to any vehicle at their workshop; with him, there was no room for unauthorised profit.

Owing to the nature of his job, great rapport with the owners of certain well-established workshops and readiness to help a fellow human being, Tony's friends often relied on him. Why? Well, my Tony was *the* man to get their damaged vehicles repaired quickly and at minimal cost whenever they

173

were unfortunate enough to be involved in mishaps on the road.

If a friend happened to call in distress after an accident, Tony would jump out of bed even if it was an unearthly hour and immediately take charge of the situation. He would make a couple of calls while hastily getting dressed and get things moving. Tony himself would be at the site of the accident, even before the tow truck could make its way there! Yes, to his friends, Tony was a guardian angel.

The Accident-prone Tony

Sadly, Tony often forgot his halo when driving his own vehicle. He was involved in quite a few vehicular mishaps after having consumed drink. I lost count of the number of times Tony had knocked and dented his own car, and even poor Dad's!

Most times, the mishaps occurred after Tony had downed one too many. It was not very pleasant for those of us at home when Tony, on his return, would be tailed by the irate driver of the vehicle involved in a mishap with Tony's own vehicle. The damage would predictably be to the rear end of the other vehicle, indicating clearly that Tony was at fault. He himself had taught me this when I used to prepare accident survey reports for insurance companies.

I would be compelled to settle the matter amicably with the furious driver, often paying more than the assessed cost, just to pacify him! After the departure of such a visitor, Tony would either try to defend himself with a pitiful tale or walk away sheepishly. After a few such incidents, it became the norm for Tony to do the latter.

I was greatly relieved that Tony was not injured, but of course, I could not say the same for our own vehicle. That would be an additional bill to settle. Thankfully, Tony knew people who would repair his vehicle speedily, but they could not always oblige to do it for free. Also, parts that had to be replaced, such as headlights, could not always be salvaged from other damaged vehicles of similar model; even second-hand replacements cost money!

Tony was involved in two rather serious accidents. Both the vehicular mishaps had occurred after drink, and on both occasions, Tony had been unaccompanied. He sustained a fractured clavicle in the first mishap and lacerations requiring stitches in the second. Our badly damaged vehicle was in the workshop for several weeks as a result of each of these accidents. The family members, on receiving the news and viewing the damaged vehicle, sustained shock and trauma, which only time could heal. Things would never again be the same.

My Nocturnal Ritual

Each time Tony was late in coming home after these two accidents, there would be unspoken uneasiness in the hearts of all those who waited for him to return. The children could be chided and sent off to bed, but Dad and Mum had to be reassured more tactfully that I would report to them when he returned, no matter what time. We just wanted him home, safe and sound.

I too found it impossible to sleep. I would toss and turn, alerted by the sound of any vehicle turning at the dead end in front of our house. It was to become a habit that could not be altered. When the familiar sound of Tony's approaching vehicle finally reached my straining ears, I would rush out of our bedroom to report his safe return to my anxious parents, who were presumably already asleep.

Rushing down the stairs, I would quickly open the front door. Putting on slippers, I would walk to the gate to unlock and open it. Tony would drive his vehicle, a little unsteadily, into the garage. I would pretend to be unaffected by his late return. As he unsteadily dragged himself out of his car, I would nonchalantly close and lock the gate.

Once we entered the house, Tony would try to make light conversation. Silently, I would lock the front door and head for the kitchen. While he showered, I would lay the table for him.

After warming up his dinner in the microwave, I would pour cold water in a tall glass and finally return to bed.

Tony would eat his dinner only if he felt like it. After finishing the tall glass of cold water, he would slowly crawl into bed. It never failed to amuse me how he unfailingly kissed me goodnight even if he suspected that I was fuming within.

When I was quite sure he was fast asleep, I would return to the dining room to either clear and clean the table or put away what had not been touched. Many a time, his dinner would remain untouched. If not, only half would have been consumed. I was always relieved when his plate was completely empty. He seemed to be losing appetite.

I would also check to see if the television had been switched off, for Tony would often settle into his armchair to eat dinner in front of the television. He also often forgot to switch off the television and the fan. Worse, there had even been times when he had dozed off in his armchair, with his half-empty dinner plate precariously perched on his lap. The telecast would have long been over, and the television screen would be 'snowing'! I would discover this only after having waited in vain for my goodnight kiss.

This nightly rigmarole had become a fixed nocturnal pattern in our lives. It would not have been so silent and peaceful if I had not learnt from past mistakes that any protest on my part only stirred up a vociferous storm. Another reason for my voluntary silence was that at least Tony had returned home safe and sound. I had even learnt to accept the dents and knocks to the family cars, thanks to my benevolent dad.

My Giving Dad

Though proud of the immaculate condition of his car, Dad gallantly let Tony drive his vehicle whenever Tony's own vehicle was under repair at the workshop or being serviced. My heart was always in my mouth at such times, until Tony had brought Dad's vehicle safely home. The few times that Tony had grazed or even dented Dad's car, Dad would sportingly comment, 'I bet the other car was not as strong as mine!'

Tony, touched by Dad's light-hearted manner and diplomatic handling of the situation, would look at me apologetically, and quickly reassure us, 'I promise I will get the vehicle back to tip-top condition the first thing tomorrow morning!' Thank God for workshops and their accommodating operators!

If only ailing humans, and livers, could be restored in similar fashion . . .

New Wheels for a Failing Liver

After the last rather-serious accident, Tony's vehicle, despite having been repaired, gave problems occasionally. Tony had to take it, time and again, to the same workshop for further post-repair investigations and adjustments. The further repairs came with a bill each time, and this was becoming a strain. One day, Tony voiced his feelings: 'It would perhaps be wiser to sell off the car or even trade it in for a new one,' he said. 'With so much being spent on trying to maintain it, we might as well be paying towards a loan for a brand-new, trouble-free vehicle.'

'Impossible!' I protested. 'As it is, I'm already struggling to make ends meet!'

'But don't you see? The purchase of a new vehicle would further motivate me to steer away from drink. The money I would normally have spent on drinking each month could be channelled instead towards repayment of a hire-purchase loan,' he reasoned.

I was sceptical. Tony had only just started taking the medication, barely a week back. Although he had started to return home earlier than previously, I could not say for certain that he had completely given up drinking. Just a couple of days after the visit to the doctor, I still got a whiff of alcohol when Tony returned home. I had taken a risk and remarked that the smell of drink lingered about him. Affronted by my lack of trust in him, he denied having taken even a drop. He claimed, however, that he had stepped into a pub to look for a friend. I was not convinced.

His proposal of purchasing a new vehicle, though a heavy commitment, might actually be a step in the right direction. Tony had spoken sensibly. In this way, I could perhaps motivate him; I could restrain Tony completely from drink if I agreed to the proposed purchase of a brand-new car. There would definitely be no money left to pay for drink if a hefty amount was to be paid monthly to a finance company.

Attempts to sell Tony's car proved futile, so we finally decided to trade in the three-year-old vehicle for a newer model. Tony gave me a pleasant surprise when the agreement of purchase was being prepared in the showroom manager's office. He suddenly said, 'I feel that circumstances might improve if you consent to the car being registered in your name.' I was taken aback, undeniably, but I felt a flutter of excitement.

Until then, I did not have a single asset in my name. It was Tony who had been registered as owner of our previous vehicles. He unabashedly declared in front of the manager, 'You are the best thing that has happened in my life, and anything that has something to do with you can only bring me good luck!' I was dumbfounded. He added, 'I also feel that it is the right thing to do, considering the fact that you will be the one repaying the loan until such time I'm able to take over.'

Tony knew that I had not expected him to make such a gesture. I had, of my own free will, always chosen to walk behind him. If at times, he had encouraged me to walk beside him, I did, but it would not be too long before I found myself behind him once more. As for ever walking ahead of him, I could never imagine that happening in this life!

Being subservient to Tony was entirely my own self-conditioning. During my visits to Tony's home while we were still courting, I could not help but notice that the womenfolk were treated as subordinates. They seemed to be contented with their status in life and sought neither recognition nor appreciation. It was perhaps then that I had subconsciously made a mental note not to override Tony if I desired a happy and peaceful relationship. I had no intention of upsetting the atmosphere that prevailed in the home of my in-laws, or the mental equilibrium that existed in Tony's mind.

As Tony proudly drove our new light-golden Nissan home, I wondered smugly if any other female member of Tony's family had a car registered in her name! Even the registration plate bore a number that was a combination of our birthdates!

Dewdrop and Wriggles waited excitedly at the gate to welcome the new car into the garage. As Tony drove it in, the children beamed with joy and pride. As soon as Tony got out of the car, Dewdrop and Wriggles eagerly opened the rear doors and climbed in to inspect the interior. They oohed and aahed in delight at the sight of the plush upholstery and modern gadgets designed to make driving a pleasure. Of course, they were taken for a drive in the new car almost immediately. It was a delightful ride, with Tony voluntarily making promises to spend more time with the both of them. I could only keep my fingers crossed.

New Car, New Leaf

Just a few days after the arrival of the new car, Tony suddenly suggested, 'Let me give you a hand with the tuitions.' I could hardly believe my ears! I could not imagine my Tony, never one to sit in a place for long, let alone stand at a desk for hours, confined to the four walls of a classroom. He would most definitely be a square peg in a round hole!

It tickled me as I tried to imagine the look on the faces of my bewildered students, should Tony take over the lesson. I laughed unintentionally, and Tony felt slighted. He asked in a hurt voice, 'Are you thinking that I will not be able to cope?'

I quickly replied, 'I'm sorry, Tony. I didn't mean to hurt you. It's just that you have always insisted on a job which allows you mobility. You like fieldwork, being an outdoor person . . .'

He then confessed, 'At this moment in my life, with my ailment, it would be best for me to keep a low profile. To be quite frank also, I have always felt guilty about hardly having given you a helping hand. You have always been at my side, seeing to it that my reports on accidents and thefts were completed without a hitch and submitted on time, but I've never played a role in your career. I would now like to assist you if it's all right. Please give me a chance to do right by you.'

I realised at that moment that if I did not accept Tony's proposal to assist me in the classroom, it would hurt him no end. Even worse, it would probably shatter his self-esteem. I asked him when he could report for duty.

Tutor Tony

It was a slightly nervous Tony who stepped into the classroom the next evening. I had prepared my junior-most class for their new tutor. I thought it would be the wiser step to take, for the senior students, who were being prepared for a forthcoming major public examination, might find the sudden change of tutor rather unsettling. Also, I had once observed Tony giving instructions to a group of young children at a family sports meet, and he was very much at home with them. The children, for their part, had taken to him immediately.

As expected, Tony got along fairly well with the 13-year-olds where general communication was concerned. However, when it came to actually imparting knowledge, Tony was at a slight loss. At Tony's request, I stood silently at the back of the classroom all the while, to ensure things went smoothly. As soon as he signalled to me, I stepped in and did the necessary. As the session progressed, I was the main tutor, holding court while Tony stood at hand to help any student who seemed to have a problem. This was not the way it had been planned at all. I wondered for how long Tony would accept the role of subordinate tutor.

Gallantly, Tony roughed it out in the classroom a couple of times more before calling it a day. I sensed the students' unvoiced relief! They, for their part, had tried to understand Tony's different approach and co-operate with him as best they could. However, one could not help but sense the underlying tension. Tony, as was his style, wanted to accomplish the maximum in the minimum possible time; children need to be handled with much patience and understanding. Besides, they were not all of the same calibre. It had taken me more than two decades till then, to understand these young minds, each one a gem in his or her own way.

The students might not have learnt much during the few days' trial, but Tony obviously realised something. I was touched when he suddenly paid me a compliment. He confessed, 'Only after stepping into the classroom and trying to fit into your shoes have I realised what a mountainous task you carry on your small shoulders. It's truly a wonder that you have never complained each time you start a new course of tuitions for five different levels at the beginning of each year!'

Tony then marvelled at what I had managed to accomplish at the end of each tuition year, admitting that although he had sometimes felt irritated when the telephone rang constantly as parents expressed their heartfelt gratitude at the success of their children, he was also proud. He sheepishly added, 'Now I know why students queue up outside our house at the beginning of each tuition intake!' He gave me a very warm hug and told me, with tears in his eyes, 'Sweetheart, I am very proud to be your husband.'

I wished he would hold me like that forever.

Illogical Logistics

The new car that we had purchased was an automatic one, but Tony still found it rather painful when it came to getting into the vehicle or alighting from it. Though he would not openly admit it, it was obvious from the grimace on his countenance. I was therefore surprised as well as concerned when Tony announced that he had met up with a cousin in the logistics line and wanted to give a shot at assisting him whenever there was an opportunity to deliver goods. He would have to get into and alight from a higher vehicle—what was he thinking?

This particular cousin of Tony had kept a rather low profile, as far as I could recall, owing to some misunderstanding that had cropped up among the members of his family and those on my in-laws' side. Puzzled, I queried, 'Tony, why the revived interest in this relationship with the very same cousin that you did not have much respect for in the past? I just don't understand this move.'

He replied, 'I've decided to let bygones be bygones and give priority to at least some form of occupation for the moment. This cousin has been pretty successful and needs reliable staff in order to expand. It's not easy to find dependable assistants, and I thought it would at least be better than just sitting at home, brooding until opportunity knocks.'

'You know you should not be straining your leg. Driving an automatic car itself seems to take its toll on you,' I protested.

Tony reassuringly said, 'I promise not to overexert myself. I sincerely want to try to contribute financially, to help curb the family's dwindling finances.'

Tony told me that he had made it very clear to his cousin that he would only be navigator to the new driver, who was not too familiar with the locations of certain towns in the south. Tony, during his time as adjuster, had mastered all the routes. He had also made it known to his cousin that he could not carry heavy loads, owing to his bad leg.

What could I say? I made a mental note to discreetly call this cousin and request him not to put too much strain on my ailing Tony. I was, however, relieved that Tony would at least have a change of scene with the new job. He had become rather restless after the classroom episode. Besides, we could most definitely use the extra income.

Recklessly Recalcitrant

When Tony was out one day, I optimistically called his cousin. His wife answered the phone. When I introduced myself to her, she good-naturedly told me that her husband had gone to the market. She then dropped a bomb—he was out buying meat that Tony had requested her to cook, with lots of spice and chilli! The two men had planned to have a drinking session that evening, after Tony returned from his assignment. I felt my body go limp. She cheerfully rattled on, oblivious of the mental turmoil she had just caused.

I could not understand Tony's attitude at all! Here I was, trying to keep him alive, and there he was, digging his own grave! Didn't he care anymore? What on earth was he trying to prove? Did he secretly despise me? Was he punishing me? Dewdrop was to sit for a very major examination the following year and most certainly did not need this kind of stress on top of the pressure of studies and tuition classes. Wriggles had not even got to know his father well yet. What about the football training Tony had promised to give our Wriggles?

What about the promises that Tony had made to me about spending more time with me after he had discovered how bravely I had endured the load of tuitions and the challenges of bringing up the family, often single-handedly? Had they just been mere words whispered into the air, only to be blown away easily? Where was the essence of his love? Sure, sure, he loved me, but it was obviously not strong enough a love to overcome his weakness! Oh, God! What great sin had I committed that I was being tormented so?

Suddenly, I heard the same voice on the other end of the receiver asking me if I could perhaps join them that evening too. I wanted to shout and scream, 'Join you? What on earth for? I know, I know, you want me to join in the fun of watching a man destroy himself and shatter his family! You want me to witness how Tony drinks enough to ravage his liver further and make himself sick enough to qualify for a liver transplant! You want me to join you so that for sure, my marriage is ruined and my children perhaps will be left fatherless?'

Then I realised that this kind woman, obliging enough to cook delicious 'liver-ruining' food for my husband, probably had not the slightest inkling of his physical condition. Tony might have shown his cousin and his wife his bad leg, but I doubted that he had shown them his ravaged liver! It was not fair on my part to vent my anger and frustrations on this accommodating soul. I politely declined her kind invitation to watch my husband self-destruct.

I pacified myself. After tuition classes were over that night, I would wait for Tony and confront him. I had every right to—I was unfailingly spending a hefty sum on the purchase of medication to salvage the still-not-ravaged part of his liver, but all in vain. These expensive capsules were most definitely not going to serve their purpose if the captain of my already threatened domestic ship kept throwing caution to the wind and courted tsunamis at every possible port! God help this exasperated ship-hand!

On Tony's return late that night, I pulled him up. The rest of the family knew that I had a battle to wage, and they had retired for the night, perhaps secretly relieved that their services were not required at the battlefront.

Tony, reeking of liquor, entered the house in a daze. He had not driven home but had been given a lift by the kind, hospitable cousin who perhaps thought it wiser not to get down even to say hello when he saw how upset I was. He drove off hurriedly, with a screech of tyres.

I braced myself to confront my beloved 'enemy'. Tony smiled sheepishly, knowing full well that he most probably had to give me a walkover. Myriad questions targeting his foolhardiness and tardiness were at the tip of my tongue, the answers to which I already knew, but still sought to seek, to justify the myriad accusations that I could no longer contain, even at the risk of losing my only recently awarded status of Wonder Wife! Fortunately for Tony that night, the brewing storm of a battle had to be put on hold—nothing would have registered in his alcohol-clouded mind.

The next morning, as soon as Dad and I had sent the children to their respective schools, I confided in Dad, 'I need to confront Tony, preferably in complete privacy.' As soon as we reached home, Dad and Mum drove off to the market, leaving the battlefield clear.

I was still fairly worked up, having been unable to get any sleep the previous night. Soon, I heard water running in the upstairs bathroom, indicating that the enemy was finally up and about. I had seldom been vociferously aggressive, but today, it was imperative that I should be so.

The Angry-Wife Ambush

As soon as Tony came out of the bathroom, he yelled out as he normally did after his morning shower, for his coffee. I answered from downstairs in a tone that surprised even me—I curtly told him, 'If you want coffee, come downstairs and get it. I'm not bringing it upstairs to you!'

He was taken aback and asked very politely, 'Is everything all right downstairs? Are Mum and Dad at war again?'

Oooh, the impudence! How dare he? Their battles were harmless, non-family shattering episodes! I could feel my blood beginning to boil already! Biting my tongue, I answered sarcastically but firmly, 'For your information, all is fine with them, the children, and even the dog!'

Sensing that a storm was brewing on the not-too-distant horizon, Tony, clad only in his damp towel, slowly descended the stairs. He walked to the dining table and poured himself a mug of coffee. He sensed very correctly that I was not my usual accommodating self.

Still holding his mug, he slowly walked into the living room. He was bleary-eyed and clearly in pain—his left leg was pitifully swollen, and I could barely refrain from running to him, to comfort him.

Quickly but silently, I reprimanded myself for forgetting that I was to take him to task. It was not going to be easy, however, for my beloved enemy, with his still-ruffled hair, looked so vulnerable and rather helpless. He made for his usual armchair and sank into it, obviously relieved to take the weight off his feet. Now, I had to strike.

In a voice steeped with sarcasm, I asked Tony, 'So, my darling husband, how is your new career progressing?' Before he could answer, I asked him point-blank, 'What is more appealing and interesting—the change of scenery as you direct the driver of your cousin's vehicle along roads familiar only to you, or the thought of the merrymaking that will follow, complete with hot spicy meat and free-flowing booze?'

Tony, stunned, immediately lost the fetching bleary-eyed look and glared hard at me. If he had been able to stand up without any difficulty, I was pretty sure that he would have made a lunge at me, to shake me back to normal mode—the subservient, docile, unquestioning lesser half.

Unable to do so, he clutched tightly the arms of his throne, willing himself to at least stand up and tower over me, before giving a slamming, majestic retort. He managed to finally stand up, but before he could give me a verbal lashing to put me in my place, the sound of Dad's car pulling up outside the gate was heard. I was secretly relieved, for I had been spared the volley of words, at least for the moment.

The Fleeing Foe

An hour and a few telephone calls later, Tony was dressed and gone. His mug of coffee was left on the table, only half-finished. He had neither eaten a morsel nor touched his medication. He meant, perhaps, to get back at me in this manner. He knew how much I loved him, and this was his way of hurting me—by blatantly refusing to try to rectify his ailing condition. Well, at least now he knew that I was aware that he was not keeping to his promise of total abstinence from drink.

Technically, I ought to have been a smug victor in the battle just fought; why then was there a foreboding prevailing, one with a timbre of imminent tragedy? With a heavy heart, I trod through the remaining hours of the day, performing my daily chores in zombie-like fashion.

It was one of the longest days in my life. I was not looking forward to the late evening either, for I was certain that the captain of my most threatened vessel would try to punish me by returning home extra late. I did not feel in the least inclined to try to telephone him and patch things up, as I used to in the past, just to make the day pass more pleasantly for the both of us.

I had observed this practice often, for Tony spent many hours on the road, and I felt it was not safe for him to drive with a troubled mind. I was astonished at my surging reluctance to clear the air—I had obviously reached the stage where I felt that nothing was ever going to make him give up this self-destructive habit. Why even bother to try?

Laying Down Arms

However, that evening proved me a little wrong. Tony came back early and, after a shower, sat down to have dinner with the family, me excluded. I only ate after classes were over at 9.00 p.m. He retired early that night, even before the children had finished their homework.

Concerned, I stealthily entered our bedroom and tiptoed in the dark to where he lay, seemingly asleep. As I turned to leave the room, Tony called out to me, weakly. I was completely taken aback. Something was not right at all! I hastened to his side, and he reached out for me. I pulled away gently and went to quickly switch on the light.

As I returned to where he lay, on his side of the bed, I saw bloodstains on the pillow! This time, they were bigger and more gruesome. Open-mouthed, I looked at them and then at him, questioningly. Tony looked away, feeling awkward.

I turned his face towards me, firmly. His eyes were bloodshot, and there were dark circles around them. His lips were parched and he looked haggard. I had not seen him look this bad before. I sat down beside him. I knew there was something troubling him, but even if I listened, what good would it do? Yet I could not move away—he was a part of me, and he was in great pain.

With a heavy heart, I asked him, 'What's troubling you? What's on your mind? Please tell me.'

He disclosed hesitantly, 'I've not been feeling too well the whole day, right from the time I left the house in the morning.' Then he added, 'Although I have high regard for the physician whom we consulted, I strongly feel that we should seek a second opinion.'

I wondered, to myself, 'What about? To confirm that your liver is ravaged or to assure you that you can safely continue drinking indefinitely?' Mentally fatigued, I debated whether to be cruel to him and put him in his place, or indulge him and make the necessary arrangements, which would inevitably involve more time, effort, and money, not to mention further heartache.

Considering that I had already given him a piece of my mind that morning and fully aware that he had found it rather difficult to reveal what had been troubling him, I said, 'All right, I'll see what can be done.'

'Thank you,' responded Tony, feeling relieved. I left the room with a sigh. I could not help feeling that I was going to be dealt an even bigger blow in the near future.

The Second Opinion

The captain's latest request was entertained first thing the next morning. I was hastened by the sight of more appalling bloodstains that had made their gruesome appearance during the course of the night. With my heart in my mouth, I enlisted the help of a close friend, also a physician, to furnish me the particulars of the best gastroenterologist in the country.

I soon got feedback that it was near impossible to be granted consultation by this accomplished doctor at such short notice. Thankfully, by a stroke of good luck and a personal request made by our concerned physician friend, an appointment was fixed for the following week, in the capital. It had been arranged for the morning hours as I was unable to cancel my classes in the afternoon.

The next few days seemed to drag, capped by nights which were far from peaceful. Tony's symptoms became more marked, and one could not help but feel that dire times lay ahead for Tony and the whole family.

The day before the appointment, I cautioned Tony, 'You have not been entirely dry, and your appointment with the consultant is tomorrow.'

Irritated that I had checked him, he remarked, not very subtly, 'If you're going to keep nagging me, I may not even keep the appointment!' Knowing full well that he was quite capable of doing just that, I decided to hold my tongue and keep my fingers crossed. I did not want to risk Tony not keeping the crucial appointment, probably *the* very appointment that would be the turning point in our lives.

Even on that night, Tony came back smelling of alcohol. I consoled myself, thinking that perhaps God wanted the consultant gastroenterologist to get a really true picture of my very adamant captain.

The Disturbing Drive Up

The following dawn saw me getting silently into the backseat with Wriggles. Tony drove sullenly, with Dad seated beside him. I had requested Dad to accompany us, in case Tony had to stay back for any tests. I was in no state to drive home alone, with Wriggles. I had not slept for many nights. Also, I needed moral support. Wriggles had missed school that morning, encouraged by his father. I suspected that his presence had a soothing effect on Tony.

Fortunately, traffic that morning was not heavy, and we reached the capital in less than two hours. Tony headed towards the hospital and parked the car. After breakfast at a nearby shop across the road, Tony and I proceeded to locate the consultant's clinic in the hospital. Meanwhile, Dad entertained Wriggles in the lobby, answering his many queries about the visit.

We had to wait for almost an hour after we had registered at the counter of the very busy hospital. I also submitted the medical report on Tony, prepared by the physician we had first consulted. Tony and I hardly spoke to each other. I did not trust myself not to provoke him. God alone knew what he was going through just then. I had to give him some space, but I secretly treasured hope that after this visit to the esteemed consultant, our threatened ship might just be steered towards calmer waters, and the captain and I would be able to communicate more amicably.

Finally, Tony's name was called out by a nurse. Wriggles was thrilled to hear his father's name called out loud and clear! Tony turned to look at me, his eyes pleading that I accompany him. I went willingly, for I needed to know exactly what was wrong, how much was wrong, and what could be done to salvage Tony's future, *our* future.

The Definitive Diagnosis

The professor was a very mild-mannered gentleman. He examined Tony for a few minutes and then proceeded to explain the whole situation clearly but firmly. Looking at Tony straight in the eye, he began, 'I'm afraid you're on an irreversible path. Nothing can be done to repair the damage already incurred. We can only try to save what is left of your liver, and to do this, you must abstain totally from drink. You must not even take a drop of shandy! If you do, you will surely be heading for disaster. There is still some hope if you give full co-operation. This will, perhaps, give your liver a little time to restore itself.'

The professor also advocated psychiatric counselling in that very hospital, the first appointment for which could be set for that afternoon itself. I was in a fix, for I had classes later that day, back to back, and the drive home would be no less than two hours. I pictured myself making numerous frantic calls to my students to cancel the first two sessions, little realising that I had not even brought with me my contact diary!

Tony's rude scoff at the suggestion of him being referred to a psychiatrist brought me back to harsh reality—Tony practically glared at the startled professor, declaring, 'What? Are you saying that I may be mentally unstable? I assure you I am not mad!'

With that, Tony made for the door, leaving me torn between meekly following him and dutifully listening to what the much-acclaimed professor had to say—we had been so fortunate even to have been granted an appointment made at such notice!

Reluctantly, I chose to do the former, but I was requested by the well-meaning professor to stay behind for a minute. Tony heard the professor call me back, and he turned around to ask the professor what he had to say to me alone. The professor replied, 'Only your wife seems to be prepared to hear me through.'

Tony stormed off, while I remained. The professor told me as gently as he could, 'Your husband is sailing downstream, very swiftly.' I must have looked troubled, for he continued, 'He might have a slightly longer life if he stops drinking completely, with immediate effect. This is something which I myself doubt he will do—I'm very sure that he consumed alcohol even last night.' Of course, he was right, but I could not bring myself to utter a word. He added, 'I am quite upset at your husband's attitude, for I have read the earlier medical report from the previous physician, clearly stating that he had been advised to completely stop drinking alcohol, even beer.' The professor then asked me, 'Have you tried talking to your husband, reminding him of his responsibilities towards his family?'

I put my head down, for I felt my tears ready to flow. Did he actually doubt that? Had he himself, a medically knowledgeable man, managed to get through to his patient, my husband? Yes, Tony definitely needed psychiatric counselling, but who was going to convince him? I looked up again and saw the sudden light of realisation in the professor's eyes. It had dawned upon him what a battle I had been fighting till then, and was still trying to.

Even more gently, he said, 'I'm so sorry. I truly sympathise with you and wish you all the best.' I could see in his eyes that he was doubtful if I could succeed. I thanked him, and with a sigh, I left the room.

As soon as Tony saw me outside, in the lobby, he mockingly asked me, 'So has the great gastroenterologist succeeded in brainwashing you? Do you also believe that I actually need psychiatric counselling?'

Lost in Anguish

I did not answer. What did my opinion matter anyway? Would he ever accept the fact that the problem he considered a small one, thus far, had actually grown to a probably unredeemable degree? Could he not even see in the slightest what his behaviour was doing to the other members of the family? What answers could I give to the questions that Dewdrop and Wriggles unfailingly asked me regarding his promises to abstain from drink? They questioned me, in frustration, each time he staggered into the house, partly because of intoxication and partly because of the pain in his swollen leg.

Dewdrop had often pointed out, 'A father who loves his children as dearly as Daddy claims he does will not punish his children like this, compelling us to witness his pain—a pain which has been brought on by his own doing. And to make it worse, he goes on doing it even though he knows it's hurting us to watch him suffer!'

Wriggles would add, 'Ma, make him stop! Tell him that we can't take it anymore, please, Ma!' They often challenged me to place the cards on the table, to make Tony aware that I would no longer accommodate his selfish attitude.

My heart bled—I knew that I owed it to our two children to make Tony realise how they truly felt about his indifference towards the pain he was unconsciously inflicting upon his loved ones, but how I could I do so without causing a fiery battle at home? As it was, whenever I hinted, even most diplomatically and tactfully at the problem, Tony would threaten, 'If you don't stop nagging and checking me, I shall leave this house right now! I shall kill myself! I shall drive recklessly, maybe into the sea . . . You are making life really unbearable for me! You have even turned my own children against me! You're a devil!' I could only stand rooted to the ground, utterly dumbfounded.

Words like these, hurled cruelly and insensitively, shattered me and had me questioning my own good intentions. Had I really hurt him so much that he saw me in such a demeaning light? Had I not, in actual fact, told our two children time and again that they should always respect their father and picture him only in his sober state? The father they often saw, after he had had a few drinks, was a lost soul who often said and did things he never would have said or done if not under the influence of alcohol.

I had pleaded with them both, 'Please try to understand that Daddy is going through a trying phase in his life, and he cannot get through it without our unfailing support. I am fully aware of how you both feel. Perhaps you think that I am not doing my part to pull him out of this rut, but I have to tread very carefully. You see, he has reached a very volatile mental state. I dare not make a wrong move at all. It could have tragic consequences. Please bear with me.'

My elderly parents fully understood what turmoil I was experiencing, and silently watched, comforting me when they felt it was called for and giving me space when I needed it. They neither forced their opinions on me, nor begrudged counsel when I sought it.

Both Mum and Dad had tried, in their own way, to make Tony see sense. Each had gone up to his room separately and had given him counsel after he had had a late-night drinking session, hoping to make a breakthrough. Alas, it had been to no avail. In fact, his response would be quite predictable. Full of remorse, he would say, 'I'm really sorry. I know how much tension I'm causing. I promise that things will change from now onwards.'

Such a morning and noon would be peaceful, and hope would dare to fill the hearts of all those at home. When the children returned from school, they would be pleasantly surprised to see their beloved father at home and their mother actually cheerful. Sadly, such a morning rarely preceded a similar evening. All it took was one phone call for Tony to take flight again.

Fiercely in Denial

With all these thoughts going on in my already anguished and fatigued mind, I almost did not hear Tony make a nasty remark as we walked past the psychiatrist's consultation room. We were on our way out, heading towards the car park, when Tony, his voice laced with sarcasm, glared at the nameplate on the door and said, 'No, I'm *never* going to give *you* the pleasure of *my* company!'

Dad, Wriggles, and I were swiftly steered out of the hospital, towards the car, by a fuming Tony. He was finding it difficult to restrain his anger. He probably felt sore because his ego had been shattered and battered. He kept muttering under his breath, 'Stupid woman! You've made me waste my time and energy, compelling me to visit a lousy consultant! That man simply over-reacted!' He swore, 'There is nothing at all wrong with me!' Then turning around, he glared at me accusingly, saying, 'I bet you collaborated with our physician friend as well as the gastroenterologist to frighten me into giving up drinking completely!'

I walked, blinded by tears, to the car. I was at wits' end. There was nothing else I could do but surrender to God. My father looked at me, sympathy written all over his face. He was worn out too.

Wriggles got into the back seat with me and turned my face towards his, questioningly. He needed no answer. He held my hand in his own little one, comfortingly. He knew better than to speak when his father was in such a foul mood.

It was a rather quiet but speedy drive to the next town, with Tony at the wheel, still muttering occasionally. As we were about to exit from the town hub, Tony pulled aside and alighted. I was surprised. It was too late to stop for lunch, for I had barely an hour to reach home and enter the classroom. He then announced, 'I have to meet up with a friend, regarding business. I will find my own way back.' Without wasting a second, he got out of the driver's seat and defiantly strode off. Even if I had protested, would he have complied?

Trudging Through the Day

My mind was in turmoil. Would he never learn? It looked like all the effort that had been made to arrange for and keep the appointment with one of the country's leading consultants had been sadly in vain. Dad took over the wheel, and we completed the rest of the journey in silence, three weary soldiers who had lost the battle they had set out to win.

The rest of the day dragged on, Mum having her hundred and one questions as to the success of the mission painfully answered by Dad. Dewdrop, on her return from school, hurriedly entered the classroom, anxious to know if we were anywhere close to victory. One look at my face and she guessed the entire chapter—a case of labour lost.

I really wonder how I coped in the classroom that foreboding day, but I knew that it was something that I had to keep at, no matter what, no matter how. If, in the past, I had ever toyed with the idea of cutting down or even giving up tutoring, I could never, even remotely, dream of doing so now. My fate had been sealed. If anything, I realised that this would be the only way I could raise my two young children. We had nobody at all to turn to, other than Mum and Dad, our two greatest support pillars.

Standing My Ground

When Tony returned that evening, classes were just over. He staggered into the house and loudly demanded, 'Give me the key to my car!' Of late, I had taken to keeping the key because there had been too many untoward incidents of careless driving after Tony had consumed drink.

I protested, 'I'm sorry, but I don't think you're in any state to drive.'

Tony lost his temper and shouted, 'I didn't ask you for your permission, but for the key to my car! I have promised a good friend that I will attend his birthday celebration, and I intend to keep my word.'

Seething with anger, I thought, 'Just look at how much it means to you to keep your promise to a mere friend! When it comes to keeping your promise to us, your own family, you have no conscience whatsoever!' Still, I controlled my temper and tried to be diplomatic. I suggested, 'Why don't you have a wash, rest for a while, and then see if you still feel up to it?' I was hoping in my heart that he would have an early night instead.

I seemed to have pressed the wrong button, for Tony grew furious and threatened, 'If you don't hand over the key to me right now, I will smash the windscreen of the car with a hammer!'

Numbed and exhausted after what had been an endless day of anxiety and frustration, I retorted, 'If that is what you want, I will personally hand you the hammer. You will actually be doing me a great favour, for then I will no longer have to worry about you driving around for a while!' Tony was taken aback, but perhaps not half as much as I. I had never responded so vehemently! I was undoubtedly at the end of my tether.

Tony, bewildered, limped quietly past me. He sat on the bottom step of the stairs and removed his socks. Then turning to Dewdrop, he said, 'Get me a glass of cold water.' Dewdrop, still shaken up, took a minute to register her father's command, before running off to the kitchen. She soon returned, holding a tall glass of cold water.

Tony took a few sips, pausing in between. He appeared lost in thought. Then Dewdrop was summoned to take the glass away. After this, Tony slowly ascended the stairs. When he finally reached the upstairs, he went to relieve himself in the toilet and finally entered our bedroom. I heard the door shut and the lock click. I would have to sleep on the sofa that night.

The next morning, when Tony entered the bathroom, I quickly rushed into our bedroom to get a change of clothes for myself. I was most grateful that we all shared a common bathroom upstairs. At times like this, it was truly a blessing! As I approached the dressing table to get my hairbrush, my eyes wandered to Tony's pillow. There were foreboding stains of blood on the powder-blue pillowcase! I felt weak in the knees. Which physician could I take my stubborn, ailing Tony to now?

Lost in my world of despair, I did not hear Tony enter the room. When I turned round and saw him standing, I noticed a trickle of fresh blood at the corner of his mouth. He was a pathetic sight, and my heart bled for him. What on earth would make this adamant husband and father see light? Why was he so intent on destroying himself when he had every reason to live?

I silently walked towards the door, to leave the room. Words no longer seemed to have any impact on the captain.

We were sailing on choppy seas, and it seemed to be even more threatening in the direction that the foolhardy captain was heading.

Ceasefire

Tony blocked my path to the door of the bedroom. With a pleading look, he reached for my hand to stop me. I wondered what he had to say this time. Clearly, he was also aware that the bloodstains were an ominous sign. He asked, 'Will you do something for me?' I did not reply, but I looked at him questioningly. He continued, 'Will you please accompany me later this evening to a charismatic prayer session? Someone told me about it, and I think I would like to attend the prayers. It might help . . .'

This was unexpected. The beseeching look on his face, however, was enough to convince me. I replied, 'If you want me to go with you, I'll only be able to do so after tuition classes are over. It may be rather late.' He squeezed my hand in gratitude.

It was a rather quiet day that unfolded, but once again, hope rekindled in my heart. My eyes fell on a brass placard that had adorned my bare classroom wall for two decades. I gazed at the praying hands in gratitude and reread the inscription above them: 'More things are wrought by prayer than this world dreams of.'

After classes were over that late evening, I had a quick wash and prepared to accompany Tony to the charismatic prayer session. Tony was already dressed and waiting. Dewdrop would have loved to accompany us to the prayer session, but had to prepare for her end-of-year examination. It was almost bedtime for Wriggles, who was already in pyjamas. We told the family not to wait up, for we had no inkling what time the prayer session would be over.

Although not of the same faith, I respected Tony's religion as I did all others. As mentioned much earlier, Tony too was tolerant of all faiths. Perhaps now he had to concentrate on one particular faith, and if the need arose, I would spiritually prepare myself to embrace the very faith that would enlighten Tony and restore both his physical and mental health. I would stand by him, no matter what, as would Dewdrop and Wriggles. We loved Tony, and that was all that mattered.

When we entered the premises where the prayer session was being conducted, I was overwhelmed by the continuous chanting of prayers by all the believers and would-be believers surrounding me. Truly, it was a different experience altogether.

As we stood close to the front, I saw Tony close his eyes and lose himself in prayer. I tried to do the same, but my curiosity would not let me close my eyes. I needed to look around for evidence of prayers that had been answered. Was there anybody else in the congregation whose fate was similar to Tony's and mine? If there was, had that person experienced any hint of a possible miracle?

As I looked around, my gaze returned to Tony, who seemed to be swaying slightly to the rhythm of the chant. As I watched, the swaying grew more vigorous. Was he so overwhelmed already? Suddenly, all those who were in a similar state were called up to the front, where the priest and his assistant beckoned them singly.

Each one who was thus affected was made to kneel down while the priest laid his hand on his or her head, after which he or she seemed to return to normal. I was intrigued by what each one of them had experienced. I wish I knew!

When Tony had returned to normal, I asked him, 'What happened? What did you feel? Did you feel any different?' He, however, ignored all my questions; his attention was elsewhere.

Cheers with the Priest

I saw Tony push his way towards the priest, who was still helping a few more affected persons return to normal. I felt sorry for my poor Tony as he desperately made an attempt to speak to the priest, who was too busy to pay him any attention. Many others also sought the attention of the dynamic priest.

It suddenly dawned upon me that it was going to be a very long night. I hoped it would not be the beginning of many such nights. I was feeling tired already. Fatigued, I found a seat a little distance away. Tony finally managed to get the attention of the busy priest. A few words were exchanged, and beaming, Tony walked to where I was seated. The revered one had been invited to join us for supper after charismatic prayers the following very late evening.

Over a supper of fine seafood in a Portuguese restaurant, Tony and the priest got to know each other better over beers! Wasn't there any other beverage in the world that could foster friendship between the ranks of faith? I did not know whether to laugh or cry, believe or doubt.

I was completely left out of the religious camaraderie. By the end of that supper, it was agreed, on Tony's persistent requests, that he was to accompany the priest on his proposed rounds in the districts, strengthening the faith of those who were lost. This mission had been scheduled to take off within the next few days, but only upon confirmation by a phone call from the priest.

I realised by the end of that supper that nobody was going to enlighten me on the exact happenings during the charismatic prayers, or how the priest was going to help my ailing Tony, who was desperately reaching out for him. The fact that the priest also enjoyed beers was against the family crusade to save Tony.

In all fairness to the priest, he probably was not even aware of the precariousness of the situation. Being a subservient wife, I had found it hard to intervene when Tony, during supper, had only casually mentioned that he was trying to cut down on his drinking. Within me, I was controlling the urge to scream loudly at the beer-guzzling priest, 'My husband is not supposed to touch even a single drop of beer or any alcoholic drink! Every drop he takes is causing further damage to whatever is left of his liver! Each and every drop is pushing him nearer to his grave!'

After we had settled the bill for supper, Tony and I drove the priest back to his quarters. Tony chatted away animatedly while driving, happy at the prospect of accompanying the priest on his routine mission. Gallantly, he offered, 'Father, I'll drive you anywhere you need to go, in my own car. I'll even pay for petrol!'

The priest remarked, 'Your wife may also need to use the car, don't forget.'

Tony merely dismissed this remark with 'That's not a problem. She can always use my father-in-law's car. Don't worry!' Having said this, Tony suddenly sensed that I might not be too happy and quickly looked behind, where I was seated in silence, to declare, 'She is a very understanding and supportive wife.' I was neither impressed nor flattered. There was a great issue here that had to be resolved.

When the priest relinquished the seat that was rightfully mine, I refused to budge from where I was. What was the point? Even if I were to sit in front, beside Tony, was he going to give me the respect that was due to a devoted wife? Despite my willing attendance at the prayer sessions and the supper, I seemed to have been invisible to my husband. This caused me deep anguish, for I seemed to be the only one who wanted to save Tony. Tony himself did not seem in the least inclined to save himself!

The only time Tony seemed anxious about his health was when he saw blood in front of his eyes. His bloodshot eyes, a gradually distending abdomen, wasting muscles, and two swollen calves did not seem to alarm him in the least. He chalked these down to insufficient sleep, lack of exercise, and bad eating habits. Medical experts had attributed them all to excessive drink. I was close to being trounced.

Tony was more cheerful during the next few days and spoke excitedly about his proposed visits to the districts with the priest. He had always enjoyed travelling and relished all projects that involved this. He eagerly awaited the call from the priest. In his eagerness, he failed to notice my detachment. I was sceptical about the whole affair; I feared that each evening would end with a drinking session.

Each time that Tony was out, he would call home to ask, 'Has the priest called? He is supposed to give me the agenda for the proposed visits to the districts.' Each time, I had to answer in the negative. A few days passed in like manner. Tony could not hide his disappointment.

Feeling sorry for my Tony, I finally took the initiative to make a call to the elusive priest. I asked him, 'Father, do you remember the request that my husband so earnestly made? Will you really be including him in your missionary visits? He has his heart set on accompanying you.'

'Yes, I do remember his request most clearly.' The priest added a little hesitantly, 'But I have learnt from certain relatives of his that he actually has a drinking problem. I really do not see how I can help him overcome it. I have too much on my hands already. I suggest that you take the problem to some nuns in a convent nearby. I believe that they can recommend herbal remedies. They have a fair bit of experience in dealing with alcoholics.'

Dismayed, I thanked him and put the receiver down. It was going to be extremely difficult conveying this message to Tony. He would surely be shattered. He was.

A Forlorn Christmas

Christmas season had unfailingly brought joy to the family in the past, complete with a Christmas tree and all its cheery trimmings in the living room. However, it did not seem to lift our spirits much that year.

My Tony looked shattered, dull, and aged. He did not feel up to lending a hand with putting up the tree. He would normally be even more excited than the children, insisting on adding even more ornaments to the already over-decorated tree.

This time, Dewdrop put up the tree. Before she embarked on decorating the tree, Dewdrop asked her little brother if he would like to give her a hand. Wriggles did not need a second invitation to help adorn the artificial Christmas tree, bought a couple of years earlier. Excitedly, he asked his sister, 'You mean you will actually let me hold the colourful glass baubles? And the silver bells? And the—'

'Yes, yes, and yes! Now will you help me or not?' His sister groaned in mock exasperation. I had not bought any new ornaments, for we were on a budget. Still, Dewdrop had bought the fairy to adorn the top of the tree with her own pocket money. She took the fairy, glittering white and with gossamer wings, to Tony and said, 'Daddy, I insist that you, with your own hands, put this fairy right at the top of the tree. Only then will I turn on the twinkling fairy lights!' Tony managed a weak smile and obliged, but his eyes lacked lustre.

There were still two weeks more to Christmas, and Dewdrop tried her best to cheer up the family. Her cousin Ritchie and his mother, Sil, had just flown in from New Zealand. Shiv had stayed behind to run the family business. Besides, he was still seething over the New Zealand episode with Tony.

Mother and son were on their way to the north of India for a holiday and were spending a few days with us en route. Delighted at being reunited after almost three years, Dewdrop and Ritchie often worked as a team to plot against the unsuspecting but equally mischievous Wriggles.

Christmas holidays were an excuse to have fun, and there was a much-welcomed ring of laughter in the house as the three children got themselves in and out of trouble. Ritchie was flying off to India in a couple of days, and he meant to leave with an impact. While they were with us, our troubles temporarily faded into the background. It was only when Tony struggled up the stairs or left bloodstains in the washbasin that we realised, with a bang, that all was not well.

God alone knew that we needed some cheer and smiles in the family. Sil and Ritchie kept us on our toes, but both were fully aware that the entire family was still focused on Tony. Sil often put an arm around me and the children comfortingly, but she was at a loss as to what exactly to say.

Sil and Ritchie soon departed for India with some of her relatives. They were going on a conducted tour of the north, a tour which Sil had much looked forward to. They left with the promise to return on the eve of Christmas.

The atmosphere at home turned sombre again. Tuitions were still on, but on a small scale. It was holiday season, and only revision classes were being conducted. Dewdrop was busy revising in preparation for the forthcoming year, when she would be sitting for her O levels. Wriggles, fearing that I might pull him into the classroom and set him some gruelling assignments, tried hard to look busy each time I looked in his direction.

Dad, Mum, and I were extremely concerned about Tony's deteriorating health. He felt cold very early in the evening itself, and he could not bear to have the fan on, even at the lowest speed. It was hard to believe that this was the same man who could never feel cool enough, even when the fan was switched on at maximum speed. Now, he would lie on his reclining chair with a blanket on, in front of the television, a far cry from the robust man he had once been.

Christmas was usually spent at Tony's father's house, with relatives and friends pouring in to join in the merrymaking and feasting, which lasted throughout the day. This year, however, there would only be immediate family members present, for the grand old man had passed away in the earlier part of the year.

Tony seemed to have grown increasingly distant from his siblings over the previous months, and I could not help feeling that he might even forego the yearly obligatory visit to his father's home. Nature took its course, and Tony fell ill a few days before Christmas itself. Finding it rather difficult even to get up, Tony lay in bed nearly throughout, covered with a blanket up to his neck. I decided to serve him meals upstairs, in our room, even though he had protested. He said it made him feel like an invalid, but we dared not risk letting him descend the stairs, for fear he might fall and injure himself.

Sil and Ritchie were rather alarmed at the sight that greeted them on their return from India. Never had Sil seen the youthful, ever-active, and optimistic Tony so incapacitated. She remarked, out of Tony's earshot, 'What has happened to the man who, practically single-handedly, made all the arrangements for my marriage to Shiv?' What answer could I give?

Christmas Eve had usually seen Tony hurrying his wife and children to church for midnight mass, after which it was off to his father's house, for blessings and family reunion late supper. That year, things had certainly taken a very different turn.

Very early on Christmas Day itself, Tony made a call to his eldest sister-in-law to tell her that he was not up to visiting them. He conveyed greetings from the family to them all and said he would catch up with them later. Following this, he called his other siblings, conveying the same message.

I had wrapped up a few presents for the three children, bought at Tony's request, several days earlier. Now, he told the eager children to open their presents. Dewdrop, Ritchie, and Wriggles rushed to the base of the glittering Christmas tree to claim their gaily wrapped gifts.

Tony watched them delightedly from his reclining chair, his illness momentarily forgotten by all in the living room.

It never failed to amaze me how, sometimes, Tony, my full-grown commanding captain, transformed into a bubbly little boy savouring every moment of childhood glee. It was a heart-warming sight for him and the rest of the family. I felt tears threatening to flow down my cheeks. Why did I have this strange feeling that I might never have my complete family at Christmas again?

Angry with myself for having such pessimistic thoughts, I turned away to see if the table had been laid for a small family breakfast. Tony had also requested that Mum and Sil cook whatever the children enjoyed eating that day. That year, we spent a quiet Christmas at home, without even turning on the fan. Together, with Tony blanketed on his reclining chair, we watched a few Christmas specials that were telecast that day. The domestic atmosphere was rather subdued but pleasant and peaceful, until the phone rang.

A Disastrous Boxing Day

Tony's cousin with whom he had embarked on the logistics stint suddenly called on Christmas evening to convey the season's greetings and to request Tony and the rest of us to join him and his family for a small celebration the following evening. Tony responded warmly and replied that he would discuss it with me and then get back to him.

I declined the rather sudden invitation for I was in no mood to celebrate. Besides, I had only a few days left which were free of tuition classes, and I needed every minute I could get my hands on to clean up the house thoroughly. The new year was fast approaching, and there would be a fresh intake of students. With nobody to assist me, I had to start immediately and work systematically in order to get the house spick and span before the new year. Sil wanted to help, but she had to visit some relatives before returning to New Zealand in about a fortnight. Anyway, Dewdrop and Wriggles were willing and available.

Tony insisted on going by himself. 'I'll take a bus. The pain in my left calf is too much for me to be able to drive comfortably. Also, it will not be economical for me to take the car,' he decided.

I protested, saying, 'You aren't exactly as fit as a fiddle, and you know that.' Still, he was adamant about making the trip. Whenever he reached such a degree of stubbornness, it was futile to try to make him see sense. Who knew this better than I?

Later that same evening, Tony made a request. He said, 'I do not want to go empty-handed to my cousin's house. Could you please buy some fresh tiger prawns that I could take with me as a gift for the family? His wife could cook them in a style that they all enjoy.'

I protested, 'Tiger prawns cooked in chilli and spice do not do justice to an ailing liver, Tony. I'm sure you'll partake of the dish, and it will not do you any good.' Once again, my pleas fell on deaf ears.

That midnight, Dad, Mum, and I drove to the wholesale market to purchase the requested tiger prawns. Tony had insisted on choice prawns, and these were usually available only between midnight and 2.00 a.m., when fresh haul was supplied to the market. We successfully made the purchase, and the captain's wish was fulfilled.

Early the next morning, my sickly, pale Tony and the fresh, juicy tiger prawns boarded the bus that would take him to his cousin's hometown. He decided to leave early to give his cousin and wife a helping hand with the preparations for the celebration that same evening. He had indicated that he might decide to stay back if the merrymaking continued till late. I was about to protest, for that might entail further drinking, but Tony silenced me with 'Don't worry unnecessarily. I know how to take care of myself.' I could not help feeling that my Tony was going to fall even more ill on his return.

The Beginning of the End

That evening, as Dewdrop and I were facing the challenge of cleaning the windows in her room, the phone rang. I was tired and irritable when I got off the window ledge to answer the phone. The voice at the other end of the receiver was that of a stranger. She asked for me by name, and when I acknowledged that it was me she was looking for, she implored, 'Please come quickly to the hospital!'

When I asked her which hospital she was referring to, she mentioned the one in the same town that Tony had left for that morning. I was stunned at first, and then I asked, 'Why?'

She replied, 'Your husband is very ill, and he is calling out for you from his bed.' Dazed, I asked her what had happened. She briefly told me that he had injuries on his body and legs, resulting from a fight. On the verge of panic, I asked her how this had come about. She said that she could not tell me more except that she had been stopped by him when she was passing by his bed in the hospital ward. He had mumbled to her my name and telephone number, begging her to quickly call me.

My head in a whirl, I put the receiver down and made arrangements to leave immediately. Dewdrop, who had been standing next to me throughout the telephone conversation, held my hand tight, and said, 'Ma, I want to go with you, please.'

Sil and Ritchie had just arrived home after visiting some relatives. Her cousin, who had dropped them home, saw the family in a state of distress and kindly offered to drive us to the hospital where Tony had been admitted. Sil insisted on accompanying us and sat in the front passenger seat, while

Dewdrop and I sat behind, close together, fearing the worst. Sil tried to look at the situation in a lighter vein, saying, 'I'm sure it's not that bad. Tony might have just had a slight fall somewhere.' I was sceptical.

Throughout the hour-long drive, I had a gnawing feeling that I was falling into a bottomless pit. I hardly paid any attention to what was being said; I just wanted to get there as fast as possible. When we finally reached the hospital, I felt a sense of impending doom. We rushed to the casualty department and inquired about Tony at the nurses' station. One of the nurses rudely directed us to the male ward on the third floor. Dewdrop and I rushed up the stairs, while Sil and her cousin remained behind.

Hit and Hurled

We finally located Tony's bed and were shocked at the sight that greeted us. Tony had sustained a laceration on his forehead and was bleeding from his lower lip. There were also abrasions and bruises on his arms and legs. His lower left leg, especially, was hideously swollen, with the veins threatening to burst. He had not been attended to at all! What kind of a hospital was this? Tony was shivering and calling out for me and the children. The thin blanket that had been thrown over him was almost falling to the ground and had large stains of blood! I looked at his trousers, which (where not covered with blood) were mud-splattered.

What on earth had happened to my poor Tony? I was utterly confused! As I approached Tony, I realised why the nurses had been so callous towards him—he was reeking of alcohol!

When Tony saw Dewdrop and me, he immediately looked relieved. He asked me in an agitated manner, 'Why did you take so long to get here? Do you know how long I have been waiting?'

I replied, barely being able to hide my frustration, 'I came to know only about two hours ago that you were in hospital and that too from a total stranger! She rang me up and gave me the shocking news.'

I tried to control myself but could not hide the fact that I was devastated and appalled to learn that he had been involved in a fight. I asked him, 'What really happened? How could it have happened when you were supposed to be with your cousin and family?'

With some difficulty, he tried to explain. 'I was waiting for a taxi to return home earlier this afternoon. I had to stand for quite a while along the side of the road, and my leg was throbbing with pain. When I finally managed to get a taxi, I quickly got into the front passenger seat. I settled in comfortably while the taxi driver drove to the taxi stand. Once we got there, the driver told me to vacate the front seat. Of course, I protested. My leg was hurting badly, and I needed to sit where there would be no danger of my swollen leg rubbing against anything or anyone. It was then that I turned and saw a man waiting. He looked furious, and his hand was impatiently grasping the handle of the front passenger door!' Tony stopped to catch his breath; he was getting worked up at the very memory of the incident. Dewdrop and I dared not interrupt him.

Tony continued, 'When I looked questioningly at the man getting impatient, he got heated up, loudly claiming that the driver had already promised him the very seat that I was occupying. I then alighted to prove to that unreasonable character that my leg was truly swollen! I wanted him to know why I badly needed to sit in front, all by myself.' Tears began to flow down Tony's sunken cheeks at this point. Before I could hand him a tissue, he swiped them away with his hand and continued.

'It was then that another two men suddenly appeared. They were ready to put up a fight! The man who wanted my seat was apparently their comrade. Anyway, there was an exchange of angry words, and this led to a scuffle. I can't remember for sure who hit whom first, but I had nobody on my side at all! The taxi driver became frightened and quickly drove off, leaving me at the mercy of the three bullies. Together, they assaulted me, finally pushing me into a monsoon drain near the taxi stand.'

Tony stopped for a moment, his tears again threatening to flow. Then swallowing a lump in his throat, he went on, 'Before pushing me into the drain, they took my cell phone, wallet, watch, and briefcase, all of which were gifts from the children and you . . .'

Tony painfully continued, in speech that was rather slurred, 'Slowly, I managed to crawl out of the monsoon drain and get the attention of a passer-by. He helped me to the nearest police station. I cannot recall what happened there. They say that I collapsed just as I was about to step into the police station. When I opened my eyes, I found myself here, in this hospital.' Dewdrop and I were too shocked for words.

When Tony had asked for us, the rather curt nurse told Tony that they had no idea whom to contact on his behalf, for there had been no personal documents on him when he had been brought in for treatment. Finally, in desperation, Tony had called out to a woman who had been observing his frantic disposition. This, then, was the kind soul who had telephoned me.

Myriad Questions

I then asked Tony a few questions which had been plaguing me right from the start of his explanation. Why had he left his cousin's house so early that afternoon? Had he not been invited to a celebration that was to be held only later that same evening? Why, if truly he had needed to come home earlier than planned, had his cousin, the obliging host, not accompanied him to the taxi stand and waited with him till he had found transport home? This had been the practice in the recent past, when Tony had been working with him. If he had been too busy, could not his young and able son have done so? Something was amiss, and I did not like the situation one bit.

Tony was reeking of alcohol, which meant that a drinking session had been in progress just before the ugly incident. I was furious, for Tony's cousin surely had more sense than to treat a sick relative like that! I had a nasty suspicion that events had not exactly taken place the way the captain had just described them. Tony did not take kindly to my questions, and he looked the other way. I, for my part, could neither control myself nor hide the fact that I was not fully convinced by what he had just told us.

I stood in front of Tony, waiting for some response to my questions, but he looked away from me. Directing his words only at Dewdrop, he bellowed, 'Get me out of this hospital!' He did not wish to be at my mercy after I had asked all those questions. 'I want to go home right now!' he insisted.

Dewdrop herself was in a state of shock. What could the poor child do? I proceeded to the nurses' station to ask how I could go about getting my husband home. The staff nurse told me that Tony could only leave the hospital in an ambulance for he was bleeding non-stop. The doctors had not dared to attempt to stitch up the open wound for fear of aggravating the bleeding.

Discharged at Own Risk

Unfortunately, there was no ambulance available. I asked if I could take him back home in my own vehicle. The staff nurse said I could, but only after I had signed a 'discharged at own risk' form. The kind staff nurse continued, 'I advise you to get your husband immediately admitted to the general hospital in your hometown. The doctor who examined him when he was brought in unconscious disclosed the fact that his condition is rather serious. He suspects that he has cirrhosis of the liver. His blood refuses to clot.'

Shaken up and close to tears, both Dewdrop and I ran downstairs. We consulted Sil and her cousin, who willingly agreed to take Tony back with us in his car. I was most relieved. In the meanwhile, I called Mum and Dad to update them.

All the way home, Tony held on to Dewdrop, who was seated between us in the backseat. He was covered with a bloodstained blanket. He did not even want to look at me. He probably regarded me as an enemy after all the questions I had asked. I was only human, and there was darkness all around me where Tony was concerned.

The past few months had not been easy, either. I had often been at a loss as to where my husband was or what he was doing. All I knew was that Tony was slowly drifting away from me. I did not like what was happening; I felt as if my whole world was about to collapse. Sensing my hopelessness, Dewdrop slowly slipped her left hand into my right, drew nearer to me, and whispered reassuringly, 'I'm here, Ma, always with you.' I squeezed her hand tight, in gratitude. Her right hand was holding her father's left. My soldier was brave and loyal.

As soon as we reached our hometown, Sil's cousin drove straight to the general hospital. It was almost 11.00 p.m. then and the staff at the casualty department was not very receptive.

Sil and her cousin left for home to get some clothes and toiletries for Tony. Dewdrop and I were left on our own to try to get medical attention for Tony as quickly as possible. We were not very successful. Fortunately, one of Tony's friends arrived as soon as he had got news from Dad. He tried his best to use some influence to help Tony.

There were some other emergency cases, but the doctor agreed to attend to Tony first. He told me that there was not much that he could do other than admit him for observation and possible transfusion.

The Hostile Husband

Tony was not very cooperative when the doctor questioned him as to how he had sustained the injuries. He mumbled some answers which were rather vague, and this turned the doctor off. He commented rather harshly, 'Alcoholics are the most difficult patients to treat.' I did not know where to put my face when the rest of the attending staff looked at me. I fought back tears of shame.

As Tony was being wheeled out, he attempted to get out of the wheelchair, pushing away the attendant and nearly stumbling in the process. Fortunately, his friend managed to get hold of him. I blindly followed the attendant, who was leading the way to the male ward. Dewdrop walked beside me, true to her word.

Each time I tried to approach Tony, he glared at me. I was beginning to feel frightened. Dewdrop could sense the growing hostility in her father towards me. She felt very disturbed but confessed to me later, 'Ma, you know all those questions you asked Daddy at the other hospital? The answers to which you badly wanted?' I nodded. 'Well,' she continued, 'I had exactly those very questions running through my head!' I was greatly relieved.

By the time Tony had settled in for the night, it was 2.00 a.m. I thought I would stay behind in the ward with Tony, but his friend advised me to take Dewdrop and go home. He remarked that we both seemed to be on the verge of collapse. Anyway, Tony had been sedated, and his bleeding appeared to have lessened.

Sil, who had arrived just a few minutes earlier, arranged Tony's clothes and toiletries in the locker beside his bed. She then suggested we all go home and return the next morning.

I nodded in agreement. I really needed to shut my mind off everything for a while, and I was sure my Dewdrop was worn out.

Discharged at Own Risk, Again

Early the next morning, I got a call from the general hospital informing me that my husband was insisting on being discharged, much against medical advice. I was at my wits' end.

With a heavy heart, I proceeded to the hospital to see what could be done. Tony, as I had expected, was in a foul mood. He was upset that he had been left there, even for one night. He implied that I was reluctant to be burdened with him. I decided it would be futile to even try to explain that he had been admitted for his own good. I regretted, however, not having stayed behind to look after him myself. He had often remarked in the past that nothing he did ever seemed good enough for me. Was it not actually the other way round? As I signed yet another 'discharged at own risk' form, it dawned upon me exactly how great a risk I was taking! Had I any choice?

When we got home, Tony appeared relieved that he was again in familiar surroundings. He remarked, 'The medical staff at the general hospital really treat patients most shabbily. It is very degrading the way they handle a patient! It's not only the doctors who think they're so high and mighty—the attendants themselves are so insensitive and arrogant!' I wondered if he had perhaps over-reacted. I could not help but think that the captain himself had been quite grouchy and harsh in his speech and mannerism. The fact that he had reeked of alcohol could not have been much in his favour either.

Tony was glad to see Sil and the three children, with whom he even tried to crack a joke or two, making light of his recent physical assault. Sil tactfully tried to extract some information but failed. All of us at home were painfully in the dark as to what had actually happened the previous day and afternoon. Tony chose to remain tight-lipped, refusing to disclose more than what he had already told me in the hospital in his cousin's hometown. No mention was made at all about his cousin, or the celebration that was supposed to have been the highlight of and reason for his visit that day.

The details of what truly happened that fateful day remain obscure until today.

Tony struggled upstairs, assisted by the children. He mostly lay in bed that day but made frequent visits to the bathroom. Each time he rinsed his mouth, there was blood in the washbasin.

This was a regular scene for the next few days. As he grew paler, the hostility in him lessened. He, who had once insisted on eating his meals downstairs only, now had no choice but to have his meals brought upstairs. Sil and I even had to resort to feeding him in bed, like an invalid. He had to be propped up with pillows, and he always needed a thick blanket to keep himself warm, despite the fact that the fan had not even been switched on!

Sometimes, his embarrassment was overwhelming, and he would keep apologising for all the inconvenience he was causing; at other times, he was simply too worn out to protest, finding it difficult to swallow even a few spoonfuls of soft diet. We tactfully suggested that it would perhaps be wise to seek medical advice again, but such a suggestion would only upset him and arouse aggression, making him weaker afterwards.

A Dismal New Year

Tony's first breakfast on the morning of New Year was oatmeal in warm milk, served to him in bed, by me. He was barely able to swallow the cereal, and he looked frightfully sallow. He was sinking slowly but surely.

When not with Tony, I went about my chores, trying to keep my mind occupied. I really wondered fearfully what the year had in store for the family.

Tuitions were to begin for the year in a few days' time, on the very day that schools reopened. Dewdrop would be sitting for her O levels in ten months' time, while our Wriggles would be in the fourth year of primary school. Sil and Ritchie had less than a week left with us before they left for New Zealand. Dad and Mum both looked anxious and fatigued, not knowing what to make of Tony's condition. It was definitely going to be a trying year.

The telephone kept ringing, for parents were eager to sign their children up for the new intake. The constant ringing of the telephone was good indication that tuition was in demand, but I wondered, for the first time in my working life, if I would be able to cope.

How was I going to manage it all if Tony did not show any sign of improvement? Sil's presence had been a blessing, and Mum was wonderful in her own way, but how were we going to manage after Sil's departure for New Zealand? It was obvious that Tony was in dire need of medical attention, but he was just too obstinate for his own good.

Finally, defeated, the weary captain sent for me. When I entered our bedroom, a rather sheepish Tony requested, 'Could you please get me admitted into a private hospital—one where I will be treated with dignity and respect?' That was the request we had all been waiting to hear, a request from Tony himself, for medical attention!

Immediately, steps were taken. Tony did not have medical insurance. We collected all the cash we had at home, but it definitely was not going to be enough. Private hospital charges were stiff. Thankfully, Mum came to the rescue; she insisted that I withdraw some of the savings she had in her personal account. My brother, Shiv, had sometimes sent cash tokens to Mum and Dad on their birthdays, anniversaries, and when business was fairly good. The withdrawal was to be done first thing the following morning, and the money to be used for the treatment of her beloved son-in-law.

Sil obligingly helped me to pack a few of Tony's personal requirements again. Tony, with my help, slowly dressed and descended the stairs. He hugged the children and made them promise to visit him later that evening. He then turned to Mum; only their eyes spoke. She knew that he greatly appreciated the fact that she would be handing over some of her savings with the hope that his suffering might be reduced. She hugged him and wished him a speedy recovery.

Tony then got into the car, not without difficulty. Dad drove, while I sat in the front passenger seat. I did not trust myself to drive in that lost state. The pale and battle-worn captain was soon admitted into a prestigious private hospital in the heart of town.

The Languishing Liver

This time, he was treated far better. The physician who attended to him was respectful and accommodating. He too, however, insisted on my presence when he described the exact nature of Tony's liver cirrhosis. He emphasised that Tony should not even think of having a drink ever. His condition was now critical despite the fact that he was still occasionally trying to make light of it.

As soon as the physician had left the room, Tony told me that he was now fully aware of how seriously ill he really was. I wondered. For a few minutes, neither one of us spoke. We were each lost in our own thoughts. Then realising it was almost noon, I asked Tony, 'Would it be all right for me to go home for a little while? I shall return with the children, a little later.'

He asked, 'Are you going to cancel tuition classes?'

I replied, 'Don't you remember? There are no classes until schools reopen, next week.' He looked relieved for me. I was touched. I continued reassuringly, 'I'll return with the children in a short while. You just make sure you get some rest, please.' Tony's meals were to be provided by the hospital, prepared strictly according to the dietician's instructions. I dared not serve him anything that might upset his already fragile condition. I gave him a peck on the cheek and left for home.

On the way home, I stopped at Tony's brother's restaurant. I informed both Tony's brother and his wife that Tony had been admitted into the private hospital just a stone's throw away. They were both busy as business was brisk during the holiday season. I did not hide from them Tony's actual condition and told them also what had happened the previous week when he had gone to visit their cousin. I did not wish to be later accused of hiding the truth from them.

I stressed, 'It is most necessary for him to completely give up drink if he wishes to lead a healthier life. What he needs most right now is moral support from his entire family.'

'Is his condition serious?' asked Tony's eldest sister-in-law.

'Well, he is stable now, but we cannot take anything for granted,' I replied. They were sympathetic and told me that they would inform the rest of the family. I thanked them and drove off.

I had done my duty, and I hoped that Tony's elder brother would take a positive step towards bridging the rift that had developed some time back. I was quite sure that Tony had taken to drinking more because of the unhappy relationship between the two. Tony had a tendency to turn to drink to forget any pain or stress that overwhelmed him.

An Unsolicited Send-Off

When I returned to the hospital with Dewdrop, Wriggles, and Ritchie later that day, I was surprised to see two strangers in Tony's room. The two women were praying over Tony, and when they had finished, they looked with pity upon Dewdrop and Wriggles. They did this after they had confirmed with me who Tony's children were. They drew closer to my two startled soldiers and hugged them. Ritchie and I looked at each other, a trifle confused yet amused.

After they had left, I asked Tony, 'Who were those two women? I don't remember having seen them before.'

Tony answered, 'They are members of the church.' What he told me next shocked my entire being: 'A priest himself came in earlier to pray over me, and for me!'

I was stunned. Was this not what was done only when someone was fast approaching death? Indignant, I made a mental note to check with my in-laws as soon as possible.

Tony, for his part, laughed it off. He remarked, 'Many people are going to be rather disappointed, I'm afraid. I intend to be up and about very soon, living a normal, healthy life!' This remark of his was like a welcome ray of sunshine on a gloomy day. It was just what I needed to keep me going, keep me believing that all was going to be fine.

Later that evening, Tony's eldest brother and sister-in-law turned up at our home. Wearing rather solemn expressions, they reminded me that they would always be there for me if anything untoward should happen to Tony. I was astonished at their sudden burst of sympathy and assurance, for it had been a long time since they had shown any concern for us. I thanked them politely, though taken aback at the pessimism displayed. I enquired, 'Are you aware that a priest visited Tony today and prayed over him?' Tony's brother replied that he and his wife had requested the priest to do so. I queried further, 'Isn't such a visit made only when a person is on his deathbed?' They remained silent.

I pointed out, 'Tony has been admitted merely to have his injuries attended to. The assault on him last week has aggravated his condition and weakened him. He will be in hospital for only a day or two at the most. It is true, yes, that his drinking has to come to a complete stop. If he manages to give up drink completely, he will slowly but most certainly be on the road to recovery.' I had nothing more to say, for they knew then that I had considered their move rather premature and audacious. My Tony, my captain, was not one to give up so easily. He was going to make it. He *had* to.

The next morning, I left early to see Tony. I needed to be reassured that he was truly going to get better. The pessimistic attitude of certain members among my in-laws had slightly dampened my confidence. Now, it was all in God's hands and, of course, sheer determination on the part of the captain to steer well away from alcohol, never, ever to sail in that direction again.

While driving, I could not help thinking, 'One does not even have to actively consume alcohol to be destroyed. Even we non-drinking members of the family are slowly but surely sinking, just watching Tony waste away. Why do people even drink alcohol? Especially when they don't know when to stop courting death so that others may live? Will Tony finally see the light?'

Acceptance

On reaching the hospital car park, I parked the car and made quickly for the lift. When I reached the floor where Tony's room was, I got out of the lift and was pleasantly surprised to see his physician just leaving his room. On seeing me, he signalled to me to stop. He came towards me and started, 'There's not much more I can do for Tony. It is pointless keeping him here. It is up to him now to completely abstain from alcohol. You, as his wife, have to be very firm about this. All blood tests and scans reveal that Tony has cirrhosis of the liver, and it has reached a rather serious stage.'

This was not the first time that I had been told of the nature of Tony's ailment, but somehow, this time, it was beginning to frighten me. When the first physician that we had consulted mentioned a condition of the liver, I had imagined it to be an ailment that could be treated. Why did it now sound as if it was beyond medical treatment, even terminal? It was not a kind of cancer, was it? Surely, it was not! But then again, was this not the irreversible path that had been pointed out by the gastroenterologist in the capital? My head was in a whirl. Had this doctor told Tony himself what he had just told me?

The defeated look on my face made the kind doctor turn on his heel and escort me back into Tony's room. There, he reiterated what he had told me minutes earlier, but this time in front of Tony himself. I guessed he must have realised that

Tony was not one who was going to heed his wife. It must have dawned upon him that Tony would surely not have reached such an advanced stage of liver impairment if he had only heeded his loved ones' pleas in the first place.

Tony was pleased to be told that he could go home. I, however, had some reservations. As I cleared his locker and helped him to dress, I kept thinking, 'A few more days of hospitalisation would undeniably have cost more, but it would have emphasised the seriousness of his ailment. At least while in hospital, there is neither temptation to drink nor telephone calls that challenge his resolution not to.' What was I thinking? He couldn't stay in hospital forever, could he? I could only pray very hard that this time, at least, the captain would adhere very strictly to all that the doctor had advised.

The bill having been settled, we drove home. Tony sounded determined to kick the drinking habit. I fervently wanted to believe him.

Convalescing at Home

The family members were surprised to see Tony home so soon. I told them that the doctor thought it would be better for Tony to rest comfortably at home. He mainly needed lots of rest and a significant change of lifestyle. The adults were pensive. The children helpfully escorted Tony upstairs, happy that they could spend their last few days of the school vacation with Tony.

Dad, Mum, and Sil soon expressed the very fears that were haunting me. We could do no more than pray for the best.

Two days passed with the family giving Tony full attention, attending to his every need. I was kept busy answering the telephone and preparing the tuition schedule for the following week. Dewdrop and Wriggles browsed through their new textbooks and gathered the necessary stationery for the new academic year. New school shoes had to be purchased for Wriggles, whose feet had outgrown the earlier pairs.

Sil and Ritchie needed to do a bit of shopping too, before returning to New Zealand. As we were about to leave for the mall that evening, Tony requested, 'Please get me a tracksuit. It's rather chilly in the evenings.' My Tony felt cold despite the fact that the fan was not even switched on. I made a note to purchase two tracksuits, besides at least another six underwear, for I had discovered that morning that Tony was starting to soil his underwear. I was unsure if this was due to his ailment.

Sil and I decided to give the children an outing that evening, with dinner at any restaurant that they liked. We wanted to cherish the memory of that evening, for only God knew when we would meet again. Dad and Mum urged us to take that much-needed break, promising to see to Tony for a few hours. We shopped and laughed at the hilarious antics of Ritchie, who adroitly slipped on a pink lace negligee when the salesgirl had her back turned! Wriggles, inspired by the laughter, decided that he did not want to be left out. Wishing to imitate the cheeky

New Zealander, he attempted to try on a lacy black number, much to his sister's uncontrollable giggles. I brought him rudely back to earth with a resounding smack. Before having dinner, we picked out two sets of tracksuits for Tony. Despite the fact that we were on a tight budget, I made sure that they were of good quality. Only the best would do for the captain.

Another Emergency, Another Hospital

When we got home later that evening, Sil and I hurried the children off to bed, for we wanted to spend a little time together while she sorted out her shopping and clothes. They were to be packed into her travel bags, and she welcomed some help. It was almost 1.00 a.m., and we were still busy packing when we heard Tony's voice. I rushed out of the bedroom downstairs, and I was alarmed to see Tony groggily descending the stairs, his pants soiled! Sil was right behind me. Tony wore a dazed expression and did not seem to be aware of his incontinence. I immediately escorted him to the bathroom downstairs, to get him cleaned up, while Sil dashed upstairs to get his towel and a fresh pair of pants. I could not believe what was happening! My Tony had always been so much in control of his personal appearance and grooming. I was badly shaken up.

Sil knocked on the bathroom door and alerted me to the fact that Tony's bed sheet needed to be changed. I grabbed the towel and quickly dried Tony, not wanting him to catch a cold. I helped him into a fresh pair of pants and then, leaving him in Sil's care, I hurried upstairs to change the bed sheet in our bedroom. I was appalled at the sight of the heavily soiled bed sheet. This had never happened before. The previous two days had revealed only slight soiling of his underwear, which I had dismissed as part of his being ill. Now, however, he seemed completely incontinent. This could only be an ominous sign that the captain's health was deteriorating.

I peeled off the bed sheet and noticed that the mattress too had been slightly stained. Fortunately, just that morning, a maid had been sent on trial, by an agent. This was because I feared that when Sil left, in just a few days, my elderly parents and I would not be able to cope with the household chores, cooking, and attending to the children's needs. Dewdrop too would be very busy with classes and tuitions for her core subjects. I had to reserve energy for my duties in the classroom as well. Tuitions were to commence just after that weekend. With all these thoughts going on in my head, I almost forgot that the maid had kindly offered to be woken up if there was any emergency. Well, this definitely was an emergency!

The maid quickly came to assist me. While she attended to the soiled bed sheet, I cleaned the mattress with some strong disinfectant, wiped it dry, and turned on the fan at full blast. Pulling out a fresh bed sheet from the linen cupboard, I handed it over to the maid and ran downstairs to see how Tony was faring. He lay on the sofa, with Sil's pillow under his head. He looked sallow and he was groaning. I battled on whether to get medical help. Sil suggested that we let him rest and decide in the morning. It was almost 3.00 a.m. then.

The next morning, Tony appeared rather motionless and barely responded. I called his physician friend again. This time, I was advised to send him to another reputed hospital, located on the outskirts of town. We had to call for an ambulance because Tony would not co-operate at all. Mum accompanied Tony in the ambulance, while Dad and I made another trip to the bank after I had packed some of Tony's personal belongings into a bag. Once the money had been withdrawn, we rushed to the specialist hospital.

This time, Tony was wheeled into the intensive care unit, owing to his altered state of consciousness. Mum's face was ashen when she saw us walk into the reception of the casualty department. She could not explain what was happening. All she knew was that her beloved son-in-law was too ill to be admitted into the normal ward. Dad walked slowly behind me, his legs aching, while I hurried to the intensive care unit, anxious to know what was happening. 'Is Tony's condition that critical?' I wondered, as I half walked and half ran.

I soon got my answer. Tony was connected to a life-support machine, with a few intravenous drips running simultaneously. I stood there in a state of shock. I simply could not believe my eyes! What was happening to my robust 'I'll *never* fall ill!' captain? This could not be happening! It was like a nightmare. My legs went weak, and I felt myself go cold.

Dad had caught up, and he laid his hand gently on my trembling shoulder. We went nearer, and I held on to Tony's bed for support. 'You have to be strong, girl,' Dad softly said. Yes, I had to be strong, very strong. Dad too had never thought he would see Tony crumble. We stood there silently for a few minutes, just looking at the floundering captain.

The staff nurse on duty looked at us with sympathy. When she learnt that I was Tony's wife, she gently said, 'Your husband is in a coma. The specialist will soon arrive to attend to him.' I had myriad questions to ask, but nothing would come out of my mouth. Dad too was dumbfounded. We just stood there helplessly, feeling utterly useless.

The doctor arrived and rushed to Tony's bed. The staff nurse furnished him with all the details he required. He flipped through some pages in a file, all the time wearing a look of anxiety. He then asked me a few questions on what had taken place during the hours before Tony's admission. I told him all that had occurred, not forgetting the frequent bleeding from Tony's mouth and the more recent incontinence. The doctor then assured me, 'Your husband will be out of his coma within the next twenty-four hours, but he will need to undergo endoscopy, which is a surgical procedure.'

I was greatly relieved that Tony would soon regain consciousness. The doctor could then do what was necessary; all I wanted was for the captain to get back to the helm—it did not feel right for me to be manning our ship. He was the captain, and I had extracted from him the promise that he would never let go of my hand, which I had put so trustingly in his. The doctor left after he had given the staff nurse all necessary instructions on how to handle Tony's case.

Dad and I went to join Mum, who was seated in the waiting area. We told her what the doctor had said, and she too heaved a sigh of relief. The staff nurse from the intensive care unit soon came to where we were and recapitulated Tony's current situation, reassuring us that all was under control. Looking at me, she comfortingly offered, 'Your husband's condition can still be treated.

'It is not as bad as cases where the patient vomits basins full of blood. That,' she stressed, 'is when the situation is beyond salvation.' I shuddered at the very thought!

I remained with Tony in the hospital, while my weary parents returned home. Later, Dad would return with Sil and the children, who were all anxious to see Tony. Meanwhile, I walked to the payphone and made a few quick calls to inform Tony's siblings that he had been admitted into the intensive care unit of the specialist hospital just on the outskirts of town.

Recounting and Reflecting

Having done my duty, I sat down to gather my wits. The events of the past ten days had been rather sudden and extremely trying. I either sat, brooding next to Tony's bed, or paced the corridor mechanically. I wondered, 'When will he come out of the coma? It is so painful and frightening to see my Tony connected to all these formidable-looking gadgets with graphs fluctuating across the screens!'

As I paced the floor, I became a little angry, thinking, 'Our marriage was not supposed to be like this at all! Hospitals were not on the agenda! Neither was Tony's drinking! What has happened to all those dreams I dared to dream? Have they all vanished?'

My life had reached a stage where I could not afford to dream at all. It was enough if I could just pay the bills and give the family a fairly comfortable life. If Tony could actually just stop drinking, the rest of our lives would perhaps be a little more peaceful, even happier. I might then be able to secure a brighter future for my two children. I was weary and my mind, stressed. I reminded myself, 'I must not give up! I *cannot* give up! I have to open the classroom door soon for the fresh intake of students, and when I do, I shall have to insist on an advance payment of fee. I may even have to increase the fee a little. After all, I am worth my salt, and many seek me out. This hospital is good, but treatment is expensive. Mum's savings have almost all been depleted, and if surgery is on the cards, more funds will have to be raised . . .'

The specialist hospital was strict about advance deposits and would not allow credit. I was duty-bound to make sure that the captain was provided with the best. Up till then, I had been lenient on my collection of fee, trustingly leaving it to the convenience and integrity of the parents. Now, however, I would have to be firm about upfront payments, although some parents might find it a strain to pay at the beginning of each month. I had to be practical—there was no other way to pay the impending hospital bills.

While all these thoughts were racing through my head, Dad reappeared with Sil and the children. I realised with a start that four hours had passed! I had not touched a drop of water or a morsel of food since the time that Tony had been admitted, yet strangely, I felt neither thirsty nor hungry. When Sil saw me, she firmly told me to eat something as soon as I got home. The children would remain with her in the hospital until Dad or I returned again. There was nothing I could do for Tony while he was in the intensive care unit. What I could do, and had to, was to raise the necessary funds for the looming surgery. When Dad and I got home, I had a quick bite and sat down with my anxious parents to think of ways to secure the money required.

On our return to the hospital, we learnt from Sil that two of Tony's siblings had visited. They had been enlightened on his condition and had spoken a few words of comfort to Dewdrop and Wriggles. I looked at my two soldiers and saw how anxiously they were watching their father's face, every minute. I could sense them both wishing fervently that he would quickly open his eyes so that we could all go home and put this nightmare behind us.

Poor bewildered Wriggles could not understand much of what was happening, but Dewdrop, several years older, was more aware of the seriousness of the entire situation. Ritchie, who had always engaged in playful boxing and wrestling bouts with Tony, could hardly believe that it was the same energetic and youthful uncle who lay motionless on the white hospital bed, with tubes connecting him to formidable equipment.

Feeling that they had been through more than their fair share for the moment, I suggested that they go home, while I stayed behind with Tony. They left only after I promised to inform them the moment that Tony opened his eyes. I gave them my solemn word, for that would be a piece of news that I would be most delighted to announce.

Conscious Again

An hour or so after the rest of the family had left for home, the nurse on duty noted that Tony was slowly coming out of his coma. 'Look,' she said, 'his eyes are twitching. This means that he is soon going to come round.' This observation gave me a renewed surge of strength. If earlier, I had harboured any reservations at all about raising the tuition fee, I now became determined to do so, even if some parents protested! It had been three years since the last time I raised the fee anyway. I had been in the tutoring line for over two decades, and my students had always done well.

My resolution was further fuelled when Tony opened his eyes. I held his hand and squeezed it, willing him to respond. He was still too weak to even acknowledge my presence. The doctor walked in just then, looking less anxious than before. A quick survey of the vital sign readings was done, after which he looked at me and confirmed that Tony was definitely regaining consciousness. I excused myself for a while, rushed to the pay phone, and called home to give the good news.

Dad said that they would soon be on their way. I hurried back to the intensive care unit, eager to know if there had been any further progress. The doctor was still examining Tony. He then spoke to me positively about the endoscopy, suggesting that it be done a day or two after Tony had fully regained consciousness. He also proposed, 'Let Tony be transferred to a normal ward until the endoscopy. He will no longer need such close monitoring, and this will also help reduce expenses.' I nodded appreciatively.

As soon as Tony came out of his coma, he asked for some water. My heart ached when I saw how parched his lips were. Earlier, we had been advised not to give him any water to drink but merely wet his lips. Now, the nurse smilingly allowed me to give Tony sips of water. As he slowly sipped the water, his eyes wandered round the room full of electronic gadgets. He was confused, but it was too soon for me to explain to him what had happened. As I watched him sip water slowly, I could not help recalling how much water my captain used to glug down each day. He would start every morning with almost half a litre of cold water! What a contrast this was. Tony looked very dehydrated lying on the bed. 'Never mind,' I consoled myself. 'Once he is on the road to recovery, he will regain a healthy glow.'

The nurse on duty suddenly called for my attention, bringing me back to earth. She was going to move Tony out of the intensive care unit to a normal male ward, and she needed to be advised on the class of ward preferred. I asked for a room with only two beds, which would allow Tony more privacy. He would also be able to watch television. I dared not ask for a room with single bed, for I had to be sure that there would be sufficient funds for other hospital expenses incurred. Tony was transferred out within minutes. He looked relieved to be away from the life-support equipment that had earlier surrounded his bed. I gently squeezed his hand—I was relieved too.

Hope Rekindled

On entering the room allotted, I found that there was no other patient there. I was pleased, for at least we could have some privacy. I put a few of Tony's personal effects into the locker and side cabinet provided. A few minutes later, the doctor entered the room. He spoke cheerfully to Tony. He was happy to see that Tony's condition had improved, and he slowly explained to him how he had been brought in for admission. Tony gave him a smile, indicating that he had understood what had been explained, but still rather weak, he soon fell asleep.

The doctor then turned to me and explained, 'Your husband requires endoscopy because he also has oesophageal varices, which is a complication of liver cirrhosis. Oesophageal varices are just like varicose veins in the oesophagus and stomach. They have developed in him because of the increased blood pressure between the gut and his damaged liver. I plan to perform endoscopy to insert a flexible scope into Tony's oesophagus and guide it all the way down to his stomach to locate these oesophageal varices. I shall then suck each varicose vein into a ring at the end of the endoscope and place an elastic band around the base of the varicose vein. These elastic bands are supposed to kill off the aberrant varicose veins. Should these varices be left unchecked, a spontaneous rupture and bleed could be torrential and potentially fatal.' He stopped to see if I had understood all that he had said. I had, and now horrified, I knew what the staff nurse had meant by 'the patient vomits basins full of blood'.

The doctor continued, 'I shall also be supporting this surgical procedure with drugs that will further reduce the risk of bleeding.' He then emphasised, 'Banding the varices is not a 100 per cent guarantee against bleeding. However, I believe it will significantly reduce the risk of a torrential bleed. The final decision is up to Tony and you. I will only proceed to perform this procedure with your complete consent.'

I was in a daze as I took in all this information. However, I still managed to put forth a few burning questions. Earlier, I had been too traumatised to ask them, but now that something concrete was going to be done to steer Tony towards recovery, I found my tongue. I queried, 'What caused Tony to go into a coma in the first place? Why was his pillow always bloodstained? Why was there often blood in the washbasin? Was it due to a lack of vitamin C, as Tony always maintained? What about the swollen legs, distended abdomen, and sallow complexion?'

The doctor patiently provided me with answers. He spoke clearly and slowly, starting with 'Tony went into a coma because his damaged liver was unable to detoxify toxins such as ammonia from his bloodstream. These toxins, over time, had accumulated to a level high enough to impair his consciousness. Tony's damaged liver was no longer able to produce clotting factors, blood constituents which are necessary to prevent bleeding. This lack of clotting factors made his gums bleed easily.' Now, I understood why there were stains in the washbasin and on the pillow!

The doctor continued, 'The bleeding gums had nothing to do with the lack of vitamin C. Tony's damaged liver was also unable to make certain proteins that are essential in the blood to keep bodily fluids in balance. Without those proteins, Tony's blood has been retaining excess water and salt. Thus, a lot of fluid has accumulated in his abdominal cavity and legs. The sallow complexion is yet another sign of his failing liver—it is no longer able to break down bilirubin, a yellow pigment that is a by-product when red blood cells are broken down. This yellow pigment has instead been deposited in the skin, thus giving Tony a sallow complexion.'

'Doctor, thank you so much for enlightening me on what has been happening to Tony, and in his body. Only now do I understand what is going on. All that matters now is that the banding is done successfully,' I implored.

'I shall definitely try my best. Every patient is to be given the best possible treatment,' the doctor assured me.

When the doctor left the room, I was not without company for long. The children soon walked in, followed by Dad and Mum. Their excitement and happy chatter awakened Tony, who slowly sat up in his bed. As they walked towards him, joy written all over their faces, Tony reached for them. Mum shed silent tears of relief, while Dad sat down on a chair to slowly absorb all that had happened. How tired he must have been, driving up and down from our home to the hospital! It was a good half-hour's drive each way.

All eyes were focused on Tony—we had much to be thankful for. After the children had spent a few chirpy minutes with their father, the nurse entered the room to check his blood pressure and give him his medication. Dad and Mum suggested that they leave for home then, for the children had to pack their bags and prepare for school. It would be the first day of the scholastic year the following morning. That meant the rest of us also had to be up early. I, however, chose to stay a little longer, to make sure that the captain was comfortable enough. Also, I just needed to spend a little time alone with him. I had felt so left out of his life for so long I simply had to know if I still mattered to him.

After the children had left with Dad and Mum, it was suddenly very quiet. I switched on the television for Tony, at his request. Then he looked around for something to read, but there was nothing. I told him that I would get him a copy of the daily newspaper when I came to see him the next morning. He requested, 'Could you also bring me the Christmas issue of *Reader's Digest*? It came with Season's Greetings cards enclosed, for the new year.'

I gently reminded him, 'We are already into the new year! Why do you need those cards now?'

He stressed, 'Please just remember to bring the cards anyway. I have a few messages that I urgently need to send out.' Sensing that this meant a lot to him, I made a mental note to bring the requested *Reader's Digest* edition, with the cards, the next day. I then left to go home, for my Tony needed to rest. It had been a long day for me too, but I was grateful that it had ended on a happy note.

I woke up early the next morning, feeling more hopeful than I had felt in a long time. Everybody else at home also felt more cheerful. Dewdrop and Wriggles were a mixture of excitement and cheerfulness as they got ready for school. Both were eager to return to school after almost two months' vacation. Sil and Ritchie would be away that day, visiting a few relatives before their departure the following morning. I assured Sil that all would be fine. She had already sacrificed so much of her time, and I truly appreciated all the help she had rendered. I insisted that she attend to her own neglected matters that day.

After the children had left for school, I called the hospital to speak to Tony. He sounded cheerful and said, 'I'm feeling better. I've just had a light breakfast.' I asked if I could get him anything he particularly wished to eat, but he declined. 'When you come, please remember to bring me the December edition of *Reader's Digest*, with the cards!' I assured him I would not forget. I then got ready and, armed with a change of clothes for Tony and the requested reading material, complete with cards, I drove to the hospital.

As I walked into Tony's room, I noticed that there was still nobody else sharing the room with him. It was fortunate that this was so. It had all the privacy of a room with a single bed, and Tony was at liberty to watch any television channel he wished to. My captain gave me a very warm smile when he saw me and looked pleased when I handed over the copy of *Reader's Digest* to him. He asked about the children, and I also briefed

257

him on the happenings at home. I was in the midst of telling Tony about the impending departure of Sil and Ritchie, when the nurse walked in. She said, 'I have a message from the doctor. He wants to see the both of you in his consultation room on the first floor.' We immediately proceeded to see him.

Tony could now fully comprehend all that had happened and was still happening to him. The doctor wished to educate us on his condition and the steps that would be taken. He enlightened us on the same, illustrating his explanation with the help of charts and drawings pertaining to the ailment. This was all done in the privacy of his consultation room. Tony had a look of remorse on his face as the doctor enumerated his symptoms over the past six months and chalked them all down to alcoholic liver cirrhosis. The very mention of the word *alcoholic* made Tony hang his head down ashamedly. I noticed this and gently took his hand in mine. He responded. He knew that I was still with him, and I knew that he was most grateful for that. We could not turn the clock back, but we could steer towards calmer waters. We simply had to avoid the storm clouds that could be looming ahead, and that might beckon to him at an unguarded moment.

Tony's Solemn Promise

After discussing the symptoms, the good doctor proceeded to educate Tony on the endoscopy and banding. 'Tony,' he started, 'I sincerely hope that you respond favourably to the procedure.

Should you agree to have it performed, it is crucial that you submit yourself to a fortnightly review, take your prescriptions with religious regularity, and *not* strain yourself physically for a few months at least. Above all, alcohol is strictly forbidden—it will ruin everything that is being done to save you.

'Again,' he emphasised, 'the banding is no absolute guarantee against bleeding. It will, in my opinion, reduce the risk of a torrential haemorrhage.'

'Doctor, I'm most grateful for this chance to save my life. I'm very keen to undergo the endoscopy, and I promise both you and my wife that I will strictly adhere to all medical advice. I thank you, with all my heart.' With this, Tony and I gave our consent for the procedure to be done in two days' time.

When I got home that day, I informed the family of all that the doctor had said and of the decision that Tony and I had made. They were all hopeful of the success of the procedure. Each of us fervently prayed that our Tony would be unwavering enough in his decision to *never* touch a drop of alcohol again.

Tuitions for the year were to commence that very day, and I would have to be in the classroom from 3.00 p.m. until 9.15 p.m. As such, I could no longer be with the captain in the afternoons and early evenings. I could only drive to the hospital after 9.30 p.m., by which time the classroom should have been locked up for the night. I was not even able to see Tony the afternoon before tuitions commenced, for I had to call at my book suppliers to confirm my orders. The children, however, went with Mum and Dad to see Tony after their return from school.

At 9.30 p.m., after the first day of tuitions, I drove to the hospital to see my captain. He was happy to see me but remarked that I looked worn out. I told him that I needed to get used to working long hours again. He cheerfully told me how the nurses had been pampering him and how happy he had been to see the family earlier that evening. Before I left, he handed over two cards for me to send out—one to my maternal uncle, Uncle Raj, residing in England, and the other to Shiv, in Wellington, New Zealand. I was surprised!

Tony offered, 'I want to forget the ugly past and start a new lease on life. To do this, I need the blessings of all my loved ones, including Shiv. I need Shiv to know that I sincerely appreciate all that he had tried to do for me. I seek his forgiveness if I have hurt him, wittingly or otherwise. As for Uncle Raj, you know that I didn't take kindly to the times that he kept commenting on my drinking rather often and being irresponsible, right? Well, I need to tell him that I was blind to all good advice, and to please forgive me.' With tears in my eyes, I hugged my captain. Deep down, I always knew he was a gem, although perhaps a little unpolished at times.

I assured Tony that I would request Sil to hand Shiv's card personally to him. This card would not be sent by post; it would travel in the comfort of Sil's soft leather designer handbag. He could remind Sil to hand over the card to Shiv when she visited him with Ritchie the next morning, on the way to the airport.

The next morning, Dewdrop and Wriggles said their goodbyes to Sil and Ritchie before they left for school. The children were really going to miss them both. Sil and Ritchie had helped to remove some clouds of gloom in the past month. Those were the rare times that the sun had shone through the clouds and the house had rung with laughter. Both aunt and cousin promised the children that they would come again soon. Sil urged Dewdrop and Wriggles, 'Please give your daddy full support when he gets home from the hospital. He needs your love more than ever. Don't annoy him, all right? Don't give him any excuse to find happiness away from this wonderful family.'

I could not recall a time when the children had not given Tony their all. I did not think the world of them just because they were mine, but because of all the essence of goodness that God had so graciously bestowed upon them. If ever I felt down, it would be just a few seconds before one of them instinctively put a comforting arm around me or planted a loving kiss on my face. I thanked the Almighty for them.

As the taxi pulled away, Sil and Ritchie kept looking in the direction of Dad, Mum, and me. They waved until the driver had pulled out of the junction, on to the main road. They were going to call on Tony on their way to the airport. The hospital was located along the route to the highway and the taxi driver had been obliging enough to agree to stop there for a few minutes. After visiting Tony, they would head for the airport and soon board an international flight that would take them across the Indian Ocean, over eastern Australia, and finally, across the Tasman Sea, to touch down at Auckland. A domestic flight would then convey them to the warmth and security of their own home in Wellington, where Shiv would be eagerly awaiting their arrival. His wife and son had been away for over a month, and there would be much catching up to do. Some of the news, though, might depress Shiv greatly.

The very morning that Sil and Ritchie were leaving, while the three children were having their breakfast and pulling last-minute pranks, Sil had pulled me aside gently, to give me some sisterly advice. She urged me, 'Please don't give up. Keep striving to save Tony and make sure that the family stays united. Honestly, if I had been in your position, I might not have been able to endure the years of stress and strain that you have undergone. I know what has transpired in your seventeen years of marriage, for both Shiv and I have made trips home annually all these years. I also know that I have never seen or met any woman with your resilience. If anyone can keep this family afloat, it is you.'

Of course, there was nothing I could have kept hidden from visiting family members. My life was an open book. How would it ever have been possible to keep matters under wrap? I pointed out, 'Sil, in my heart, there has always been, and still is, the hope that Tony will see the light one day. That day will be the first day of the beginning of a wonderful life together. I strongly feel that my patience will finally be rewarded. All I want is a happy home captained by my then hopefully enlightened Tony and enlivened by rings of laughter from our two highly enraptured deckhands, Dewdrop and Wriggles!'

Sil marvelled, 'How tenaciously you hold on to the reins of optimism despite the many challenges and obstacles that have unexpectedly sprung up along the route, often in succession!' I personally felt, and still do, that any other woman, whose marriage meant the world to her would not have hesitated to do exactly the same. I agreed with my well-meaning sister-in-law, nevertheless, that I had braved enough stormy seas till then with the captain and now truly deserved to sail tranquil waters.

As she was leaving, Sil promised to keep in touch more regularly and assured me that she would tell me of Shiv's reaction on receiving and reading Tony's card. My brother is basically a very warm and loving man. I knew that he would find it in his heart to forgive his errant brother-in-law.

After Sil and Ritchie had bade farewell to Tony that morning, some of his relatives called on him. This time, there was no accompanying priest. Tony gave me this information when I called him at the hospital. He also told me how pleased he had been to see Sil and Ritchie earlier that morning. He expressed a wish to see Shiv too, one day in the near future. I was overwhelmed at the thought of these two important men in my life reuniting. I then got ready to go the hospital. I bought the daily newspaper on the way and arrived at the hospital at 10.00 a.m.

I spent a pleasant hour with Tony, much amused at the friendly banter that went on between the cheery captain and the genial medical staff. What a contrast this was, compared to the time he had been admitted to the general hospital in our town. His behaviour then had truly alarmed me, for he usually had good rapport with others, making them feel at ease. It was an inherent gift, bestowed only on a few.

I left Tony in jovial company, after I had promised to return when tuition classes were over that night. A few of his close friends also paid him a visit that afternoon, while Dad, Mum, and the children called at the hospital only in the evening. Dewdrop had to attend a tuition class after school, but she still wanted to see her father before surgery the next day. Tony definitely had no shortage of well-wishers!

On their return from the hospital, Dad confided in me, 'Tony is beginning to feel a little anxious about the procedure scheduled for tomorrow morning. He talked about it apprehensively, but is trying to keep himself occupied, watching television or reading.' I wished I could just cancel my last class for the day and rush to give him reassurance, but that was not going to remedy the situation. Also, it was a class that had just taken off for the year—how would I explain my need to reassure my husband to a batch of new students and their parents who had paid in advance for the month? The next best thing to do was to call the captain and speak to him, telling him to keep his chin up. I did that.

Immediately after class was over, I drove to the hospital to be with my anxious captain. I assured him, 'All will go smoothly, Tony. You are in very competent hands.' He felt better and more confident. We talked optimistically, and I gave him my word that I would there by his side as soon as the children had been sent to school the next morning. I then kissed him and drove home. It was almost midnight.

The Procedure

The next morning, when I entered Tony's room, he was not to be seen. I was puzzled. Sensing my confusion, a ward nurse informed me that Tony had been wheeled to the endoscopy suite just a few minutes earlier. I had hoped to be on time to see him just before he was wheeled in for the procedure. Feeling guilty that I had let him down, I waited resignedly for his return. I conditioned my mind to think positive thoughts while I absent-mindedly browsed through the *Reader's Digest* lying beside Tony's pillow.

About an hour later, a rather groggy Tony was brought back to the room. The nurse attending to him informed me that Tony would require a few hours' rest and politely suggested that I return in the afternoon. Heeding this well-intentioned piece of advice, I decided to drive back to the heart of town and settle matters with my book suppliers. This would keep my mind occupied until Tony was able to receive visitors.

That afternoon, I received a call from Tony himself. He sounded all right but said that he was anxious to see the family. I told him that I was just about to start tuition class but assured him that Dad, Mum, and the children would call on him as soon as the children had come back from school and had their lunch. I myself would only be able to see him after 9.30 p.m. I did not tell him that it was important for me to collect all the fees that day, to be able to settle the cost of the procedure. The last thing I wanted in the world was for him to worry at this stage. It gave me much strength, however, to hear his voice over the telephone. Now, surely, there would be tranquil waters and sunny skies.

The family went to the hospital as promised. On their return, the children were chirpy and thrilled that their father would soon be home. Wriggles and Dewdrop had been pleasantly surprised with chocolates from Tony, who had requested a hospital attendant to buy them from the gift shop on the ground floor. It looked like life was going to be sweet again.

Tony had expressed to the family, 'I yearn to be in the comfort of home, surrounded by my loving family. I don't want to miss a minute of it. I hope the doctor will soon let me go home.' It warmed my heart tremendously when I heard this. Of course, I would approach the doctor the very next day and ask when Tony could be discharged. I would also have to make sure that I could fully settle the hospital bill by then. I had collected a fair amount of money that day, for a new third form class had taken off. The intake had been most encouraging. God was being benevolent once more; things were taking an optimistic turn.

By 9.30 p.m., I was on my way to the hospital, thinking, 'If everything goes well, I shall not be travelling this route again tomorrow night. Hopefully, Tony will be resting in our own bedroom, and when I feel the urge to see his face, I shall only have to run up the stairs, to our bedroom—what a relief! Will he ever be able to understand how merely seeing his face gives me the strength I so badly need to carry on with my increasing responsibilities? I doubt he will ever realise how much I love him. Is it only women who feel this way, or is it the sheer intensity of love that one being has for another? God, how much I love this man.'

Lost in my own thoughts, I did not realise that the traffic light had turned green, until the driver in the vehicle behind mine blared his car horn repeatedly! Startled to reality, I jerked forward and stepped on the accelerator, eager to get to my recuperating captain.

I was thrilled when I entered Tony's room and saw him walking about. Apparently, he was feeling stronger and more determined to return to normalcy. This was a promising sign. However, it was crucial that he kept a positive outlook. This mindset, coupled with strict discipline, would surely put him on the high road to maximum recovery. If he steadfastly maintained this healing formula, the journey to better health would not be too long.

I, for my part, was fully geared to give him full support in anything constructive that he desired to undertake. I was also going to love him more than ever, if that was possible. Tony smiled on seeing me, and we sat down to talk about getting him discharged as soon as we could. Seeking some answers, I took a walk with the captain to the reception area of that ward, where we spoke to the staff nurse. She advised me to call the consultant doctor the next morning and have a word with him. We were reassured when she said, 'I strongly believe that as long as Tony recognises the urgency of the fortnightly review and strictly adheres to everything else that the doctor advises, there is really no reason to keep him here.' Smilingly, she added, 'It has been a pleasure, Tony, having you in the ward. We shall miss you and your sunny disposition.'

Tony's face lit up with joy. Yes, it was most definitely time for the sun to shine on us at home too. I left shortly afterwards, hopeful that I would be accompanied home by my husband the following day.

Early the next morning, I counted whatever money I had collected as fee over the past two days. I called Tony to tell him, 'I shall be at the hospital as soon as I have checked with the doctor to see if you can be discharged. Then I shall also have to call the administration office to enquire about the payment to be settled. If the money I have in hand is sufficient, I shall come straight to the hospital. If not, I shall have to call at the bank first.' Tony understood the situation.

I made the necessary calls. The doctor said, 'I shall have another talk with Tony in his room, before you arrive. It is imperative that Tony adhere to all medical advice and requirements. I would advise you also to accompany your husband each time he attends a review.' I thanked the doctor and assured him that I had every intention of doing so, but requested that it be carried out in the morning. He understood my situation and said he would oblige. I thanked him again.

I called the administration office of the hospital and was connected to the finance department. I was enlightened on how much the total bill was, how much I had already deposited, and finally, what balance remained to be paid. I was most grateful to God that I had enough money in hand. However, our savings were all depleted, as were Mum's. I called Tony again to tell him that I would be there soon. He asked, 'How are you going to manage to pay the bill?' I chided him lovingly, telling him that it was not his problem to worry about. All he had to worry about was to get well and *remain* well.

Discharged with Guidance

With the required cash in my handbag and hope in my heart, I drove to the hospital. I had secretly wished that I could bring Tony home before the children returned from school, and now, my wish was going to be fulfilled. Their joy would know no bounds when they came home from school and saw their father seated in his usual armchair in the living room. It would also be much easier on both Dad and me, having Tony at home. I had often felt very tired after classes and could barely keep my eyes open while driving to the hospital and back again, late at night.

Dad, being the ever-willing and accommodating man that he was, had never complained. Each time he had called on Tony at the hospital, he would return with positive remarks about his condition. Mum, of course, was always asking Tony if there was anything in particular he fancied eating. As she grew older, she often felt tired more easily when working in the kitchen. Yet she was eager to please her son-in-law, taking pains to prepare dishes that he especially relished. Now, with Tony returning home, she could pamper him all she wanted. His loss of weight over the recent months had caused all of us much grief and anxiety, and I knew she would do her best to help him regain good health and maybe put on some weight! I thanked God over and over again for having blessed me with such wonderful parents.

Sil and Shiv were also on my mind as I drove to the hospital to get Tony. Sil had called to inform us that both Ritchie and she had arrived safely in Wellington. She had given Tony's card to Shiv, and it now lay in the drawer of his bedside table. He often took it out to read, and according to Sil, there was now a softer look in his eyes. It was only a matter of time before they buried the hatchet.

With this comforting thought in my mind, I parked the car and hurried to Tony's room. The doctor himself was still there, reminding Tony about what was expected of him once he was discharged. The procedure had been carried out successfully, but the aftercare was crucial. When he saw me, the doctor turned to me and said, 'I want to tell you myself that Tony will be in your care henceforth, and as such, you must help to make sure that he adheres closely to all medical advice.' Then smiling, he turned to Tony again, with 'Don't forget to collect your medication from the pharmacy before you leave the hospital and please make sure you come back in a fortnight for your review.' We thanked the doctor for all that he had done for Tony. I would never forget how painstakingly he had explained the whole procedure to both Tony and me, and how patiently he had answered all my questions on Tony's condition. Wishing Tony all the best, the doctor shook hands with us and left.

I helped Tony to dress, after which I gathered his belongings. Having put them into two small bags, I proceeded to the ground floor to settle the bill. In the meanwhile, a wheelchair was arranged for Tony. After I had settled the bill, I proceeded to the pharmacy to collect the captain's medication. There was quite a wide array of pills and capsules, packed in no less than ten little plastic packets. For one fleeting moment, I thought, 'I hope

Tony will not work himself up into a mood where he refuses to take all these medicines. He has never been one to complete any course of medicines, often abandoning them halfway.' I then chided myself, nipping my pessimism in the bud. Of course, things were going to be different now!

An attendant brought Tony down in the wheelchair, from the ward on the third floor. I met them in the lobby and informed the attendant that I would bring the car round to the entrance. I then walked off to the car park, clutching the precious bundle of medication.

As Tony was being helped into the car, I heard him promise the attendant that he would, on the day of his review, be gifting them a cake in appreciation of all that they had done for him. I smiled—what a far cry this was from the time of Tony's discharge from the general hospital. All he needed was kindness and love, two qualities that he himself had had an abundance of, before drink had taken over.

As I drove the captain back to our 'ship', I conditioned myself once again to be staunchly positive. Tony had every reason to reinstate himself at the helm of our ship, which though buffeted by many a storm, still proudly held its mast high. Together, we could still steer through the choppy seas of life, bravely and determinedly. Nothing should daunt us now.

Home Sweet Home

On Tony's return from the hospital, a long-yearned-for tranquillity pervaded the domestic domain. Tony, after what seemed like ages, was finally at peace with one and all at home. He was most appreciative of Dad's chauffeuring Dewdrop and Wriggles to and from school, tuition, and music classes. He was no longer resentful and misconstruing of Dad's sincere efforts to do his bit for the family. The captain openly gushed his gratefulness to the kitchen queen, Mum, while she stood long hours over the hot stove, meticulously brewing herbal concoctions to boost his recovery.

Dewdrop and Wriggles were thrilled when their convalescing father gathered them around him every now and then to point out an interesting fact or two when *Discovery Planet* or *National Geographic* aired on television. Wriggles would be absolutely relieved to be allowed to brush aside the drudgery of homework and instead revel in the wonder of wildlife with his beloved father, even if only for a few blissful moments. Dewdrop would, after a few minutes, dutifully return to her world of physics and additional mathematics, but I would have to subtly kidnap the reluctant Wriggles from his father's loving cocoon. Before long, after ensuring that I was gainfully occupied in the classroom, he would slowly wriggle back to his father's armchair.

Foreboding Fears

It was sheer relief to have Tony safe and peaceful at home with us. The maid who had just joined us remarked sometimes on what a happy home we had—an innocent remark, which filled me both with pride and fear. I felt proud because few families could boast of three generations living peacefully together under one roof. However, fear also lurked in my heart—fear that my Tony would suddenly get up one morning and decide that his current prescribed manner of life lacked the excitement and lustre of the past.

I tried to push such thoughts away, but sometimes, I saw a faraway look in Tony's eyes that left me wondering if the prevailing domestic ambience was enough to keep him contented. Where the rest of us were concerned, it was as if heaven had graciously descended upon us. At times, I was even afraid to be happy, afraid that I might suddenly wake up to find that it had only been a dream.

Tony had now developed the practice of waiting for me after tuition classes so that we could have dinner together. If he had already eaten with the rest of the family, he would still make it a point to keep me company at the dining table. I sometimes wished, 'If only my Tony had showered me with such attention and companionship right from the start, life would have been so wonderful and fulfilling . . . well, still better late than never.'

I thanked God, and the doctor, for the paradise bestowed. I sincerely prayed and hoped it would last.

After I had eaten, Tony would return to his armchair to sit and watch television for a while, until I made sure that the children had completed their school assignments and packed their bags. After they had kissed Tony goodnight and gone upstairs to bed, I would mark a few books and then say goodnight to the captain. The captain, however, no longer wanted to remain alone in the living room, not even to watch a wrestling match on television! Very often in the past, Tony, who was addicted to watching wrestling matches on television, would refuse to turn in till the programme had ended. Now, the same Tony dreaded being alone downstairs. I was startled; this was most unlike my brave Tony. Something was not right.

If we were in our room and I needed to go downstairs to the kitchen to fix myself a nightcap, Tony would plead with me to return to the room as fast as possible. I was truly alarmed. A warning bell rang in my head.

At night, Tony slept fitfully, holding my hand, like a frightened child. Obviously, something was troubling him. I made several attempts to find out, and finally, after much cajoling, Tony confessed that he sometimes heard his late father calling him. This worried him for he took it as a sign that his late father was beckoning to him, to join him. My captain wanted to live.

Finding Strength

Almost a week after the surgical procedure, Tony called the family together for a brief meeting. He expressed a wish for all of us, Dad and Mum included, to sit together and read a chapter from the Bible each evening, at 6.00 p.m. The captain was passionate about this request and had fixed the time so that I would be able to push the last two classes to a later slot, leaving a half-hour interval after the earlier two classes. Mum and Dad agreed, not wanting to disappoint Tony. The children were taken aback at their father's sudden request but fell in line.

The Bible-reading session started that very evening with every family member taking turns to read. At the end of the reading, Tony prayed for the good health and welfare of every member of the family, near and far, his and mine. He prayed that we might go on remembering the blessings that God had bestowed upon us and thank Him unfailingly. Finally, he prayed that God forgive us for any sins we had committed, wittingly or unwittingly.

Adjusting, Again?

The Bible reading seemed to give Tony new-found strength. He made a telephone call to the manager of an adjusters' firm in the capital, enquiring if there might be any chance of a branch being opened in our town. Apparently, this had been in the pipeline, and Tony, who had pushed away earlier thoughts of adjusting as a career again, was thinking along different lines now. I was upset, and I did not make any attempt to hide my feelings of dissent. I thought that we had been through this nightmare long enough in the past for Tony never to set foot in this field again. Tony calmed me down and begged me to listen to what was on his mind.

Taking my hand, he sat me down and started, 'I assure you that I will never repeat the mistakes I made in the past. I have learnt a severe enough lesson, and am not going to risk my life anymore. As an adjuster, at least, I was respected and sought after by those who appreciated my services. When I left adjusting and ventured wholeheartedly into other businesses, nothing came of them. I failed miserably, and the family suffered considerable financial ruin. Family relationships also were strained.

'Drinking,' he stressed, 'is what brought me down, and now that I am on the wagon, I shall be fine in this very same line, a line in which I have enough experience to manage a branch.' Looking into my eyes, he continued, 'However, I need you to be by my side, to give me the strength and confidence to start afresh.' The captain never failed to amaze me with his implicit trust in the very person he sometimes declared his nemesis.

The mornings saw Tony busier than before, making telephone calls to the key person in the capital. This gentleman seemed to be keen on taking Tony on as the manager of the proposed branch in our town. The proposed new branch was to be opened once a suitable office lot was decided on. New staff would also have to be recruited and trained by experienced staff sent to our town for a spell, by the main office. I drove Tony around in the late mornings, looking for a suitable office lot near our house. Tony wanted to be sure that I would be willing to remain in the office as close as possible to school dismissal hour.

In my weary heart, I wondered, 'How on earth am I going to cope with the impending colossal load? As it is, there never seem to be enough hours in a day! With the increased intake of students for tuition, I can barely finish marking essays in time for the next lesson. Now, the captain wishes for me to edit, perhaps even type, reports to be submitted to the head office. When am I supposed to attend to my own preparation of lessons? Who is going to take Mum to the market if Dad is not up to it? Who will accompany Dad to pay the bills at places where parking is difficult? Who will attend to any emergency that may arise at home?'

All these realities had not dawned upon the captain as he bravely took the helm. He was looking ahead, too far ahead—in his growing enthusiasm, he had failed to look behind him to see if the others on board could weather the voyage! They might have their limitations and personal needs too.

I wanted to voice out the unfairness that the captain was dishing out so 'generously', but I restrained myself. The situation was still rather delicate. I would just have to wait until he was stronger in health. This great plan for his career was giving him a purpose in life—I was not about to shatter his dreams. I also knew that within me, if I had to, I would probably bend even more than I had ever done before. I had wanted so much for us to steer towards calm seas and sunny skies, which was what the captain thought he was doing. He had merely overlooked one point—he was hurling his first mate into turbulent waters!

Several more days passed in similar fashion. The children cheerfully went off to school, after which Dad drove Mum to market. Tony and I would then step into the office at home to think of other requirements for the new branch that was to be opened, probably in three weeks from then. The manager from the main office in the capital would have to personally come down to view possible locations and then finally decide.

Tony had also been assigned the task of looking for suitable and dependable staff, preferably those who were young and willing to learn the job. Furthermore, they should be dedicated and happy to stay on for a while. He had in mind some job-seekers who were children of his friends. They had finished schooling and were still seeking employment. Tony called up the parents and told them about possible job opportunities for their children in the near future. They were most appreciative, and those whose children were keen called back. Tony explained the nature of the jobs available and advised them to get their résumés ready. I marvelled at my Tony. His recent illness had not in the slightest dampened his enthusiasm to help.

After making necessary calls and completing any other work in town, I would try to mark as many books as I could before the children had to be picked up from school. I was in a quandary; sometimes, I could barely mark three essays in an hour for it was my habit to make my students write on alternate lines only, giving me room to correct in detail the errors that they might make. It might be said that I was over-meticulous, but it was an effort that was greatly appreciated, both by students and parents. I had misgivings of 'Will I be able to be as fastidious in my grading of assignments three weeks from now?'

A glance at the clock would hurl me back into reality, and I would rush out to pick up Wriggles from school. After he had been brought home and seen to, I would be off again, this time to fetch Dewdrop. After a few precious minutes spent with the two weary children, my duties in the classroom would whisk me away for the next three hours. Then after the Bible-reading session in the living room at 6.00 p.m., I would continue classes for yet another three hours. During lessons, I would sneak into the dining room or living room whenever I got a chance, for a quick hug from whoever was within sight and a sip of tea. I needed both to feel re-energised.

A Silver Lining

The maid who had been sent by the agency was quite a capable woman. She did not need much supervision, having quickly mastered the ropes of housework the way Mum and I wanted it done. Mum usually handled the chores in the kitchen and the laundry, and the maid was trained slowly but surely to do things Mum's way. It fell upon me to train her to do the rest, which was the general cleaning of the house—cleaning of bathrooms/toilets, dusting, sweeping, and mopping. I did not take kindly to work done in a slipshod manner, and the initially reluctant-to-sweep-under-the-beds maid soon learnt that though I was small in build, I was a giant to reckon with when it came to cleanliness! Once she fell in line with my system of housecleaning, however, we got along famously.

The maid slowly began confiding in me, and it saddened me to learn how much suffering she had undergone. Her husband had been a very caring and loving man until he had taken to gambling and drinking. It reached a stage where she did not even have enough money to feed her two young daughters. Her gambler of a husband had by then also become an alcoholic, very often falling ill. One fateful day, he suddenly vomited blood. She was then left alone to fend for her girls. Leaving them in the care of her elderly mother, she had left her own country to seek employment as a maid, in ours. She said to me, 'You have much to be grateful for. Your husband has realised his folly and is trying his best to make good.' Little did she know that I sent God a thank-you prayer almost hourly!

Ridiculously Recalcitrant

On a Wednesday morning in January, the day before Tony's fortnightly review, the captain had locked himself in our room, presumably to rest in quiet. The children were at home that morning as it was a public holiday, being the first day of a major festival. I needed to get a towel from the room, so I knocked on the door. As there was no response, I knocked again, a little more determinedly this time. A panting Tony opened the door. When I entered the room, I found his bull-worker on the bed. I was shocked! Flailing my arms, I exclaimed, 'I hope you have not been trying to exercise with the bull-worker! The doctor has strictly cautioned you against any physical exertion or strain for a few months.' Tony looked at me sheepishly, guilt written all over his face. I slumped on the bed, my legs feeling very weak.

Just then, the telephone rang, putting a quick end to further confrontation with regard to the forbidden exercise. The call was from a close friend of Tony, in another town. His father had just passed away. Tony was visibly aggrieved, for he had been rather attached to the affectionate and jovial elderly gentleman. It must have rekindled tragic memories of the death of Tony's own father less than a year before. Not wishing to talk any further, Tony went to shower, after which he donned his newly bought navy-blue tracksuit. I was puzzled, for the sun was shining brightly that morning. 'Are you feeling all right? Is it not warm?' I asked him, gently. He answered that he found it a little chilly. I could not help but remark, 'Perhaps you should not have strained yourself earlier.' He looked away sheepishly.

After breakfast, Tony made a quick telephone call from the living room. Then he requested that we have the day's Bible-reading session at 9.00 a.m. We were a little surprised at the sudden change in what had become routine. It was to be the seventh reading since we had embarked on it. Putting our own activities aside for the moment, we gathered in the living room. Tony did the reading himself that morning, and he really seemed under the weather. Mum also pointed this out to me, in a whisper. I shrugged my shoulders helplessly.

I was, however, thankful that Tony, contrary to my initial fears, had been taking each and every medication prescribed, without fail. I just prayed he would continue to do so. As far as his diet was concerned, we followed it to a T. Dad drove Mum to market almost daily so that she could buy fresh vegetables, fish, and other requisites to boost our Tony's health. This was probably why she was wondering why he looked rather off-colour that morning. I attributed it to the sad news he had received earlier.

After the reading, Tony informed us, 'I shall be leaving soon for the funeral. It is to be held in Uncle's hometown, an hour away.' I was about to protest, for I did not think it would be wise for Tony to be in the open for too long at the crematorium. Just then, I heard the sharp toot of a car horn outside the house.

Tony quickly explained, 'I have already arranged with a friend to drive me to the crematorium. He will also drive me home after the funeral, so please don't worry. He was also close to Uncle, and appreciates that he won't have to make the trip out of town alone. I'll probably have lunch outside if it gets late.'

That explained the telephone call that Tony had made just before the Bible-reading session. I was at a loss—it was too late for me to intervene. He had taken matters into his own hands, obviously. Still, I advised, 'Please do *not* overstrain yourself, Tony, or eat anything too chilli hot or spicy for lunch.' The captain, displaying his irritation at my insistent reminders, assured me curtly that he would be careful. With that, he got into the waiting vehicle and was off.

I stepped outside to close and lock the main gate, feeling a tad confused. I wondered aloud, 'Is it wrong to caution a loved one against doing something that might prove adverse? Is it wrong to try to save a loved one from pain? Is it wrong to love someone so much that you wish you could exchange bodies with him until he is as close as possible to a healthy-enough state to be declared fit and then hand his body back to him again?' At least then, I could do what was necessary without having to irritate him with reminders about exercising greater caution. The family dog, Pluto, looked at me sympathetically as I made my way back inside. Having been with us for years, he knew our struggle with Tony only too well.

The Calm Before the Storm

I entered the house to attend to some unfinished chores, for there would be no tuition classes that day or the next. Schools were closed for two days for the festival. If I finished some work fast, the children and I could later watch a movie together, on television. The captain would most probably be back by then, and if not too tired, he could perhaps be enticed to join the rest of us. We needed some quality time together and a chance to unwind. A comedy would be the best bet. This thought motivated me, and I even planned to prepare a snack or two that the children would enjoy. They deserved some fun. I did too.

While I sorted out some books in the classroom bookcase, Dewdrop and Wriggles sat at their homework, eager to complete whatever they could before we sat down to a family show. While we were engrossed in our respective tasks, the doorbell rang. There was someone at the gate asking to see me. I left what I was in the midst of doing to see who it could be.

A heart-warming sight greeted me. A student of mine, dressed fetchingly in her festive best, smiled most lovingly at me. She was holding a three-tiered tiffin carrier in one hand and an attractive covered tray in the other. I was overwhelmed at this gesture of love and appreciation. The festival had decided to pay us a visit! I thanked both the beaming little girl and her indulgent father, who had taken the trouble to drive his tutor-smitten daughter to her adored tutor's house. I handed the goodies over to the maid while I stood at the gate to see the father and daughter off, waving at the child who had only just become my student but was already so attached. I had only been doing my duty as a tutor, but here she was, sincerely doling out affection for me. Children are truly a gift from God, loving unconditionally.

I entered the house and inspected the contents of the tiffin carrier and tray. Each receptacle was filled to the brim with curried chicken, glutinous rice, and spicy peanut sauce. The multi-sectioned tray held an assortment of tempting cookies. Wriggles, the resident Cookie Monster, instantly left his homework, declaring he needed to perform a customs check. He squealed with sheer delight at the sight of the cookies in enticing little shapes topped with chopped nuts, cherries, chocolate chips, and coloured rice. Knowing him, he would make it his immediate mission to taste each and every variety, and then fill his plate with those that most tickled his palate. Dewdrop would have to be quick on the draw! Needless to say, lunch was a grand affair. Of course, we set some aside for the captain to sample later that day.

Enter the Tempest

Just as we had cleared the dining table, the doorbell rang again. I went to see who it was and caught sight of a car driving off. Who had rung the bell? Then I got a glimpse of part of a navy-blue tracksuit, just beside the right pillar of the main gate.

It was Tony! Why was he holding on to the pillar? I rushed out to unlock the gate, and I was shocked to see an extremely pale Tony on the verge of collapse! He weakly called for help. I screamed for Dad, Mum, everybody!

Had Tony returned in the car that had just sped off? How could the driver have driven off the way he had when Tony apparently needed help? Then I heard Tony muttering something about his friend having had to rush off to attend to a family crisis. I was too shocked to analyse the situation any further. All I knew was that the captain was crumbling. Dad, who was supporting him as best as he could, wore an expression of grave concern. Holding Tony on the left side, I was ready to cry.

The minute we reached the bedroom downstairs, Tony slumped on the bed and implored Mum, 'Please rub balm on my forehead. My head is throbbing painfully . . .' Mum gently lifted Tony's head on to her lap and proceeded to apply the balm, rubbing it vigorously on his forehead. Her eyes filled with tears at the pitiful sight of her sinking beloved son-in-law. As I removed his shoes, Tony asked for a basin. I was alarmed. I suddenly recalled the ghastly words of the staff nurse and the maid. No, no! It could not be so! He probably needed the basin merely to spit into. What on earth was I thinking?

I rushed to the kitchen to get the basin and hurried back to the room with it. Wriggles and Dewdrop were already at Tony's side, Dewdrop holding his right hand. She said, 'Ma, Daddy's hand feels very, very cold. Is he going to be all right, Ma? I'm feeling really worried . . .'

Wriggles, unsure, asked, 'What's happening here? Why is Naniji rubbing balm so vigorously on Daddy's forehead? Is his headache very bad? Will the balm help? Will he get better quickly?'

The Descent Begins

Dismissing the children's queries, I quickly held the basin under my captain's chin, for him to spit into. He lurched forward, jerking his head. What came out of his mouth made me freeze—it was thick, red blood! More blood spurted out in quick succession, and soon the basin was a quarter full! My legs began trembling, and I felt as if I was having a nightmare. This could not be happening, no, no, no! It was simply an illusion! The children stared in horror, while Mum started to pray fervently. Dad was at a complete loss, his eyes too glistening with tears, behind his thick glasses. The maid looked at me pitifully—the inevitable had happened. *She* was not entirely shocked, having witnessed a similar sight not too long ago. We were now sisters in tragedy.

With unsteady hands, I still held the basin, my vision blurred by tears. What was happening to my husband, my Tony, my captain? Oh, God, no! We had to save him, we simply had to! 'Dad, Mum, quick, tell me what to do! Please, somebody help

Tony!' I screamed in utter despair, overwhelmed by a wave of helplessness.

The basin was threatening to overflow, and we had to quickly run and get another one. Dewdrop had to hold the basin now, while I ran to make an urgent call to Tony's doctor. The maid hurried to fetch another basin to replace the one being used, also threatening to overflow.

Wriggles was stunned at the sight of the blood, and Dad had to comfort him. Thank God Dewdrop was not traumatised. My fingers were trembling so badly I could not even dial the numbers correctly, succeeding only at the third attempt. At first, Tony's doctor could barely understand my frantic jabber. When he finally understood the severity of what I was trying to say, he declared that he would have to attend to Tony immediately. Then however, he dropped a bomb: no ambulance was available; every unit had been summoned out. We would have to wait, but by then, it might be too late.

The Frenzied Drive

Dad and I decided there and then that we would drive the floundering captain to the specialist hospital at our own risk. We quickly bundled the shivering Tony into the backseat of the car, with a blanket wrapped all around him. Dewdrop sat with him, holding the basin, as he still vomited intermittently. I sat in front, with another empty basin ready and a pillow to place under his head if he felt he needed to lie down. Dad switched on the hazard lights, and we were off. At 2.00 p.m. that day, Dad expertly weaved his way through the festive traffic and rushed for the outskirts. He, who had never driven at breakneck speed through town before, was oblivious of the occasional angry stares of other road users, most of whom were in a relaxed, festive mood. Not one of us uttered a word, each one of us deeply lost in thought and anxious. Each time Tony made a retching sound, Dewdrop held the slowly filling basin closer to his chin. Each time I heard that sound, I had an increasingly sinking feeling. Our life together was falling apart.

As soon as we arrived at the specialist hospital, Dad made a beeline for the emergency unit. I flew out of the front door and rushed to arrange for a gurney. I also requested the receptionist at the counter to inform Tony's doctor that he had arrived. I then rushed back to the car, accompanied by an attendant who was wheeling the gurney. By the time I returned from the car with Tony safely secured on the gurney, the doctor was already waiting in the emergency unit. He asked me, 'Did Tony take any alcohol or exert himself earlier today?'

I answered shakily, 'I am not sure about the alcohol, but I believe that he had attempted to exercise with a bull-worker early this morning. He also attended a funeral just hours before the vomiting started . . . He is going to be all right, isn't he?'

The doctor remained silent. He wore a grave expression as he started barking instructions at the nurses. There was an intimidating sense of urgency all around us, and I was most uneasy. Dad and Dewdrop were soon by my side, but neither said a word. What was there left to say? Our captain was no longer within reach. Suddenly feeling extremely weary, I slumped into a chair. When I looked around me, I saw many faces looking in our direction, most of them sympathetically. They must have witnessed how Tony had been rushed to the area behind the curtains of the emergency room. They must have also seen the looks of anxiety and gloom depicted on our faces.

A nurse appeared from behind the curtains and asked for me, stating that the doctor wished to see me. I quickly went to her side and found Tony groaning in discomfort. The doctor informed me that they were waiting to take Tony up to the intensive care unit, where a bay was being set up to swiftly handle his current condition. I was advised to stay by Tony's side until he was sent up to the intensive care unit. I could only nod.

There was blood dribbling down from the right corner of Tony's mouth, and tissues drenched with blood lay by his side, beside his sunken face. The basin of blood that had accompanied us all the way to the hospital lay under the trolley. Tearfully, I took some tissue from a box on the side table and wiped away the blood from his chin. Blood, so precious for the sustenance of life, was still oozing out of my Tony's mouth. Why did someone not immediately stop this loss of priceless blood? What were they doing? When, oh, when were they going to save the captain?

As if in answer to the questions that ravaged my weary mind, a nurse rushed into the emergency room, shouting out instructions to an attendant to quickly wheel Tony to the intensive care unit, where his doctor was waiting. The attendant immediately obeyed. I stepped aside to give way, and then followed the attendant. Dad and Dewdrop joined me when I stepped out of the emergency room. We all needed to know what was happening to Tony. Solemnly, we made our way to the lift and rode up to the third floor.

We were instructed to wait in the corridor while the doctor, nurses, and attendant worked on Tony in the Intensive Care Unit. We caught glimpses of the medical team urgently setting up the life-support system. The doctor then came out to advise that Tony needed immediate replacement of blood constituents such as plasma and platelets to replace lost blood. Vitamin K was another prerequisite to arrest bleeding. He also enlightened us on the fact that each unit of plasma and platelets was going to cost a considerable bit of money.

No Stone Left Unturned

I merely nodded to all that the doctor said and consented that they perform the necessary transfusions immediately. We did not have much financial reserve left, but I was not about to leave any stone unturned in our efforts to save the captain. Money could be earned again, but the captain was irreplaceable. Dewdrop squeezed my hand, seconding my decision. Dad did not say anything, but his silence indicated assent. I was not alone, and we were not about to allow our captain to flounder further. Still, it was very clear that we were now at the mercy of a tempest.

By 4.00 p.m., Tony's transfusion was underway. Plasma and platelets were being fed into his veins, to replace lost blood. A medical monitor beeped in a corner, recording his heart rate, blood pressure, and oxygen levels. His breathing was assisted by a pronged tube running beneath his nostrils. We had just been allowed into the intensive care unit, and the doctor began to gravely brief us. He started with 'Tony is also losing blood from the lower end now, so adult diapers are required.'

Locking my eyes with his, he continued, 'When Tony was first admitted to the intensive care unit a fortnight ago, I was confident that he would come out of his coma. This time, however, although he's conscious, the situation is far more dire. His bleeding just won't stop. Wherever a needle is inserted, blood trickles out persistently. I advise you to quickly inform his other relatives about the severity of his condition.' Dewdrop and I were both numbed by the doctor's words. Dad immediately slumped into a chair. The doctor gazed at each of us helplessly. He understood our plight and reassured us that he was doing his level best.

Bracing Ourselves

I willed myself to walk to the pay phone, Dewdrop close by my side. With fingers that very reluctantly co-operated, I somehow managed to dial the telephone numbers of the homes of two of Tony's siblings. With a growing ache in my heart and a lump in my throat, I struggled and finally found the words to inform Tony's eldest brother and eldest sister of his plight, leaving it to them to contact anybody else.

When we returned to Tony's bed, the screens were drawn. Two nurses were changing Tony's blood-drenched diaper. By the time it was 6.00 p.m., three diapers had been changed. He was losing blood faster than it was going in. Even the vitamin K did not seem to be helping. I sensed impending doom as I stood helplessly by the captain's bed. I dared not even hold his hand, for there were large bruises and bleeding points where needles had been inserted. My thirsty captain, in a hoarse, guttural voice, begged for water. Alas, he was not to be given even a drop—the best I could do was to dab a wet wad of gauze on his parched, cracked lips.

There were tears flowing down Dewdrop's cheeks. I could not help wondering, as I looked at her forlorn expression, how she was going to face the challenging year ahead. I shuddered to think what lay ahead for us in the course of the year, a year which had started on such a shattering note. I quickly pulled myself together and requested Dad to drive Dewdrop home so that she could have something to eat and drink, as well as freshen up. She might have to be awake the whole night. Dad understood and realised that he would have to be in charge of the situation at home. He would also have to explain to Mum and Wriggles how grave the situation was as well as prepare them for the inevitable. They had probably better come soon.

By 7.30 p.m., Tony's siblings and close friends had gathered outside the intensive care unit where he lay. Dad and Mum soon arrived with the two children. Wriggles was taken aback at the sight of so many people in the corridor, and he desperately searched for me. When he found me, he clung to me, afraid to let go. Mum had been crying, probably wondering why her only daughter had to undergo such anguish. Dewdrop was overwhelmed by the sudden show of pity that was displayed by relatives, both known and unknown to her. All she wanted was to be with her father. Wriggles too wished to go to his father's side. However, only two persons were allowed in at a time, and they too had to be herded out each time Tony's blood-drenched diaper had to be changed.

The doctor, after seeing to Tony for the sixth or seventh time, pulled me out of the group of relatives to tell me, 'It would be advisable to prepare yourself for the inevitable.' He could see that Dad, Mum, the children, and I all looked crushed, but it would do no good giving us false hope.

I felt like screaming out loud, 'It is not fair that I am the one who always has to put up a brave front! Why do I have to pretend that I am not hurt or feel pain every time there is a crisis? Why do I always have to be the pillar of strength? What about my own emotional needs? Where can I go and cry? Why is there no shoulder for me to cry on? It just isn't fair! Nothing feels right anymore! The captain is abandoning our ship—this is not how our marriage was meant to be!'

Tony's youngest sister-in-law suddenly walked to where the doctor was talking to me. She wanted to know if it was possible to perform a liver transplant. The doctor explained to her that even if the organ were available then, surgery would be impossible, for the very first incision itself could cause Tony to bleed to death. She assured the doctor that her own husband, Tony's brother, and some close friends were willing to donate any amount of blood that was needed.

The patient but weary doctor repeated, 'The gesture is most noble, but the transfusions are not doing much good.' At this point, he dropped a bomb: 'The transfusions are actually prolonging Tony's suffering. His heart is beating forcefully, but the varices are bleeding incessantly.' Turning to me, he advised, 'Please allow me to discontinue the transfusions.' I was aghast! What on earth was he saying? He continued, 'Though it seems cruel, it is the most humane thing to do. Tony is currently in great pain . . .' Feeling as if I was about to collapse, I looked for a chair. I needed to gather my wits. The tempest was determined to claim a casualty: our captain.

Resentment

By 10.00 p.m., many had come and gone—relatives from near and far, close friends, as well as workers from the restaurant which Tony had once helped his brother to manage. The strong smell of spices typical of such a restaurant clung on to their clothes, and when they walked in, you could tell at once that they had come directly from work. Tony had been popular with them, for he had often stood up to speak on their behalf. I was touched initially by their devotion for Tony, but when they clamoured to find out who Tony's unfortunate wife and children were in the crowd, I resented the pitiful looks cast in our direction when we were pointed out to them.

I suddenly felt repulsed that they regarded us as objects of despair. They were probably imagining the worst for us, expecting us to be at the mercy of society, should anything happen to the captain. The doctor's earlier advice to me to brace myself for the worst ran deeper than he could ever have thought. Yes, I had to fend for myself and mine, with great tenacity. The captain would have wanted it so.

The flow of visitors slowly ceased. It was close to 11 p.m. Only, Dad, Mum, the children, Tony's eldest sister, and a nephew remained. Dewdrop and Wriggles looked worn out, and they were confused about all that was happening to their beloved father. Was he or was he not going to recover? I had not told them yet what the doctor had advised. Now, it was time to seek the counsel of the elders—Dad, Mum, and Tony's eldest sister, who was weeping softly. Tony's eldest brother and sister-in-law had left by that time.

The doctor approached me and brought up the subject again, for it was time for more transfusion. He stressed, 'Tony can go on receiving transfusion, but all the blood that is being introduced into his body is being expelled through the anus. Nothing is being retained . . .' The doctor was also at his wits' end. He was exasperated because despite Tony's resolute heartbeat, his liver was failing fast. He had, over the past two weeks, become rather fond of the captain, and he was finding it hard to give up on the determined patient. However, he felt that it was cruel to prolong Tony's torment when his body was obviously rejecting transfusion, and no surgery could be performed to replace the crucial organ. It was best to surrender Tony to God.

Surrendering

Dad, Mum, and the children left for home when it was close to midnight. Tony's eldest sister, nephew, and I remained by his side as he bled away. Now and then, Tony uttered a few words, mainly pleading for water. I could only watch tearfully while his sister, now and then, gently dabbed a wet wad of gauze on his parched lips. The three of us stood silently by Tony's bed, leaving only when the nurses had to change the blood-soaked diapers. A few times, I stepped out of the room to pace the corridor, wondering what lay ahead. Sometimes, my sister-in-law joined me, not really knowing what to say or how to comfort me. Words could do nothing; words and pleas had wrought nothing. We would then solemnly return to Tony's bedside, knowing full well that no miracle had been written in this chapter of my life.

Matters of the Heart

At about 4.00 a.m., Tony suddenly turned his head, as if looking for someone. His sister quickly grabbed my hand and put it in his, saying that she had heard him utter my name. Then Tony, with half-closed eyes and much effort, called out my name again. Gathering all my strength and struggling to hold back tears, I gently squeezed his hand to indicate my presence. Turning to me, half-choking, he said, 'I'm sorry for all that has happened. I really tried my best . . .' I nearly broke down but held his hand tight, assuring him that I knew he had.

Deep down in my heart, however, I could not help wishing that he had tried much harder when it had come to refusing drink. Had he done so, nothing even remotely resembling this scene would have ever taken place. How I wished that the captain had steered away from approaching storms which had been so clearly indicated on his barometer. He had thrown all caution to the wind despite repeated pleas from his devastated but devoted crew.

Suddenly, Tony turned to look for his sister. I gave up my right to his hand and placed hers in his. I was stunned by what Tony had to say to her. Still half-choking, he said, 'Please make sure that my last journey is from my in-laws' home, not Father's. I have received nothing but love and respect in the home I share with my in-laws, my wife, and children. I let them down so many times, but they kept on loving me, believing in me . . .' Struggling to speak, he added in a rather incoherent voice, 'In that home, I have never known want of any kind. They have always shared my pain and cushioned my falls . . .'

My Tony suddenly seemed to have so many things that he earnestly wished to say. I was overwhelmed, for although he was in considerable pain, he was still making great effort to acknowledge the care and concern we, in our humble home, had shown him. He did not have to, for were we not his family? Why was he speaking like a guest who was about to take leave? I did not want him to go, ever.

Tony's sister shed tears and told him that she was fully aware of the devotion and love that had been showered on him by Dad, Mum, and me. It was true that Tony had lacked attention and support from his own side, except from his eldest sister. Tony had often lamented on this when he was feeling troubled, especially after problems had set in for him, pertaining to his job and drink. My anxious husband then requested, 'Please make sure that my children and my wife receive their rightful share due to me from our late father's estate . . .'

Several of Tony's siblings were having differences arising from claims after his father's demise. Tony, wishing to be heard through and through, still struggled to continue with 'My wife has worked very hard for me and my children to have enough . . . I am heartbroken that I am leaving her nothing to help her in her time of need . . .'

It had been rather frustrating for Tony, who had badly wanted to make up in some way, somehow, for the money that had been lost to the viper. Dewdrop would soon have to go for tertiary education, and it was going to be impossible for her to do this if she did not secure a scholarship or have some form of financial backing. His weeping sister promised him that she would stand up for us. I just stood there, not knowing what to say. I felt like I was watching a heart-wrenching film. This could not be happening to me.

Tony, getting weaker, looked for me again. I quickly took his hand. He beseeched, 'Promise me that you will give our children the highest education that you can. Remember, they are our biggest assets. Most probably, nobody will be there to help you, except Dad and Mum. I'm confident that they will always be there for you and our children. They, you, and our children are the best things that ever happened to me, the best gifts from God himself . . .'

I wanted to scream out loud that he too had been the best thing that had ever happened to me and that we could have overcome all obstacles, faced all challenges and come out victors if only . . .'

As I wiped away falling tears on the sleeve of my T-shirt, I released Tony's hand for a moment while I turned to reach for a tissue to blow my nose. Almost immediately, I felt my hand being replaced in Tony's. It was the nurse, telling me it would be easier for my Tony to 'leave' if I did this, for the journey ahead was not easy. He would feel more comfortable if he felt my presence beside him for as long as possible. As I gently squeezed Tony's hand, his hand responded feebly.

Final Request

Tony suddenly spoke again, looking for his sister. This time, he had only one thing to say to her, one last request: 'I wish to be cremated according to Sikh rites and my ashes to be strewn into the sea . . . Promise me that you will respect my wishes, promise . . .'

I was stunned, but I understood why. Tony had always resented the way his family members shrank away from cleaning the graves of their deceased relatives near and far, often letting it fall on him to attend to the weeding and cleaning of no less than eight graves each and every year. These graves were located in two different cemeteries, at opposite ends of our town. The family members seemed to find it a burden and made all kinds of excuses to escape this mundane task. Tony had gallantly armed himself with a spade, candles, and fresh flowers each time he embarked on this filial mission.

I had accompanied him a few times, helping to place the candles and flowers after the weeds around the graves had been cleared. Tony would finally light the candles himself, and together, we would pray for the souls to rest in peace. Dewdrop had once been present at the grave-cleaning session, and she had innocently skipped and jumped over the graves in play, merrily singing nursery rhymes. Her father had to stop her enthusiastic sport, telling her that it was disrespectful. Poor Dewdrop had found it rather difficult to understand how people who were supposedly resting in peace in another realm could be irritated by little sounds and nursery rhymes sung on earth! Shrugging her shoulders, she then snuggled to my side, asking if we could go home.

Each time we drove home after having performed this service, Tony would remark that he did not wish to burden any living member of the family with the task of attending to his grave. I used to be shocked at such callous remarks at first, perhaps because I had never had to face such a task—my deceased relatives had always been cremated according to the simplest of rites. Tony, on several occasions, had commented that cremation was a more sensible and considerate way to dispose of the deceased—land should be left for the living! He had also lauded the fuss-free rites of cremation practised by my people. I never thought that Tony had given it so much thought, but here and now, my dying Tony still wanted to do his bit for the living, with the simplest of send-offs.

Though I was overwhelmed by Tony's requests, my thoughts were running wild: Would his family members ever agree? He was making two requests that were going to quake my in-laws—his cortege to leave from our home, and that too for the cremation ground! Tony was leaving me in a tight spot. Would these requests be entertained with understanding and compassion, or would they cause a major conflict between Tony's folks and mine? It would be the last thing I needed at this tragic moment in my life! More importantly, would my beloved husband have his last wishes respected? I tried to quell the turmoil of questions within.

Fortunately, Tony's sister and nephew had heard his final requests themselves. Her tears falling freely, Tony's sister assured him, between sobs, that she would personally see to it that his last wishes were carried out exactly as he desired. On being reassured, Tony fell silent. By then, both Tony's sister and I were finding it difficult to restrain ourselves from weeping loudly. Tony's nephew was also sobbing as he stood on the other side of the bed. The nurse had discreetly left. The clock on the wall showed 5.30 a.m.

The three of us stood by Tony's bedside, watching helplessly. Tony's diaper had been changed just a few minutes earlier, the blood-soaked one having been put into an ominous-looking black disposal bag. It was one of three full bags lining the bathroom wall a few metres away. Precious blood was oozing out incessantly from my Tony's body, and my precious Tony was slowly dissipating out of my life. Silently, tears flowing down our cheeks, we stood and watched Tony slipping away. As he slowly faded away, my hand held his even more tightly, foolishly believing that I could hold him back. Turning his head to one side, Tony made some faint sounds. Then he fell silent again and appeared to be looking into space.

I kept my eyes on him, grief and fatigue temporarily replaced with sheer curiosity. What was he looking at? What did he see? Where was he going?

I wished I knew, and suddenly, my grief washed over me like a tidal wave, forcing me to whimper aloud. I longed to go with him. I held his hand more tightly than ever, but there was no more response. He had left yet again, without telling me where.

My captain abandoned ship at 5.40 a.m.

Epilogue

It was just over a day since the captain's demise. I gazed wearily at the crowd of people surrounding us beneath the scorching sun on the cremation grounds. Even with so many people around me, I felt so alone. The final rituals leading up to the lighting of the pyre had been carried out as requested, albeit with much disapproval on the countenances of Tony's siblings.

I trudged away from the pyre, feeling completely beaten and devastated. Dewdrop walked steadfastly beside me, holding Wriggles' hand. Dad walked a little behind, leaning on his stick for support. I suddenly felt two arms holding me firmly and ushering me into a vehicle. I do not even remember who this kind soul was, but the touch was reassuring and the cool interior of the air-conditioned vehicle, soothing. I rested my head on the window, weeping silently as the driver guided the vehicle slowly away from the crematorium and into traffic.

Myriad questions flashed across my sleep-deprived mind: How did this happen? Tony was a man full of sensibility, dedication, love, and compassion. Why did he choose drink at every juncture of our journey together? He, who had sworn never to come under the influence of alcohol. He, who had demonstrated deep insight about the lives of families destroyed by drink. Had I unwittingly driven him to drink? Where had I gone wrong?

How was I to even begin picking up the pieces of my life? Tony had departed in a whirlwind of events and debts, a few of which we will never learn the answers to. There was a car to keep paying for and lapsed life insurance premiums. I realised with a bang that I had failed to keep up with the payments for the past three months, owing to escalating hospital bills. What about the credit card loan? I felt immensely cornered and burdened.

What of the children? They had witnessed one parent succumb to habit and die. I had to put on a very brave and stoic front if they were to grow into functioning adults.

What of my aging parents? How much longer could they stand by me? I had to fend for them too. All their savings had been depleted in trying to help me save Tony.

Relatives had come and gone over the years, spending weeks with the family. We had some good times then, but would they now be willing to help us in our time of need? They had declared then how much they loved us and how close they felt to us. Would they feel so now?

Would Tony's people actually give the children and me our rightful share of inheritance?

What of Dewdrop's further education? Would I be able to fulfil Tony's request?

Would Wriggles ever learn to play football? Would he ever recover from witnessing his father's horrific decline? The little boy had yet to shed a single tear.

What of me? Myself? My shattered dreams?

Little did I know that my captain's demise was only the tip of the iceberg.